Mortal Temptations

"Angry goddesses, hulking demons, love scenes that will melt wax . . . A brilliant release! Kudos to Allyson James—I definitely think she has a successful series on her hands." —*Romance Junkies*

"To say that Ms. James has a knack for paranormal romance would be an understatement . . . A beautiful, erotic romance that exemplifies once again the power love has to conquer all obstacles." —*Wild on Books*

"Ms. James has a way with words . . . This book is a prime example of how to do erotic romances well." —*Eye on Romance*

"When readers stop panting and drooling . . . they will be pleasantly surprised to learn that they've picked up a little travel, Egyptology, and mythology knowledge along with the advanced sexuality seminar taught by Professor James. I can't wait to see what's in the syllabus for next term." —*Romance Reader at Heart*

"The balance of intrigue, romance, and unbridled sexual fantasies makes James's story of gods, demigods, and mortals a sizzling page-turner!" —*Romantic Times*

The Dragon Master

"Allyson James has created a delicious story you can read more than once!" —*Fresh Fiction*

"The dragons are back and ready to rumble in this high-octane series from James . . . Tops yet again!" —*Romantic Times*

continued . . .

The Black Dragon

"More dragons, please, Ms. James." —*Night Owl Romance*

"The audience will relish this compelling entry."
—*Midwest Book Review*

"Dragon fans rejoice . . . tasty and tempting reading."
—*Romantic Times*

"Never lets up, not for one single, solitary, wonderful moment . . .
Allyson James has a winning combination that makes *The Black
Dragon* a story to remember!" —*Romance Reader at Heart*

"Destined to leave a smile on your face and dragons in your dreams."
—*Romance Reviews Today*

Dragon Heat

"A unique and magical urban paranormal with dragons, witches,
and demons. Will keep you enthralled until the very last word!"
—Cheyenne McCray, *New York Times*
bestselling author of *The First Sin*

"Exciting and passionate, this story is gripping from beginning to
end." —*Romantic Times*

"[A] delightful romantic fantasy." —*Midwest Book Review*

MORTAL
SEDUCTIONS

ALLYSON JAMES

HEAT
New York

THE BERKLEY PUBLISHING GROUP
Published by the Penguin Group
Penguin Group (USA) Inc.
375 Hudson Street, New York, New York 10014, USA
Penguin Group (Canada), 90 Eglinton Avenue East, Suite 700, Toronto, Ontario M4P 2Y3, Canada
(a division of Pearson Penguin Canada Inc.)
Penguin Books Ltd., 80 Strand, London WC2R 0RL, England
Penguin Group Ireland, 25 St. Stephen's Green, Dublin 2, Ireland (a division of Penguin Books Ltd.)
Penguin Group (Australia), 250 Camberwell Road, Camberwell, Victoria 3124, Australia
(a division of Pearson Australia Group Pty. Ltd.)
Penguin Books India Pvt. Ltd., 11 Community Centre, Panchsheel Park, New Delhi—110 017, India
Penguin Group (NZ), 67 Apollo Drive, Rosedale, North Shore 0632, New Zealand
(a division of Pearson New Zealand Ltd.)
Penguin Books (South Africa) (Pty.) Ltd., 24 Sturdee Avenue, Rosebank, Johannesburg 2196,
South Africa

Penguin Books Ltd., Registered Offices: 80 Strand, London WC2R 0RL, England

This is an original publication of The Berkley Publishing Group.

PRINTING HISTORY
Heat trade paperback edition / September 2009

Library of Congress Cataloging-in-Publication Data

James, Allyson.
    Mortal seductions / Allyson James. — Heat trade pbk. ed.
        p. cm.
    ISBN 978-0-425-22970-5 (trade pbk.)
    I. Title.
    PS3610.A427M66 2009
    813'.6—dc22
                                                    2009013295

PRINTED IN THE UNITED STATES OF AMERICA

10 9 8 7 6 5 4 3 2 1

MORTAL
SEDUCTIONS

PROLOGUE

Three thousand years ago

DEMITRI really knew how to *screw*.

Val straddled him in the impossibly green meadow, feeling him deep inside her as his hips rocked like a boat on the water. He splayed his hands over her breasts, dark on white skin, his liquid brown eyes heavy. His cock was thick, twisting inside her, the best she'd ever had.

Val raked her nails down his chest, letting her claws extend and draw a little blood. Demitri jumped, growled in pain, and let his eyes flick to tiger yellow. The big faker. He loved it.

The meadow flowed under them all the way to the misty mountains, the azure sky perfect. Of course it was perfect. These were the fields of Olympus, the sacred mountain. Demitri had brought her to this forbidden place, and the sex was all the sweeter for it. Demitri had proved he wanted her enough to break the laws of his own people.

"Worth it," she moaned. "You are worth it, my love."

"Shut up," Demitri panted.

He balled his fists and thrust his hips upward, his huge cock stabbing her deep. Val closed her mouth. He was right—they should just enjoy.

Demitri's body was tight with muscle, his skin made brown by the sun. His chest was wide, nipples nestled in dark hair. He had flat abs, hips made for sexing, and the biggest cock she'd ever seen.

She loved that cock, thick and full and throbbing every time Demitri looked at her. She loved to sink to her knees, wrap her lips around his huge arousal, and suck him all the way in. She loved to lick her way around his tight balls, part his legs, and dip her tongue toward his anal star.

Demitri would groan and wind his hands through her hair. He loved whatever she did to him. Sweet man. She'd trapped him, the tiger-eyed demigod with the gorgeous body. Or maybe he'd trapped her.

Val dug her hands into his chest, this time without the claws. She could be sweet. "Come for me, lover."

The wide cock was doing its trick. Val rocked her hips, driving it in. At the same time Demitri reached between them and shoved his thumbs against her clit.

Val screamed. *This* was why she'd let Demitri catch her, why she risked death screwing him in this meadow sacred to his people. She was forbidden here, a half-demon demigoddess from another pantheon. But she came here for Demitri. She'd do anything for him.

Demitri groaned. He half sat up, his gorgeous face and beautiful lips coming to hers. She screamed again as his seed scalded her inside, the excess trickling in hot droplets between them.

She clasped Demitri's face between her hands and kissed him. She delved into his mouth with her tongue, wanting to swallow him whole.

She could. She could turn to her true form and gobble him up. He'd die in ecstasy and he'd always be part of her.

Val's heart twisted. *No, don't hurt him.*

What a strange thing for her to think. She hurt everyone. She was Valenarian, the destroyer. She annihilated adulterous men, foolish mortals who ran from the beds of their wives, unable to resist Valenarian's call. They got their just punishment.

But Demitri was different. Demitri was . . .

"Demitri," she whispered against his mouth. "I love . . ."

A blinding white light filled the valley, and the stink of divinity punched her.

"Shit." Val shook Demitri, but he basked in afterglow, his eyes half closed. A growl came from his throat, his pupils slitted like a cat's. "Demitri, we have to go. Get us out of here!"

Val shrieked as strong hands reached down and lifted her right off Demitri. Demitri's still-hard cock slid out with pleasant friction, but Val went sick with fear.

She landed on her feet and found herself facing an enraged goddess whose beauty was terrible. Val's impulse to fall to her knees and press her face to the grass nearly overwhelmed her, but she forced herself to remain upright. She was demon, she was the destroyer. She'd not bow before the Goddess of Love.

"This is my grove," the goddess said, her voice both sultry and terrifying. "Defiled by you. Now you will face your punishment."

"Demitri brought me here. *He* defiled your grove."

Aphrodite slapped her. Val spun with the blow, nauseous with pain. Her heart thumped with terror, knowing that the goddess was tempering her strength. If Aphrodite let loose, Val would be dead.

"Is that all you've got?" Val said, refusing to be cowed.

Aphrodite ignored her. "Demitri. Rise."

"He already has," Val snorted. This earned her another blow, and she wiped blood and tears from her face.

Demitri stood before Aphrodite, sorrow in his eyes. "Be easy on her. I've watched her for a while now. She doesn't understand the sadness she causes."

Val's heart wrenched. *"Demitri."*

Demitri looked at her, his eyes dark again and filled with pain. "I'm sorry, Val."

"You tricked me." The heartbreak of that overrode even her terrible fear of the goddess. "You planned to give me to her all the time."

Demitri looked away. He was still naked, still beautiful, tall and glorious in this summer meadow.

"You son of a bitch," Val cried. "You told me you wanted me, that you couldn't resist me."

"No," Demitri said, his voice tight. "You believed me because you wanted to." He looked at Aphrodite. "She truly doesn't know."

"Well, she will learn."

"What do you mean, I don't know?" Val snapped. "Don't talk about me like I'm a child. I'm a daughter of Heka. I'm the slayer of unfaithful men. They bleat to their wives that they love them, but all I have to do is crook my finger, and they come running." Val pointed at Demitri. "You did the same."

"She entices them to stray when they wouldn't have," Demitri said. "She leads them to their doom. I've seen the aftermath, the broken families, the hungry children."

"They're cheating, lying bastards!"

"She does this to innocents?" Aphrodite asked.

"She used to be a simple vengeance demon," Demitri told her. "At first she did slay only those men who ruined women's lives. Somewhere that warped inside her. Now she calls all men, whether they are guilty or not. She used to destroy for justice, now she's caught in the joy of it." He looked sad. "She does it well."

"What about you?" Val said desperately. "You couldn't resist me. You love me."

Demitri put a hand on her shoulder. It was such a warm, caring hand that she almost melted. "Aphrodite asked me to help her stop you."

Val jerked away. "No. You love me. You told me."

Demitri's eyes flickered again, tears welling inside them. "You did make me happy, but I knew it was illusion."

"No, with you it wasn't."

"It always is, Val. You've lost the capacity to understand the pain you cause. Aphrodite will help you."

Tears of rage streamed down her cheeks, smearing the blood and dirt on them. "You lying bastard, you said you loved me. I'll kill you."

Val lunged at him with claws extended, flailing against his flawless skin. Demitri deflected her with one rapid blow. Val stumbled back into the goddess, and Aphrodite's arms closed around her like a trap.

Tears rained down Demitri's face. "Take her and go."

"Demitri, I love you." Val struggled against the goddess, but it was like fighting a mountain. "I didn't lie when I told you that."

"Maybe. Which is why Aphrodite will be kinder to you than you deserve."

Aphrodite grabbed Val's face, twisted her head around. "Look into my eyes."

Val fought desperately. To look into the eyes of a goddess was death to a demon.

The goddess put two fingers on Val's eyelids, forced her to meet her gaze. Sudden, awful power washed through Val's body, and she stopped struggling. She stopped thinking, stopped doing, stopped everything.

Demitri watched Val's lovely body go limp, her red-streaked black hair uncurl down her back as though magic had kept it in its enticing ringlets. She hadn't been wrong about Demitri loving her—when they'd been alone, and Val had forgotten herself, they'd laughed and loved, argued and made up. It had been the best experience of Demitri's life.

But Aphrodite was right. Valenarian had to be stopped.

"Thank you, Demitri." Aphrodite gave him a nod, the only reward he'd get for his broken heart. "She will serve me now, and be healed."

Demitri bowed, unhappiness robbing him of words.

A flash of light, and the meadow was empty. No Aphrodite, no Val, nothing but untouched beauty. Insects hummed and birds called to one another as they floated over the flower-studded grass.

Demitri fell facedown on the ground and wept. He wept like a demigod, his tears streaming so thick and fast a little rivulet formed under his body and flowed away across the grass.

He felt a touch on his shoulder, a male hand, calloused and hard. "You all right?"

It was the voice of Andreas, his friend and companion, a demigod who could take the shape of a white leopard. Demitri rolled over and looked up at him. "No."

"Let her go," Andreas said. "Plenty more in the world where she came from. We'll show you."

"Leave him be," another voice rumbled. Demitri's friend Nikolaus stood on his other side, the man's silken black wings flowing to his heels. Both men were naked, muscles gleaming in the sunshine.

Demitri got to his feet, wiping away tears. "It was necessary," he said.

"Doesn't mean it was easy," Nico said. He wrapped a consoling wing around Demitri's shoulders.

"No." It had been surprisingly difficult. The damn woman had gotten under his skin.

Nico ran a thumb across Demitri's jaw, then slanted a comforting kiss to his lips. "We can't erase what happened, but maybe we can ease the pain a little."

Demitri looked into his best friend's dark eyes and nodded. Nico and Andreas were a mischievous, incorrigible pair, always in trouble, but they were loyal friends and companions.

Andreas, always more direct, closed his fist around Demitri's deflated cock and squeezed. Then he kissed Demitri, released him, and called his leopard form. "Let's run," he said as he changed.

Demitri's tiger flowed through him, altering his body into that of a sleek beast. He hit the ground on all fours, easily catching up to and overtaking the smaller cat of Andreas. Nico skimmed behind them, black wings outstretched, his god's body glowing.

Friends for eternity, Demitri thought. *Nothing will part us. Nothing . . .*

1

"WE need to help her, Demitri."

Demitri had returned from his luncheon with his organization of hoteliers to find the Goddess of Love waiting in his office. *Just what I need. Aphrodite wanting a favor.* You couldn't exactly say no to the gods, even if it meant destroying your life to help them.

Outside the dirt-streaked windows, Cairo seethed at a dizzying pace. Even in the heat of the day, the streets were packed with cars, trucks, buses, and tourists. Demitri's hotel was a lush, cool oasis of calm in the huge city. His office reflected the luxury of the small hotel, with lattice screens, comfortable chairs, and a tiny whispering fountain.

Aphrodite had chosen to wear a bright blue Indian sari, because she had no idea what country she was in and didn't much care. Her hair was neatly pulled back into a knot, and her nails gleamed with pale pink nail polish. Jewelry bedecked her fingers and bracelets whispered on her arms. She looked like a lovely upper-class Indian lady visiting exotic Egypt.

"If she isn't made complete, I will be required to kill her," Aphrodite finished without inflection. "The male gods of the pantheon, including your illustrious father, are annoyed with me for keeping her alive at all. I have one chance to save her or she will be put to death."

Demitri adjusted the pen tray on his desk to keep Aphrodite from seeing the pain in his eyes.

"You had her in your prison for three millennia," he said in a mild voice. "You couldn't heal her in all that time?"

"She wasn't in prison," Aphrodite said tartly. "She served me and was glad to do it. She's been obedient, dutiful, and calm. But she isn't cured and they know it."

"Why are you involving me?"

Aphrodite rose, straightening her sari with elegant fingers. "Because she's never forgotten you. Whichever way she bends in the end, she'll do it because of you."

"You're supposed to be the goddess of love, not cruelty."

"It's been three millennia, Demitri," Aphrodite said, throwing his words back at him. "You couldn't get over her in all that time?"

"You know time to gods and demigods is different. No comfort of memories fading, no dwindling to nostalgia."

"I know that. What do people in this century say? Oh yes, 'deal with it.' The ultimate end is much more important than your feelings, wouldn't you say?" She smiled at him, the dazzling smile that led so many to believe she was gentle and good. "Since your very existence may depend on it."

She headed for the door, but Demitri stepped in front of it. "Don't walk out through my hotel. Mortals can't take you, you know. I don't need my customers passing out in the lobby."

Aphrodite preened. "Very well, Demitri dear." She patted his cheek. "Do as I say, and you will live. So will she." She turned toward the window, catching the sunlight and making it bright, brighter, then glaring incandescence. "The other is important to the plan. But she must not know. It is most important she doesn't know what he's really for . . ."

Demitri screwed up his eyes as Aphrodite vanished in a blinding flash. The light returned to normal, the office looking slightly dingy in contrast with her absolute beauty.

Demitri sighed and raked his hands through his hair. Aphrodite's plan was twisted, but Demitri knew it would be effective. Val would live or die, succumb to temptation or resist. Either way, Demitri would be heartbroken all over again.

He'd normally turn to his friends Andreas and Nico to grumble about his problems and ask for their help, but the two men had gone. They'd fallen in love, completely and finally, and had returned to New York with their ladies, the lucky bastards. Demitri was happy for them and wished them well, but he missed them. They'd been best friends for eons, and now he felt utterly alone.

Aphrodite was returning Val to him, the woman he'd loved but could never have. He'd have to face her alone, without the loud-mouthed support of his friends. And he'd have to let her go at the end, once more facing a world of hurt.

Perfect.

~ ~ ~

THE man from the hotel was definitely following her. Val walked through Cairo's darkened streets, intent on a carpet shop she'd visited earlier that day. She heard his footsteps directly behind her now, the bulky male with his short haircut standing out among the native Egyptians. She smiled. He didn't know much about stealth.

The man had tawny hair and green eyes and a great body, and he was Val's assignment. The dossier on Leon Dupree had indicated that his perfect match would be found in Luxor, and Val had to get him there and together with the young woman.

Aphrodite, for reasons known only to herself, had suggested

Val stay in Demitri's lovely little hotel in Cairo while carrying out her task. Leon Dupree would end up there, and it would be more convenient, the goddess said. Aphrodite's "suggestions" were more like direct commands, and Val obeyed, as she always did.

Demitri had blatantly avoided Val since her arrival, which was fine with Val. She'd thought she'd be able to face him with the numbness she'd grown used to, but when she saw him two days ago—for the first time in millennia—pain had pierced her heart. The feeling surprised her, the first that had broken through her emotionless state in a long time. She'd never forgotten the beauty of Demitri's big body and his coffee brown eyes, and he hadn't changed one bit.

Val adjusted the scarf she'd thrown loosely around her red black curls as she stopped in front of the carpet shop. Demitri didn't need to worry. He'd broken her all those years ago on Mount Olympus, and then Aphrodite had crushed anything that was left of Valenarian the demoness. Now Val served Aphrodite, and her errand here was to help her goddess, nothing more. If Val repeated that often enough, she thought, she might even believe it.

The man behind her stopped when she did, and she smiled again. Not stealthy at all. She went inside, but her stalker didn't follow.

The shopkeeper who came out of the back was not the assistant who'd waited on her earlier that day. He was Egyptian, not very tall, in a dark, well-made business suit, but he wasn't human. Val saw his god-aura superimposed on his human body, not one of the higher gods, but strong enough to hurt her if he chose to.

He took one look at Val and hissed. "Demoness."

"Not demoness," she corrected. "Customer. Your assistant put aside one of the cashmere rugs earlier for me."

"Which one are you?" the small god went on. "What do you want from me?"

"To buy a carpet. So, why are you here selling them instead of attending banquets with the gods?"

For some reason people liked to tell their troubles to Val. Perhaps it was the way she smiled that made them soften and spill their guts. She'd done this with wronged women when she'd been a vengeance demon, and the ability came in handy now that her job was to coax lovers together.

The little god's stance relaxed, and he sighed. "There isn't much else for me to do. For ages I guarded a tomb on the banks of the Nile, but a Greek goddess, she destroyed it. Some archaeologists took away the mummy, and no one has summoned me in a long time."

"So you decided to set up shop in Cairo?"

"From here I can help guard families and homes, as I did of old. No one has statues of Bes anymore, but they buy carpets."

Val nodded sagely. "And you put your protective magic on the rug. Interesting."

He stiffened again. "You are a vengeance demon. That's what I smell."

"Used to be a vengeance demon. That part of me is dead. Now I'm sort of an assistant." Aphrodite had told Val that her job of bringing together those in love would cure her, but Val didn't feel cured. She felt empty, drained, unfulfilled.

She touched a carpet, feeling through the wool a frisson of benign magic, warm and comforting. Strong. Bes would never be on the same level as Isis, but he had steadfast strength.

Bes gave her a look of horror and lunged at her. "No, don't touch it!"

The hangings at the door burst apart, and the square-shouldered man came barreling in. "Keep your hands off her."

Leon Dupree spoke English with a curious accent, all long vowels and slurred consonants. His face was red with fury, fists bunched in violence barely contained.

He rushed in to protect me. The thought astonished Val, and she felt a stirring through her numbness. *He's not for you, remember.*

Bes backed away, his eyes wide. "My hands are not on her."

"It's all right," Val said quickly. "He was afraid I'd damage the rug. That's all."

Leon glared at Bes in deep suspicion. "You're sure?"

The man was wound up, his adrenaline high. Val felt a touch of the otherworld about him, though he was nothing like Bes or even Demitri. But there was something wild about him, something primal. His body was solid muscle, his hair wheat blond. His dark green eyes had seen hardship, had feared and fought and lived as he'd watched others die.

Bes was a god and could kill this mortal with the flick of his finger, but under Leon's hard stare, Bes did his best to look innocent and harmless. "A misunderstanding," he said.

"Keep the carpet for me," Val told him. "I'll return and fetch it tomorrow. Good night."

"Good night," Bes said uncertainly.

Leon gave Bes a gruff nod, then parted the curtains so that Val could walk out ahead of him.

Val ducked past Leon's body, liking the hum of his aura and the warmth of his skin. He smelled like sweat and a hint of soap and aftershave.

The evening was still warm after the hot November day but had begun to cool. Leon walked protectively next to Val, silent, solid, and gorgeous as hell.

"You're the one going on an archaeological dig, is that right?" Val asked as they walked along together. "Are you an archaeologist?"

"My brother is." Leon's green eyes fixed on her for a moment then returned to scan the streets. He walked next to her like a bodyguard, alert for danger. His blatant protectiveness made her warm. "He asked me to come out and help him if I wanted. 'Scuse my manners. My name's Leon Dupree."

"Val." She hesitated. "Valerie Stevenson." That was the neutral name Demitri had come up with for her, one that could fit several nationalities. "Your name is French, but you're not from France, are you?"

"It's Cajun."

Val mentally ran through the studies she'd done of twenty-first-century culture before she'd come on this assignment, but drew a blank. The word hadn't been in his dossier, either; it listed his nationality as "American."

"What country is Cajun?"

He gave a short laugh. "Louisiana, in the States. New Orleans and the bayous. The French settled the area a couple hundred years ago, and we're the result."

"How very interesting." Val slid her hand through his arm, trying not to reflect on the strength beneath her fingers. "Why were you following me?"

Leon shrugged, muscles on his wide shoulders rippling. "You left the hotel by yourself, and I worried for you, walking the streets alone."

"How gallant."

Another shrug, another fascinating play of muscles. "It's the way I am."

Val wished she'd stop admiring his body. He was tall, with tight abs and biceps you could bounce a coin off of. He wasn't for her; she needed to remember that. The penalty for Aphrodite's assistants falling for either party of their assignment was death. Besides, Aphrodite insisted her assistants take vows of celibacy, so even if Leon hadn't been her assignment, Val would have to keep her hands off. A vestige of Valenarian the demon stirred inside her. Not fair for Aphrodite to send Val to a hard-bodied man who had just enough of the supernatural to tempt her.

Do your job, Val chided herself. *Don't give Demitri an excuse to report you.*

Thinking of Demitri helped. The confusion and pain she still felt about him blurred her rising lust for Leon.

The shop hadn't been far, and they reached the hotel in a disappointingly short time. Demitri's inn was a small, almost Parisian-looking building left over from the nineteenth century. It was a "boutique" hotel, offering luxury for the traveler tired of the commercial chains.

Of course Demitri would own the best hotel in the city. In his human guise, he wore expensive suits and looked like a respectable, prosperous businessman. He'd tamed his silken hair into a ponytail, but Val knew what his hair looked like mussed from sex. She also knew how wild and how masterful he could be, and she didn't think all the centuries could have changed him. He'd simply grown good at hiding his true nature. He'd saved her life all those years ago, she understood that, but he'd tricked Valenarian into falling in love with him to do it.

"Do you want coffee?" she asked Leon as they paused in the lobby. Her usual modus on assignment was to befriend one of the parties involved and introduce him or her to the other, or act as mediator if they already knew each other.

Leon gave her a quick smile. "Sure."

"In your suite?"

The glance turned to one of surprise, but he didn't miss a beat. "Sure."

Val told the concierge to have coffee sent to Mr. Dupree's room, and they rode up silently in the elevator. Demitri had given Leon one of the largest rooms, at the top of the hotel, a suite with four bedrooms and four bathrooms and a central sitting room with a fountain in the middle of it.

"The suite's too damn big for just me," Leon said when he opened it with a key. "But it was all Demitri had. I expected he'd stick me in the basement somewhere when my brother asked him to put me up. I'm getting it gratis, though, so I'm not complaining."

Val unwound her scarf and shook out her hair. "Demitri can be generous."

"Hospitable, we'd call him where I come from. I keep meaning to thank him, but I never get the chance. He seems real busy."

"Oh, yes, Demitri is always busy."

The coffee arrived, and Leon took the tray from the waiter and arranged the cups on a table. The waiter looked curious, but Leon ushered him out and shut the door in his eager face.

"How do you like it?" Leon asked.

"You mean my coffee?" Val slid off her shoes, sank into a big chair, and tucked her feet under her. "No sugar."

"No sugar it is."

He poured a cup for her and ladled hunks of sugar into his. He handed her the coffee, his deep green eyes lingering on her lips, then her breasts. He didn't leer, didn't demand. He was simply a man enjoying a look at a woman.

When Leon turned away, Val let out her breath. His sweatshirt was tight against his broad shoulders and biceps, and his jeans cupped his ass in a satisfying way. The old Val wanted to rub up against him and purr.

"Tell me about this Louisiana place," she said as he sat down.

Leon rolled his coffee cup in his hands and started spilling his story, just like Bes had. Val liked Leon's voice, deep and slow, his accent so different from anything she'd heard before. She could imagine it whispering his lady's name in the dark, telling her how he wanted to pleasure her. Valenarian would have been on this man in a heartbeat. Valerie could only sit back and let him talk.

Leon told her how he and his three brothers had grown up in a small house in a small town called Fontaine, which was south of a place called New Orleans. His father had died when they were all little boys, and his mother had raised them alone.

As he talked, Leon relaxed, stretching out his long legs and crossing them at the ankles. He told her about driving swamp boats in the bayous and wrecking one on an alligator, he and his dog paddling like hell for shore; his teenage years tinkering with boats for a guy and loving it—until the guy got drunk and started whaling on Leon.

"Why did he do that?" Val asked indignantly.

Leon shrugged. "He was a drunk. He'd done that kind of thing before, but he'd never attacked me until then. At least I was big enough that I could take him, but I worried because I sometimes brought my younger brother Remy to help. We didn't go back after that."

"Did you take vengeance on him for hurting you?"

"Vengeance? Nah, he didn't know what he was doing. We felt sorry for him. He died a couple years later."

Valerie knew that some people did feel compassion toward those who hurt them. She always found it odd, this forgiveness, and she strove to understand it.

"Tell me more," Val encouraged.

Leon went on about how he'd graduated from high school and joined the army so his mother wouldn't have to keep feeding him. He'd trained as a medic, gone to Afghanistan twice, and come home the second time to find the damage Katrina had done to his old stomping grounds, people having to leave their lifelong homes, their lives forever altered.

"Who is this Katrina?" Valerie asked. "She sounds terrible."

Leon laughed. "A hurricane. Flooded my mama's house and tore down so many in my little town. Our house is still standing, but we had to rebuild it from the ground up." He paused. "I guess we get so caught up in our own troubles we forget other people don't know everything about them."

"You have so many troubles."

"Everyone does. But I got my three brothers and my mom."

His brother Remy, was the smart one, and they'd all worked to send him off to a good school. He'd won scholarship after scholarship, and now was a postdoc at the University of Chicago, becoming an expert in Egyptology. Val heard the pride in his voice.

"He's out here on a grant now," Leon went on. "Digging up stuff in the Valley of Kings down by Luxor. He said they could always use a trained medic, and I don't have anything to do anymore, so I figured why not? Also he wants me to—" He broke off suddenly, clamping his lips shut.

"Wants you to what?"

Leon looked at his empty coffee cup. Val felt his reluctance, which meant that they'd come to the most interesting part of the conversation.

Leon looked up at her, his mouth still closed. He was strong, resistant, which only intrigued her more. Val continued to smile at him. She wanted to know everything about this man, wanted to wrap her arms around him and slide her hands into his conveniently placed back pockets.

Leon got up, poured himself a little more coffee, then sat down on the floor next to her chair. He put his back against the chair and stretched out his legs, his warm bulk oddly comforting.

"Wants you to what?" Valerie repeated. "I won't tell."

Leon studied his coffee some more, then gave up. "He's worried about some things going on at the dig. He says it might be nothing, but sometimes tools disappear, or pieces of pottery, or other little things. And then people walk away and never come back. Nothing happens to them or anything, they just decide they don't want to stay. Remy thinks it's weird, and he wants me to keep an eye on things."

"A long way to travel to help out a brother."

Leon shrugged. She liked his shrugs, especially when his shoulders brushed against her knees. If she dared, she could stroke her fingers through his hair, find out how rough or smooth it was.

"I did two tours in Afghanistan, kind of got used to the Middle East. I like it, actually, and I wanted to see part of it that wasn't a war zone. So I came."

"It was good of you."

"Haven't done anything for him yet except stay in a posh hotel. A friend of his knew Demitri and got me put up here until it's time to go to Luxor."

"Which is when?"

"A couple of days. I came a little ahead of schedule to do some sightseeing."

"I might go to Luxor, myself," Val said. "It's been a long time since I saw the skies above the temples of Karnak."

Leon smiled at her. "I think I'd like that."

When he smiled, his whole face warmed and his eyes went dark. His lips turned up, the lower the slightest bit fuller than the upper, a man's lips, which she hadn't touched in centuries.

Leon slowly pushed himself up until he sat on the edge of her chair. He studied her in silence a moment, then he slid his hand behind the nape of her neck, leaned down, and kissed her.

Val knew she should jerk away, put herself across the room from him. He wasn't for her. He was for the woman down in Luxor Val had to lead him to.

But Val couldn't make herself push him from her. The tiny part of her that was still Valenarian whispered, *Have this. Just a taste. When he meets the woman and falls in love, he'll forget you.*

Leon's lips were like silk. Smooth and warm, they parted hers, his tongue dipping inside her mouth. His hand was firm on the back of her neck, fingers teasing her curls. Valerie leaned back and ran her hands along his hard shoulders, loving the feel of man beneath the shirt.

Warmth flushed her body, her nipples hardening to little points inside her blouse. She felt loose, watery, hot. His body was heavy against hers, his arms strong, his lips gentle but not leaving any doubt what he intended. He wanted to have sex with her, the friendly sex of two people far from home finding themselves alone together in a hotel.

His fingers slid down her blouse to undo the first button. She closed her eyes as hard fingertips touched her bare breast, finding and catching on the point of her nipple.

"No," she groaned. "I can't."

"Why not?" His breath was hot on her lips. "You got a boyfriend? Husband?"

"It's not that."

"What then? Do I smell bad?"

Val wanted to laugh. "No. That is, you smell good." She put her nose to his bare neck and inhaled. He was all kinds of good, and for fun she put out her tongue and licked him.

Mistake. He tasted salty and nice, and she wanted to lick him from head to toe. She wanted to open his jeans and see what kind of cock he had and how it tasted. Judging from what pressed her from behind the fabric, it was a nice one, thick and long. She imagined it was dark with a rush of blood, the tip smooth and cool.

"I won't push you, *chere*," Leon said in her ear. "We'll take it slow if you want. Get to know each other better."

Val put her hands on his chest, tears flooding her eyes. "We can't. I can't—ever. I'm sorry."

Leon's eyes flickered strangely, a flash of that otherworldly thing she'd sensed in him. "Well, since my mama raised me to be a gentleman . . ."

He slowly unwound himself from her and stood up. Tension thrummed through his body, a virile male who'd been about to let loose tightening up again.

Valerie got up with him but couldn't resist running her hands along his chest. She *wanted* him, and not like Valenarian would. Valenarian the demoness would have him on the floor, extending claws to shred his clothes. She'd press him flat on his back and impale herself on his rigid cock. No talking, no getting to know each other, just straightforward, fulfilling sex.

But Valenarian was gone, suppressed behind too many layers of Aphrodite's brainwashing. The woman Valerie wanted Leon naked, but she wanted to slide her arms gently around him, to get to know his body and let him get to know hers. She wanted it slow, nice, memorable. She wanted him to want to see her again when it was over.

Valerie rose on her tiptoes and kissed Leon on the mouth. He moved his lips in response but didn't hold her.

"I'm sorry," Val said. "I should have told you right away, but I so enjoyed talking to you."

He put his hands on her shoulders and gently pushed her away. "You didn't have to pretend you'd have sex with me to get me to talk to you."

"I didn't pretend. I really do want to have sex with you. But I can't. It's forbidden." Val ran her fingertips down his chest again, feeling his heart beating beneath his skin. She couldn't tell him the whole truth, because that, too, was forbidden, but she could tell him part of it. "I'm a celibate, you see. I took a vow never to have sex with any man, no matter how much I might want to."

2

THIS was a new one on Leon. *Not tonight, darling. I'm celibate.*
Leon stepped back and studied her, a gorgeous female with curly dark hair streaked with red. He'd thought the red was dye until he'd seen it close. The color was natural and beautiful, red mixing with black like weavings of silk. Her eyes were dark, not brown, but such a dark, intense blue they looked almost black.

Kissing her had been dizzying. She knew how to kiss, knew how to use her hands, knew how to make his cock sit up and dance.

"So, are you a nun?" She didn't dress like a nun, even if she wore a long-sleeved loose tunic and pants, clothes that covered most of her skin.

"Priestess," she said. "A priestess of Aphrodite."

Leon started to laugh. "You can just say no, sweetheart. You don't have to come up with excuses. I can take it."

Valerie gazed up at him with beautiful eyes he wanted to drown in. They were like the night sky just before darkness took over.

"It wasn't my choice to serve her, though I can't pretend it's been horrible. But she insists on having her priestesses celibate."

"Aphrodite is the Goddess of Love, right? Like Venus."

"Venus is the name the Romans gave her, yes. She prefers Aphrodite."

"And the Goddess of Love wants you celibate. Isn't that a little backward?"

"Love is for others, and herself. Not for her priestesses. We must remain pure to do her work."

"Right." Like mythical goddesses talked to people all the time.

"I don't know why you're surprised," Val said. "You aren't quite human yourself. I haven't decided what you are, but you have some supernatural in you."

Leon wanted to back up yet another step, but he held his ground. The one thing he hadn't let her pry out of him was that he and his brothers were shifters. He'd been taught to keep it quiet from the time he'd been a little boy. The rest of humanity wouldn't understand their special gift, and no one could ever know.

Leon understood better when he got older. People didn't like people who were different. Those who didn't fit the mold were either shunned, driven out, or hurt in some way. Didn't matter how strong or magical he was—normals would try to hunt him down if they knew.

"Keep that to yourself," he said. "I don't need it blabbed around, and neither does my brother."

Val smiled. Damn, she had a sexy smile. His blood started heating all over again, just when he thought he'd calmed down.

"Your secrets are safe with me, Leon Dupree." She touched his chest again. Why did he suddenly envision her raking her nails down his bare skin while she rode him? He felt his eyes flicker into an animal's and back again.

Val lowered her hand. "I should go."

"You don't have to. We still have half a pot of coffee."

She twirled one curl around her finger. "You want me even if we don't have sex?"

"Doesn't mean we can't be friends." Did he really mean that? Or did he want to try to convince her to thumb her nose at her vow of celibacy and get between the sheets with him? He wasn't sure. He also wasn't sure how much he believed she was a priestess of Aphrodite.

He thought for a second she'd say yes. Then she shook her head, taking on a look of regret. "I can't." Another touch on his chest. "You are too tempting. If I stayed, I'd want to eat you up."

Yes. He pictured himself spread-eagled on the bed with her mouth all over him. She'd lick his skin then take his cock and suck him down deep.

"Perhaps I'll see you at breakfast tomorrow," she said. "Good night, Leon."

Damn. He forced the fantasy away, wishing his erection wasn't pounding so hard.

"Yeah, right. Breakfast." He walked her to the door and opened it, surprised he could move normally with the huge thing throbbing in his pants.

Val paused at the door, rose on her tiptoes again, and pressed a light kiss to his lips. Smooth and sweet.

"Thank you," she breathed.

"For what?"

"An enjoyable evening. And thank you for worrying about me at the carpet shop."

"You never told me what that was really about."

"Yes, I did. Or Bes did. A misunderstanding." She tapped the tip of his nose, then turned around and walked toward the elevator. Her hips moved enticingly, making him want to close his hands around that slender butt and drag her back.

She waved again as the stepped into the elevator, then the doors closed, and she was gone. Leon slammed the door and locked it, then swung around, shoving his hands through his hair. His army buzz had grown out some, nowhere near the long mop he'd worn as a kid, but he had enough hair to pull in frustration.

"Damn it." His erection wouldn't die, and his imagination wouldn't stop thinking about her naked, licking him, kissing him, rubbing her body on his. It had been too long since he'd had sex, the last time being about six months ago.

Shit. Maybe he should take a vow of celibacy, too, and live in a monastery raising grapes or something. No, he'd bury himself on Remy's dig and forget all about women and his needs.

It never worked out for him anyway. Women liked him, but something about him put them off, and he'd never developed a lasting relationship. They wanted his body, not the rest of him. Maybe it was the way his eyes went weird when he got excited or angry, the one shifter part of him he couldn't control.

Leon realized he was standing in the middle of the room, hands on his head, sweating. His body wanted to change, to relieve his frustration by becoming a snarling animal. He held himself back. He might wreck the place, and he couldn't pay for it. And that would make Remy look bad.

Leon kicked off his shoes, got some towels from the bathroom, and stripped off his clothes in his bedroom. This was one of four bedrooms, each as opulent as the others. A huge mirror in a delicate wooden frame reflected the sumptuous bed and beautiful paintings on the walls.

It also showed a naked Leon leaning his butt on the bed, his sand-colored hair a mess, his eyes yellow. The mirror reflected his enormous, angry cock, which moved a little with each heartbeat.

Leon didn't have any lube, not having had the foresight to pack any, but it didn't matter. He wet his palm with his tongue and closed his hand around his aching erection.

~ ~ ~

DEMITRI watched Val exit the elevator on her floor and walk to her room. No, *sashay* to her room. She made the simple act of walking down the hall enticing.

Her hair looked curlier than when she'd arrived yesterday. Was it the heat of the city on the river? Valenarian the demon's hair had always been tight corkscrew curls, lovely ringlets that had tumbled over her body. The few times he'd seen her after she'd become Valerie, humble priestess of Aphrodite, her hair had been nearly straight.

Valenarian was gone, he reminded himself. Demitri had trapped her and Aphrodite had erased her, leaving Val alive with a new, softer personality.

At least that's what he'd believed until Aphrodite said there'd been incidents. Valerie hadn't remembered them when questioned, but Aphrodite suspected that Val had seduced a few men on her assignments, had sex with them, then erased their memories. She wasn't certain and couldn't prove it, but the other gods had started grumbling that Aphrodite had been a fool to keep Val alive. Most of the male gods were touchy about demons whose purpose was to murder adulterous men.

Demitri made himself turn away from Valerie, not confront her. He'd been waiting to see if she'd come down after his waiter told him the interesting tale of her going to Leon Dupree's suite. His tiger's senses didn't smell sex on her, only coffee, but she had been up there a good long while.

"Demitri." Her sultry voice sounded behind him.

Demitri turned reluctantly.

"Is everything all right?" she asked.

Her eyes were innocent, blue now when they'd been black eons ago. Since her arrival, she'd never once shown a memory of anything between her and Demitri—correction, between Valenarian and Demitri. She and Demitri might have been old friends getting reacquainted—no more, no less.

"Everything's fine," Demitri said. "How about with you?"

"My room's lovely, thank you."

"You went out tonight. Why?"

"Shopping. You have no need to worry. Your friend Mr. Dupree made sure I returned without harm."

"You went to his room."

"For coffee." She closed the distance between them, reached up, and straightened Demitri's tie. Just the touch made him want to back her against the wall, to furrow her hair, to press his tongue into her mouth.

"Really," she said. "Coffee only."

Demitri looked into her beautiful eyes. Had they darkened since she'd been here? He couldn't tell.

"You don't have to worry about me, Demitri." Val stepped away from him. "I've been living all these years without a single hitch. I've brought a lot of love into the world."

"So I hear."

"I was merely doing my job. You can go back to bed and stop following me."

"I wasn't following you."

Her brows arched. "No? Your room isn't on this floor, is it?"

"I had business on this floor. It's my hotel."

"That is true. I suppose that means you can go to any floor you wish." Val smiled sweetly. "Good night, Demitri. Sweet dreams." She turned back to her bedroom, opened the door, and went inside. Demitri glimpsed the large bed and her clothes folded neatly over the backs of the elegant chairs.

He could go in after her. He'd been charged to keep an eye on her. He could stay with her, learn her again, make damn sure she didn't do anything to Leon Dupree. But he couldn't interfere. Aphrodite had made that clear. No matter how much it killed him, he had to let Val choose her path, even if it meant her death.

His eyes moistened, and he looked away before she could see. "Good night." He closed the door for her then rested his fingertips against it.

Wiping his eyes, he turned around and took the elevator up to the very top of the hotel, where he'd given the best suite in the house to Leon Dupree.

~ ~ ~

LEON groaned. His hand moved faster, stroking his cock in a rapid, even rhythm. The mirror showed a man bulked with muscle, his eyes a wild yellow, a hard red cock appearing and disappearing between his fingers.

He imagined Valerie touching him, Valerie taking him into her mouth and sucking in hard, quick jerks. Leon squeezed his fist, imagining how her lips would feel around him. He dipped his other hand behind his balls, feeling them tight and hard. He stroked them, letting an animal growl escape his throat.

Val was so damn beautiful. He loved how her hair curled around her fingertips when she touched it, loved how her eyes darkened, the blue becoming almost black when he'd kissed her. The cleavage he'd glimpsed under the button he'd undone was soft and lickable. She hadn't worn a bra, which was fine with him. He'd wanted to open her shirt, lower his tongue to her breasts and taste them all over. He'd take her nipples into his mouth one at a time, suckling until she groaned with it.

The frustration of having to let her go made him stroke faster, pull harder. Lamplight shone on the droplets of sweat on his shoulders and neck. The hair at his groin had twisted into tight, damp curls, sandy brown and coarse.

"Val," he groaned. He felt the buildup of his climax—the movement of his balls, the need to thrust, the mindless darkness of it ready to release. "Val, sweet woman I want to fuck. *Damn*, do I want to fuck you."

Here it came, the roar, the release, the darkness—

Someone banged on the front door. The knocking was loud, insistent.

Leon's cock slipped out of his grasp, and he grabbed a towel to catch any mess. But the moment had passed, too late. The tingling faded and frustration took its place. *Hell.*

Leon dropped the towel and jerked on his pants. "Just a minute." Barefoot and bare-chested, unsated and still throbbing, he strode through the living room and yanked open the door.

Demitri the hotel owner stood in the hall, hand raised to knock again. Demitri wore a pristine tailored suit and tie, and had his hair pulled back into a neat tail. He was shaved and washed and manicured, and was obviously not impressed with Leon scruffy in jeans and bare feet.

"Something I can help you with?" Leon asked, his breathing still heavy.

Demitri raised his brows and looked him up and down.

"I was working out," Leon said. "Trying to stay in shape."

Demitri gave him a brief, unconvinced nod, then hoisted a small overnight bag. "Pipes broke in my bathroom, and I will have to stay up here until it can be fixed. It's an old building."

His words were stiff, not apologetic. Leon opened the door wider, stepped out of the way. "It's your hotel."

"I'll use one of the bedrooms and be out most of the time. You'll never see me."

Leon shrugged. "Like I said, it's your hotel. I've bunked with twenty guys in the same room before. I think I can handle someone staying across the hall."

Demitri gazed at him for a while longer as though wanting to say something more, then he turned on his heel and marched to the bedroom opposite the one Leon had taken. He opened the bedroom door and started to go inside, then swung back around to Leon.

"Valerie Stevenson was up here."

Shit. "Yeah, we had coffee."

"I know. I spoke to her in the hall downstairs."

Leon moved his hands in a *what about it?* gesture. "Is something wrong with that?"

Demitri wouldn't meet his gaze. "She and I used to be lovers. A long time ago." He sounded sad.

"I promise you we just had coffee. She told me . . ." Leon hesitated, wondering if Val had been bullshitting him, if she would have a good laugh at Leon's expense. "She said she was a celibate priestess."

Demitri nodded. "That is true. She is celibate." He put an emphasis on the word *celibate*.

"Don't get riled. As you saw, she left. A lady says no, I don't push her."

Anger flickered through Demitri's eyes, terrible, vast anger that wasn't necessarily directed at Leon. "Keep it that way." He turned on his heel, stalked into his bedroom, and slammed the door so hard it rattled.

Leon blew out his breath. He stood there a minute, staring at the blank closed door, then he turned to his own bedroom. The unused towel lay across the bed, mocking him for his missed release. He didn't need it now. His hard-on had shriveled in the face of Demitri's angry stare.

The encounter had been interesting, not just because Demitri had revealed his past involvement with Valerie. When rage had flashed across the tall man's face, his coffee-colored eyes had flickered for an instant to gold yellow, his pupils becoming slits. It might have been a trick of the light, but Leon knew better. Demitri, the uptight owner of a luxury hotel, sometimes spent time in the shape of a wild cat.

~ ~ ~

I need to remain in control.

Demitri lay awake, sweating and staring at the ceiling. Leon Dupree had been masturbating, his claim he'd been working out feeble at best. Demitri had smelled the sex on him, the frustration, the sweat.

That made Demitri believe more than anything that Valerie had walked out without touching the man. If they'd had sex, Leon would have been sated and heavy-eyed, not keyed up and needing to release.

Demitri imagined Leon stripping off and pulling his swollen cock through his fist, stroking and pumping to ease the pain. Demitri had done that often enough when memories of Val overwhelmed him.

He eased his hand to his own cock, feeling it throbbing and hot. Val had loved Demitri's cock. She'd known how to lick it and suck it until Demitri had been mad with passion. He'd taken on Val all those centuries ago to help Aphrodite, thinking he did a good deed, but he'd fallen for Val very fast. Even now he couldn't look at her without his body tightening.

Let her go. It was over, and now he needed to save her life.

The creak of Leon's door across the hall made him open his eyes. He heard soft footsteps then another creak, this one of a mattress.

Demitri slid silently out of bed. The footsteps hadn't been Leon's, and Demitri's cat senses knew a third party had entered their suite.

Without bothering to dress, Demitri stepped naked into the tiny hall between the rooms and eased Leon's door open a crack.

~ ~ ~

LEON awoke to someone getting into bed with him. Instinct made him rise up and pin the intruder to the mattress, his hands locking around a slender neck.

He jerked away when his night vision showed him Valerie's pointed face, dark eyes, and riot of red black curls. She lay beneath him, smiling her sweet and sultry smile, her eyes glinting in the dark.

"Hello, lover," she purred.

3

"VALERIE?" Leon sat back on his heels. "What the hell?"

Valerie arched up to him. "You can be rough, lover. I don't mind."

She was a lush armful, soft and sweet. She wore a fine-linked gold chain around her waist, all the better to loop his fingers through.

"What the hell are you doing here?"

"I'm sorry I said no earlier." Valerie ran her fingers hands down his bare torso, her nails lightly raking his flesh. "I had to make sure of you."

"Demitri's asleep in the next room."

"Is he?" She gave him a wicked smile. "Do you want to wake him up so he can watch?"

Holy shit. "Are you drunk?"

"Not drunk, lover." Valerie lifted her naked body to his. "I need you, Leon. It's been so long, a lifetime of loneliness, and now you want me."

"Just a minute. You and Demitri fed me the same shit about you being a celibate. What is that about?"

"Don't worry, I'll explain everything. You told me all about you, and I'll tell you all about me." Val sucked her lower lip between her teeth. "But first we're going to fuck like there's no tomorrow."

Leon hesitated, but his body throbbed. Why argue? A beautiful woman had just jumped into his bed and started rubbing herself all over him. Why not take what she offered? This was what he'd wanted to happen, wasn't it?

He let her drag him down and kiss him, her tongue plunging deep into his mouth.

"All right, then," he whispered.

~ ~ ~

SHE gave him the best sex of his life. Deep, grunting, satisfying sex. They tried many positions, Val proving she could be creative. The covers tumbled to the floor, the bed shook, and the room got hot.

She straddled him, rocking on him while Leon held her firm breasts in his hands. He didn't protest when she backed out and took his very erect cock in her mouth and played until he came. He was hard again almost right away, and he entered her from behind, her butt in the air while she screamed into the bed.

Sex and more sex. She didn't get tired. She was on top of him again, their bodies pressed together, face-to-face, when Leon finally fell asleep.

He woke alone to the sun trying to penetrate the heavy window shades. He lay spread-eagled on top of the empty bed, stark naked, pin dots of sunshine dancing across his skin.

He listened hopefully for a running shower, looked around for Valerie's clothes. Nothing. She was gone, and he was alone. "Damn."

He got out of bed and into the shower, where he leaned against the wall, shaking, while hot water blasted over him. It had been years since he'd had a sex hangover, but he was exhausted and drained. Valerie had been one hell of a partner, though he'd probably never have the pleasure of her again.

His sense of profound regret surprised him. He hadn't come out here looking for love, he'd come to help his brother, maybe to find a more permanent job so he could send money back to his mother. Anyone as exotic as Valerie wouldn't want to marry a Cajun boy anyway. She was used to staying in boutique hotels, buying expensive carpets, dating hotel owners, and all he had was a houseboat on a bayou. Leon was a diversion from boredom for her, that was all.

Leon snapped the shower off, dried himself, dressed, and strode out into the suite's sitting room.

Demitri was eating breakfast at a table spread with a white cloth. An empty plate and silverware waited in front of the chair across from him, and dishes of food and a basket of bread rested in the middle of the table. Demitri read a newspaper, and he turned a page without looking up.

"I ordered breakfast for both of us," he said. "Do you mind?"

Leon had planned to head down to the dining room, hoping to see Valerie there. But maybe it was better if he didn't. If Leon talked to Val again, he might do something stupid, like ask her to come to Luxor with him. Besides, Demitri was his host and had gone to the trouble of ordering the breakfast. Not only that, Leon had just had sex with the man's ex-girlfriend.

"Thank you." Leon sat down and reached for a roll. There wasn't any butter, but there was hummus, which Leon had discovered he liked.

"Did you sleep well?" Demitri's voice rumbled from behind the paper.

Leon chewed and swallowed. "Pretty much."

Demitri folded the paper and threw it down on the table. His face was dark with anger. "I know you had sex with Valerie."

Not much use in denying it. "Yes." He licked hummus off his fingers. "You told me you two broke up a long time ago."

Demitri scowled. "You have no idea what you've done."

"I have a pretty good idea." Leon spooned more of the tasty paste onto his bread. "If you want to throw me out of your hotel, you can. But she snuck into *my* room and hopped into bed with me. I didn't seduce her. She pretty much seduced me."

"I know. I saw you."

Leon froze. "What, are you saying you watched?"

"For a time, yes."

"Well, shit, why didn't you just take pictures? Maybe a video?"

"I wouldn't record without your consent."

A weird answer, and the man wasn't even embarrassed. "Thank you for small favors."

"Val is still very beautiful." Demitri closed a tight hand around his coffee cup. "Though the chain around her waist was new."

"I don't like discussing ladies I've been with, all right? Call me an old-fashioned boy."

"You should not have been with her at all; that is the point," Demitri said angrily. "You should have resisted her."

"What for? She wanted me, I wanted her, and you said yourself y'all were quits a long time ago."

"Because of her vows."

"That priestess of Venus shit? She fed me that because she didn't want to do it right then. She was letting me down easy. I figured she changed her mind and came back."

Demitri shoved back his chair and stood up. "No, you fool. She truly is a priestess of Aphrodite, and she could be punished for sleeping with you. Severely punished."

The man quivered in rage, his face dark, his eyes flicking to tiger yellow. "How severely?"

"She could be killed."

"Killed?" Leon got to his feet. "Christ on a crutch, why?"

"She was forced into service to Aphrodite for her past misdeeds, allowed to live if she took the vows and did what she was told. I was supposed to keep an eye on her while she was here, make sure she didn't do what she did with you."

"Then why the hell didn't you come in and stop her?"

"Because . . ." Demitri trailed off, his expression unreadable. "I was commanded not to. I was to observe, not interfere, and report what temptations she could not resist."

"You'd report her? Even if it meant she died?"

Demitri looked away. "I'm bound to obey."

"Fuck that. I'm not letting you get her killed. I can't believe you'd hate her that much for breaking up with you."

"I don't." He looked back at Leon, his eyes weary. "I loved Val with all my heart."

"Then help me find her and warn her." He started for the door.

"You must stay away from her. Let me deal with Valenarian."

Leon turned. "What did you just call her?"

"Val. Valerie."

"No, you called her something else."

"She used to be Valenarian. She took the name Valerie when she turned to her new life."

"Whatever she's called, we need to find her."

He continued to the door, but faster than Leon thought the bigger man could move, Demitri got in front of him and blocked the exit. "You're not going anywhere."

"Get out of my way," Leon said.

"No."

Leon's anger flared. He hadn't been angry in a long time—he'd suppressed almost all emotion to keep from going crazy. His anger blazed out now and felt good. "Get out of my way," he said, very quietly.

Demitri's body grew and brightened, stretching to the ceiling of the high room. Leon squeezed his eyes shut as the light grew, the room heating like the desert floor.

He opened his eyes as Demitri threw back his head and roared. The man's face elongated into a big cat's, tiger stripes flushing his body. His muscular arms changed to the squat shape of a tiger's, his shoulders and haunches becoming powerful. His body rippled with fur, and a tail sprang from his buttocks with a sudden spurt.

Demitri landed on all fours, and Leon faced a huge, yellow-eyed, hot-breathed tiger.

Demitri was bigger than a normal tiger. He must be something more than a shifter, but Leon didn't yet understand what. Demitri's lips curled back from huge white fangs.

"All right, kitty, kitty," Leon said. "If that's how you want to play."

Leon kicked off his shoes and started pulling off his clothes. He'd learned how to get rid of clothes fast when he was a kid, running up and down the bayous at night with his brothers.

Once he was naked, Leon swiftly brushed the tiger's shoulder. By the time Demitri swung his claws at Leon, Leon had leapt out of range.

Leon concentrated, seeing, feeling, hearing, smelling the tiger. He sucked its essence into himself, learning it, making it part of himself.

His eyes changed first, the world becoming convex and sharply defined. Then his face and his teeth, fangs curving outward, long and powerful. Then, with a long shudder, his body became a tiger's. He landed on his clawed feet and swished his tail, every bit as large as Demitri.

Yeah, boy, anything you can be, I can be, too.

Now the dominance contest would begin. Demitri was used to being alpha—that fact screamed itself to Leon in his stance, his body language, the way his eyes never moved from Leon's. Demitri snarled, nose wrinkling as he took in Leon's scent. Leon snarled back at him, not about to look away.

Leon didn't consider himself the alpha, the leader, but he wasn't a follower either, not one of the pack. Leon was a shifter, not a were-anything, and he didn't take on the politics of packs and their leaders. Tigers were mostly loners, but even among them there were the strong and there were tigers that couldn't make it. When two tigers entered one territory, only one tiger left.

Demitri struck first. His ears went back, and his front paw came out with a lightning-fast strike. Leon danced out of the way, deflecting the blow with a strike of his own. Demitri hit out again, his teeth bared, the powerful paw coming down again.

Leon knew Demitri wanted him to fall on his back, to expose his soft underbelly and throat. The gesture would mean that Leon conceded to Demitri's dominance, leaving it up to Demitri to let Leon rise or rip out his throat.

Not going down, Leon thought with glee. This was fun. He rose on his hind legs and lunged. He got Demitri in a lock, Demitri trying desperately to get his teeth on Leon's neck.

The two cats fell to the floor in a crash of limbs, rolling over each other. Both tried to get hind claws up to slash bellies; each tried to twist around to get hold of the other's neck.

Leon sensed that Demitri wasn't trying to kill him. Demitri's strikes were savage, but the cat was holding back. Demitri wanted Leon to obey.

Leon had never been good at obedience—just ask his commanding officer. He gave Demitri as good as he got, letting the man know he could kill if he wanted, but like Demitri, he was choosing not to.

Adrenaline surged, and Leon growled with the joy of it. He hadn't done anything this fun in a long time. Demitri's eyes were flat with anger—he wanted to control, to tame, and Leon wasn't about to let him.

"Oh, goddess," came a female voice at the door. "*Two* of you?"

Leon rolled away from Demitri and back to his feet. The tigers faced each other, panting, while Val watched in shock from the doorway.

"Demitri?" she exclaimed. "Where did you get a twin?"

Demitri snarled one more time, then morphed back into his

human form. Leon thought about Leon, his man shape, his true self, and a little more slowly flowed into it.

Valerie was staring at them, her hair flowing in a straight wave to her waist. "Leon? You're a tiger, too?"

"I'm a shifter," Leon said when he found his voice again. "I can take the shape of different animals."

Valerie's gaze roved Leon's naked body then Demitri's, her tongue coming out to brush her lower lip. Leon never noticed his nudity after he'd shifted, his animal brain not understanding the embarrassment of being unclothed. But he felt the heat of Valerie's gaze as she roved it appreciatively down his body. As Leon watched, the curls of her hair wound slightly tighter.

"Val," Demitri said in a warning tone.

Val gave him a deprecating glance. "I'm celibate, Demitri, not blind."

Leon reached for his shirt. "This has been fun, but I need to talk to Val."

"About what?" Valerie asked.

"Last night."

"There's nothing to talk about," Demitri said, tight-lipped. The man didn't bother to dress. He was nearly seven feet tall and built like a wrestler, with sun-bronzed skin flowing over big muscles. Black hair dusted his chest, and a thatch of black curled between his legs. The hair brushing his legs and arms was also dark, but streaked with gold—the tiger in him.

Leon buttoned his shirt and reached for his jeans. "There's everything to talk about."

Demitri had his hands on his hips, scowling at Valerie. "Tell me your version."

"My version of what?"

"Your version of coming up here and seducing Leon. Damnation, Val, you know what I'll have to do." He looked anguished.

Val frowned back at him, lovely today in a light blue tunic-looking thing. Leon wasn't a man who much noticed what a woman wore, but he liked that Valerie favored flowing, light-colored clothes that brought out the blue in her eyes. Her eyes looked very blue this morning; last night in the dark they'd been almost black.

"What are you talking about? I told you, Leon and I had coffee, then I went to bed."

"And then you had sex."

Val looked perplexed. "No, we didn't."

"Don't play innocent, Val. I saw you."

"How could you have? I was in my room asleep all night." Val looked at Leon in confusion. "Are you playing some kind of trick? Did you tell him that because you were angry I *wouldn't* stay?"

"You climbed into my bed, Val," Leon said, keeping his voice gentle. "We had sex." Heat flared through his veins. "Great sex."

"Well, you were mistaken. It wasn't me."

"No mistake." Leon went to her and put his finger under her chin. Her eyes softened, and he wanted to dip his finger inside her red, moist mouth. "It was you, *chere*."

She shook her head and stepped back. "It couldn't have been, Leon. If it was dark, and you couldn't see, you can't be sure."

"I have the night vision of a cat," Leon said. "So does Demitri, I'm guessing. It was you, darlin', unless you have an identical twin." He ran his gaze over her body. "Really identical."

"Well, I don't." Val started to say something more, then she stopped, and her eyes widened. "A twin. Oh, no, that can't happen, can it? It isn't possible."

"What isn't possible?"

Demitri looked grim. "Valenarian has been coming out to play."

Before Leon could ask what the hell that meant, Val put her hands to her face. "No, Demitri. No, I swear it."

Leon stepped between them. "Do you mind telling me what you two are talking about?"

Val's eyes flooded with tears. "Valenarian, the destroyer."

"The what?"

"I swear to you, Demitri, I didn't do it on purpose," she said. "I remember nothing but leaving and going to my room."

"It doesn't matter," Demitri said. "Whether you remember or not, the demon is getting loose, and Aphrodite is right. You know what has to happen."

"Stop." Leon glared at them. "Tell me, in plain English, what's going on."

Tears streaked Val's cheeks. "The punishment for what I've done is death. Demitri is right. She has to be stopped."

She bowed her head, all hope in her eyes gone. Leon stepped in front of her. "Like hell," he said.

"There's nothing we can do," Demitri countered.

"You said you two used to be lovers," Leon said in anger. "Does that mean you cared about her?"

Val looked at Demitri almost fearfully. "He hated me. He did what he had to do in order to imprison me."

"Not exactly," Demitri said.

"What does that mean?" Leon asked. He felt like he did when he was trying to get two of his brothers to make up after an argument.

Demitri's eyes darkened. "I fell in love with her."

"You gave me to Aphrodite."

"I had to. I promised I'd help her, and you were out of control. You had to be stopped."

"Like now."

Demitri inclined his head.

Leon growled. "So, what, you're just going to turn her in again?"

"I have to," Demitri said in a hard voice.

"No, you don't. I don't see Aphrodite hanging around here. How's she going to know if you don't tell her?"

"Leon." Val's voice was soft. "She'll discover it. I'm tied to her. She already knows and will come for me."

"Not if we help you. What's wrong with you, Demitri? If you

loved Val, if you still love her, give her another chance. I'll go to my brother's dig and never touch her again." Another pang of regret.

"I helped Aphrodite because she has a hold on me," Demitri said. "A big one. She kept my father from destroying me when I finally left my mother's people. He viewed me as an abomination and spared me only after Aphrodite's intervention. I vowed I'd help her in return."

"Vows," Val said sadly. "They make life difficult."

"I don't believe you two," Leon broke in. "You're going to turn her in, and *you're* going to let him?"

"We don't have much choice," Val said. "And if Val is coming out to play, as Demitri said, she has to be stopped. Even if it means I have to die."

4

LEON looked furious, but Val couldn't explain. Demitri understood. Demons and demigods didn't die like mortals, but the gods could kill one on a whim. Or they could eradicate a demon who was a threat to humankind, like they wanted to with Valenarian.

"We'll go to Luxor Temple," Demitri said. "Leon has to go to Thebes anyway—we can travel together on my plane. We'll make supplication to Aphrodite there." He looked at Leon. "You will be a witness."

"Like hell I will."

"You have no choice," Demitri said in a hard voice. "Pack your things. We leave this afternoon."

~ ~ ~

IN the end, Demitri had his way. Val knew he would. Demitri might put on a show of being a civilized businessman, integrated with the mortal population of the world, but he was still a demigod who liked to have control of things. He wasn't above using his powers, not to mention brute force, to get what he wanted.

Leon didn't exactly give in. Val could tell Demitri was surprised at his resistance, but Leon said forcefully that the only reason he was going along was to make sure Val was all right.

Demitri took the copilot's seat next to his pilot, which left Val and Leon uncomfortable on opposite sides of the cabin. Val glanced over at Leon, who was staring out the window, his duffel bag planted firmly on the seat next to him. Leon was harsher looking than Demitri, with sandy brown hair just growing out from a close cut, his green eyes slanted in an exotic way. He wasn't as tall as Demitri, but he was built, solid, as she'd observed before.

When Leon had poured out his heart last night, Val had found a man of honor who loved his family and missed them. He felt he could best help them by getting out from underfoot and finding something constructive to do. She guessed that when he found a way to make money, he'd send most of it back to his family.

When Leon had kissed her, Val had almost given in. Almost. His lips had been silken soft, warm, comforting and exciting at the same time. It had taken all her strength to get up, walk out, go to her room, and stay there.

Except she hadn't stayed there, if Leon and Demitri were telling the truth. Valenarian had gotten a taste of Leon and decided she wanted more, much more.

Val's heart constricted. Valenarian could have killed Leon or hurt him irreparably. There was a reason Aphrodite didn't want the demon loose in the world. Val didn't necessarily want to die, but she feared the loss of control over Valenarian even more.

Val also regretted that she didn't remember sex with Leon. He probably made love like the wild animal she sensed inside him. He was a lot like the Demitri she'd fallen in love with long ago. Demitri of today didn't like her, didn't want her here. She saw that every time he looked at her.

Like now. Demitri gazed at her around his seat, his eyes yellow with his tiger's anger. Valerie didn't flinch, meeting his stare until he turned away.

The Nile unrolled beneath the plane, the wide strip of blue and the deep green of cultivation contrasting starkly with the yellow white desert beyond. They flew over cliffs where nothing grew, the winter sky overhead bright, almost painfully blue. Settlements clumped along the river, growing more dense around the city of Luxor. Luxor was the tourist mecca for those who wanted a glimpse of Ancient Egypt—the mighty temples of Karnak and Luxor, the Valley of Kings, Tutankhamun's tomb, the Ramesseum, and other wonders. Here somewhere, Val thought as they landed at the airport east of town, was the woman Leon was meant to be with.

Demitri's friend who had set up Leon to stay in Demitri's hotel owned a hotel himself in the heart of Luxor. It was another boutique hotel situated near the mighty Old Winter Palace, and had been housing tourists in Luxor for more than a hundred years. Demitri hired a car to take them there, the driver navigating around everything from tour buses to farmer's carts to a string of donkeys.

Val expected Leon to shoulder his duffel bag and be off across the river to find his brother as soon as they stopped, but he silently followed them into the hotel. Demitri's friend Karim was an Egyptian, not a supernatural. Val knew right away that he was an ordinary human being—simply a man in a buff-colored suit with an affable smile. His well-dressed, pretty receptionist gave them keys to three rooms on the same floor and sent for someone to help with the luggage.

Not long after, Val was unpacking when Demitri entered her room, followed by Leon.

"What are you going to do now?" Leon demanded as he closed the door behind them.

"We wait," Demitri said. "As soon as the moon is full, we take Val to Luxor Temple and see what Aphrodite wants to do."

"Can I point out that this is Egypt? Why does a Greek goddess have a temple here?"

"She doesn't." Val sat on the end of her bed and rested her weight on her hands behind her. "But there are certain sacred spaces in the world that all pantheons honor. One is here in Luxor Temple. If I make supplication, Aphrodite will answer."

"I still say we don't tell her," Leon said. "It happened once, and it won't happen again."

Val felt his gaze linger on her body, and she realized her position thrust her breasts out provocatively. Demitri was looking at her, too, and she sensed his pheromones from across the room.

Her own desires started to stir. Having two gorgeous, hard-bodied men looking at her on the foot of the bed was making her warm. Her nipples started to tighten, her skin to tingle.

"Stop that," she said.

Demitri raised his brows. "Stop what?"

"Both of you stop looking at me like you want to lick me all over." Her heart beat faster as she suddenly pictured herself stark naked with both their tongues lapping her body. "I shouldn't have said that."

Leon's eyes had gone greenish yellow, and Demitri shifted his stance. Their thoughts were moving along similar lines, she could tell. Whether each man included the other in the fantasy, she didn't know, but she suddenly hoped they did. Licking her, then she licking them back, maybe all three of them licking one another.

She fanned her face with her hand. "Is it getting hot in here?"

Leon reddened. "Maybe we should go for a walk."

Val jumped to her feet. "Excellent idea. Luxor is beautiful, and the weather is just right today."

"Perhaps we should go to Thebes instead," Demitri suggested. "Find his brother."

"The west bank is nice, too," Val said. "We could look at some of the tombs." Tomb paintings and dry lectures from archaeologists should take her mind off things.

They decided on the west valley, and Demitri's hired car and driver took them there over the bridge south of town. Val sat in the front next to the driver, her body still humming from her brief fantasy. In the back, Leon and Demitri remained quiet.

Leon's brother Remy was working in a remote area of the Valley of the Queens, nowhere near the tombs of the famous pharaohs: Tut, Seti, Tuthmosis. Remy and his team lived in a house near the base of steep cliffs near the entrance to the valley, a few miles from the cluster of hotels that lined the road. The Egyptian couple who kept house for the archaeological team told them that Remy had gone to his excavation, about a fifteen-minute walk. The three of them followed the path to the base of the cliffs, where people swarmed determinedly over the ground or gathered under awnings to pore over bits of stone. They found Remy in the largest of the open-air tents.

Remy Dupree looked much like his older brother, though his hair was a little longer and a little more bleached by the sun. His eyes were the same shade of green, and Val felt a whiff of the supernatural on him. He was a shifter, too.

There were differences, however. Remy was deeply tanned from spending all day outdoors, and he seemed more lighthearted, more prone to smiling and laughing. His eyes weren't haunted like Leon's, but then Remy hadn't seen war and brutal death like Leon had. Leon had spared Remy that by working hard and sending Remy to school, where he could bury himself studying the past. The realization made Val want to stand a little closer to Leon, to feel his warmth.

"We're working on the tomb of a prince," Remy said after he'd given Leon a bear hug and been introduced to Val and Demitri. "A pharaoh's son who didn't live to become king. The tomb was robbed eons ago, of course, but there are plenty of scraps left to thrill an anal archaeologist." He laughed a hearty, booming laugh, and Leon softened enough to grin at him.

"Look around if you want," Remy said. "I have a lot to do before dinner, and then we can talk. As long as you stay out of the marked off areas, you'll be fine. We have a cooler full of water and sodas if you need them."

He breezed off, his feet crunching on the hard-packed earth.

Val adjusted her scarf over her head and stepped out from under the awning, her sunglasses cutting the worst of the glare. The sky blazed bright blue, and sun shone on the white- and dun-colored cliffs. Demitri walked purposefully toward the excavation, speaking in easy Arabic to the Egyptians working there.

"He says we can go into this one," Demitri said after talking to a man standing by one of the dark openings that no one showed much interest in. "He says they've finished in there and uncovered good paintings. He thinks we're tourists."

"We are." Val ducked into the shadow of the tomb, happy to be out of the sun. She slipped off her sunglasses. "At least I am. I haven't been to Egypt in centuries."

"Centuries?" Leon's surprised voice fell flat against the narrow passage.

"The last time I was here was in the time of the Romans. Cleopatra was touring the ancient monuments, showing off her interest in Egypt's great past. I tried to warn her not to pit herself against Octavian, but she wouldn't listen."

"Did you have a hand in that debacle?" Demitri was farther down the passage, heading for the dark opening at the bottom. A string of electric lights hung above them, burning a steady path.

"Of course not. I was there to help one of Cleopatra's maids, who was able to slip away from the chaos and marry the soldier who loved her. *She* lived happily ever after."

Valerie felt the weight of Leon's stare. He gazed at her then Demitri beyond her, his expression fierce.

Demitri made it to the bottom of the passage, stepped into the dark room beyond, and flicked on a light there. Val heard him swear, and she hurried to join him. Leon ducked in behind her.

"Shit," Leon echoed.

The chamber was covered with pictures. Hidden in the earth for thousands of years, the colors were fresh and clean, unworn by wind and weather. Red, green, gold, and silver paint covered the walls and ceiling, the images orderly and even. What had made Demitri swear was that every scene was an erotic one.

Osiris impregnated Isis; gods strode across the wall with huge, erect phalluses. Smaller humans copulated across the next level of the wall, fertility being the theme of the entire sequence.

"I don't think this will cool us off," Valerie said.

"Why not?" Leon put his hands on his hips and studied the paintings. "It's not really porn, is it? That one is impossible." He pointed to a woman standing on her head with her legs wide open, two men with incredibly long penises spilling seed into her vagina.

"Exaggerated, maybe," Demitri rumbled. "The theory is possible." Both men looked at Valerie, and she flushed.

"Stop thinking about it," she admonished them. "You're supposed to be keeping Valenarian away, not figuring out how to share her." Her cleft began to ache. "We have to keep her quiet."

"That is so," Demitri said.

She could see that he was erect, no matter that he tried to turn and hide it. She imagined his long cock, nice and hard for her, his balls warm against it. Leon's hard-on was more noticeable, his tight jeans outlining his crotch.

Mmm, let me stand between them and put my hands on both of those fine phalluses.

Val felt the raw lust of the demon stir inside her, and she clenched her fists. "It's all right for you," she babbled. "If you two need to be sated, you have each other. In fact, you probably should take each other so you'll stop looking at me like you want to drag me down to the ground."

Silence. Val looked up to find Demitri and Leon both staring at her like she'd lost her mind.

"I'm not gay," Leon said, and at the same time, Demitri said, "He's mortal."

"He's not *quite* mortal," Val said. "I'm not sure what exactly he is, but there's magic in a shifter."

Demitri didn't look convinced. Leon, on the other hand, had gone red. "I don't do it with guys. If other guys want to . . . do that, they can, as long as it doesn't involve me."

Val shook his head. "Demitri's not a man. He's a demigod. They don't have the same rules as human beings."

"So I should have *sex* with him? You got to be kidding me."

She turned away. "We're in an uncomfortable situation, which is my fault. At least you two would be able to release. No need to keep it bottled up."

Leon's glare could have started fires. "No."

Val nodded, pretending to take his word for it. She noticed, though, that his erection hadn't gone down.

"Are we finished with ancient erotica?" Demitri asked. "No wonder that old man was laughing when he sent us down here."

"I'm done," Leon said curtly.

"The paintings are so beautiful." Val tilted her head back to take in the entire room. "It's like no time has passed at all."

Leon gave the pictures another brief look then headed for the door. He ducked out and was gone, but Demitri stayed, watching Val with a strange look on his face.

She smiled at him. "We look the same, too. Like no time has passed since we last said good-bye."

Demitri's eyes softened. "I regretted what I had to do." He tucked a lock of hair under her scarf, his fingers warm. "You will never know how much I regretted it."

His touch was strong. Val still remembered everything they did together three thousand years ago, every word shared, every look, every kiss. Even with the demon suppressed, her memories of Demitri were fresh.

Valenarian had loved him. She'd loved how the sun had touched his naked body, how his muscles had moved when he'd taken her into his arms. His lips had been pure delight to kiss, to lick, to nibble.

Val remembered running her hands down his back, feeling his firm ass against the cup of her palms. She remembered how deeply he'd penetrated her. The ecstasy had been beautiful, and had grown even more beautiful when she'd started falling in love with him.

"Demitri," she whispered. She slid her hand behind his neck, under his warm hair, and rose up to kiss him.

Demitri made a faint noise in his throat and laced his arm around her back. His kiss parted her lips.

It was still there, the spark that had ignited her, the brief happiness she'd thrown away. The love. The *desire*.

"You haven't changed at all, lover," she murmured, feeling hot inside. "Why don't you spread me as wide as I can go and put that *fucking* enormous cock inside me?"

Demitri shoved her away. He was breathing hard, his eyes wide, the tiger in him changing their color.

Val gasped. The demon laughed and ripped from her. With a final chuckle, Valenarian disappeared, leaving Val weak and terrified.

Sweat shone on Demitri's face. "The full moon is in two days. During that time, I think I'd better lock you in your hotel room."

Val nodded, shaken. "That would be best."

"Let's find Leon and leave this place."

Demitri made Val walk in front of him, and she heard his heavy footsteps behind her. They left the beautiful room behind them, with its erotic reminders of what Val had lost. The blank passage was like her life now, long and empty, undecorated, while the wild eroticism of the colorful tomb was like the world she'd left behind.

As they emerged, the elderly Egyptian still stood in his place to point tourists toward the tomb. The look on his face was one of great amusement. Demitri ignored him, but Val turned to stare at him. She wasn't certain, but his eyes and smile looked very much like those of the carpet shop owner in Cairo.

~ ~ ~

"STAY here tonight," Remy said to Leon when Leon returned to the dig house. "You can bunk with me."

Leon thought about Val and the scared look in her eyes when Demitri said she had to be taken for judgment for what she'd done. They might believe all the bleating about Aphrodite and demons, but Leon didn't. He wasn't sure what Demitri really meant to do to her, but Leon wanted to be there to prevent whatever it was.

"I can't. Not yet."

Remy looked past Leon to where Val and Demitri were picking their way back toward the camp, and he grinned. "I get it. She's a fine woman, Leon. Is she with him?"

"No. At least, not anymore."

"And you're sliding in? Does she like army medics from Louisiana?"

Leon shrugged. "I don't know yet."

Remy laughed. "Well, good luck. Let me know when you want me to find you a room you can share with her."

Leon couldn't say anything more, because Val and Demitri had caught up to them. Both of them looked unhappy; Val looked worried.

"What happened?" Leon asked them as they headed back to where the driver waited with the car.

Val answered, her voice shaking. "Valenarian almost came out again. We need to go back to Luxor."

They wouldn't say anything more. Once across the Nile and back at the hotel, Demitri took Val by the elbow and steered her into her room. The doors had old-fashioned locks, needing a key to open and close them. Val handed Demitri her key.

"What the hell are you doing?" Leon demanded.

"She can't be trusted."

"Yeah? Neither can you."

Demitri gave him a cold stare. "Valenarian emerged for a brief moment after you left the tomb. Val can't control her. She has to be locked in until we leave for the temple, just in case."

"He's right, Leon." Val's eyes were very light blue, no mistaking the change in them now. "It's safer for all of us if I stay secluded."

"Why don't you go back to the dig?" Demitri said pointedly. "I'm sure your brother will welcome your help."

"No way am I leaving her at your mercy. I don't want you deciding you need to take her to this temple and do a ritual murder or something."

Demitri closed his fist on the key. "I'd never hurt her. What Aphrodite decides, she decides, but I'd never hurt Val."

"Even though taking her to the temple might kill her?"

Val interrupted. "He's doing what has to be done, Leon. You have no idea how destructive Valenarian is. She could kill you without thinking about it. She's evil and brutal and can't be trusted. I'd sacrifice myself to keep that from happening. I'm tired of my half existence anyway."

Leon lost his temper completely. "This is bullshit. Both of you are crazy. There is no Aphrodite or sacred space in Luxor Temple, and I'm not letting this nut job kill you because you had sex with me."

Val's voice remained soft and matter-of-fact. "It's not the same as a human death. I'll simply cease to be. It won't hurt me."

"I don't give a damn. I'm not letting him do it."

"You have to," Demitri said tightly. "The goddess won't allow you to stand in her way. She'll obliterate you if you do."

Leon studied Demitri's immovable face, dark eyes that glittered with both rage and sorrow. Leon didn't understand what was going on here, but he knew he wasn't going to win the argument. He held out his hand.

"Give me the key."

Demitri's eyes narrowed. "Why?"

"I don't trust you. I'm fine with keeping her in there, as long as you can't get to her."

Power rippled through Demitri, like it had before he'd changed to his tiger. A thread touched Leon like a crackle of lightning. "You know nothing of this, mortal."

"I'm not exactly mortal, as Val keeps reminding you. I'll take you on any day."

Val folded her arms and frowned at Demitri. "Give him the key, Demitri. I trust him."

"And you don't trust me?" Demitri asked softly.

"No," Val said. She turned away from both of them and slammed the door.

~ ~ ~

DEMITRI slept fitfully. He lay naked under a thin sheet, the warm air making him restless.

He was acutely aware of Val on the other side of the wall. He knew each warm, even breath she took, when she turned over in bed, when she sighed in her sleep, when her hand drifted down to cup between her legs. She didn't rub herself; she only held her hand there, as though she found the touch comforting.

Demitri as well felt the almost human aura of Leon in the room beyond Val's, the man as wakeful as Demitri. Leon didn't trust Demitri, didn't believe any of this was true. Demitri couldn't really blame him, but it didn't matter whether Leon believed or not. Aphrodite had to be faced sooner or later. Better at a place of Demitri's choosing than waiting for her to strike.

Demitri sat up, punched his pillow, then lay back down and drifted into dreams.

He dreamed of the sunny plaza in Athens where he'd met Val for the first time. He saw her across the square, dressed in a gauzy wrap and veil that left her arms bare and showed a shadow of deep cleavage. Her glorious length of red-streaked black curls spilled down her back.

Men stared at her without bothering to hide either lust or disapproval. No woman seen walking the streets in Athens was respectable, by the fact of her simply being outdoors. Dutiful wives and daughters confined themselves to the home, while men and prostitutes had the run of the city.

Demitri let Val catch his eye. When she smiled at him, he moved to her, feeling her dark aura tingle in his blood.

It was easy to persuade her to come with him to the small, whitewashed room he rented, which contained little more than his bed and clothing. Demitri let her think she enticed him there. When they both were naked, she arched against him, her nails piercing the skin of his back.

At the small bite of pain, Demitri whirled her around and pinned her face-first against the wall. Val struggled, shocked, but she was no match for Demitri's strength.

"What are you?" she gasped.

"I'm Demetrius."

"My name is Val," she said, softening against the wall. "Nice to meet you."

Demitri leaned down and closed his teeth on her ear. "I've heard you've been a very, very bad girl."

"I have." She gave him a sultry smile over her shoulder. "I'll be as bad as you want me to be, lover."

Demitri licked the line of her jaw, his cock high and hard. He'd been told to seduce her, and never had a command been so easy to obey. He lifted her and leaned her forward, maneuvering until his cock slid right into her cleft. He pinned her wrists above her head on the wall, bracing her with his weight.

"*Very* nice to meet you," she laughed. "Are you always this friendly?"

"Stop talking."

"Anything you say, lover."

It was a raw, brutal fuck, and didn't last very long. Both of them were shouting in climax within minutes, then Demitri dragged her over to the bed and fell on it with her.

Val traced his cheek as he caught his breath, her eyes flickering from midnight to a blue like the twilight sky. "Who are you?" she whispered.

"I told you."

"Demetrius." She let the name roll off her tongue. "I'll call you Demitri. That will be my pet name for you."

Demitri had no interest in a pet name, but hearing her say it made his heart beat with sudden joy. He gently kissed the lips he'd bruised before. Valenarian couldn't hurt him—Aphrodite had reinforced his magic with her own to make sure of it. But Demitri could hurt her.

He nuzzled her hair, liking how it smelled. He pushed her back on the bed and pressed little kisses from her throat to her breasts. He moved to her navel, taking time to lick his way around it.

Val whimpered when he pressed his lips to the swirl of hair above her mons. She smelled damn good, and when he dipped his tongue between her quim's lips, he found she tasted good, too.

He drank her, then rose over her and put his lips to her mouth. "Taste."

She slowly licked his lips then pulled him down to her and kissed him. They kissed for a long time, exploring, tasting, getting to know how each other felt. Demitri rolled flat on his back, and she grinned and slid herself down on the bed to study his cock.

She knew exactly how to pleasure with her teeth and tongue and hands. Demitri's hips came off the bed, and his fists ground into the bedding. Val worked him while he spread his legs for her, letting her do anything she damn well pleased.

You must seduce her to capture her, Aphrodite had ordered. *You know how to do that, Demitri, from what I hear.*

Perhaps, but Val was seducing Demitri at the same time, making him want her like he'd never wanted a woman before. He was coming in her mouth in hardly any time, and Val smiled around his cock as she swallowed him down.

Demitri collapsed, panting, but he was barely spent. "Your turn."

He pushed her down into the bed and drank her again. When he lifted his mouth to hers, he nudged her knees open and plunged his cock inside her. They made love until they both fell asleep, two half gods with the strength to pleasure each other all night.

Demitri woke near dawn to see the pale smudge of her dress against the blue-painted door, Val trying to leave the dark little room. Demitri hooked one arm behind his head and watched as she opened the door. She took a step forward then stopped.

She stilled, puzzled, then put out her hand. She met nothing but empty air, but when she tried to walk forward, she ran into the shield of Demitri's will.

"You can't go until I say you can," Demitri rumbled from the bed.

Val whirled. He saw the rage in her eyes as her body brightened. "You have no idea who you are dealing with."

"Neither do you."

"You're a demigod. I figured that out."

"That's only part of it."

"This is only part of me, too, lover."

Val unwound her scarf and wrap, tossed them aside, and became a demon.

5

V<small>AL</small> was not what Demitri expected. Her body elongated and became so bright it was like looking into the heart of fire. Her limbs were strong and supple, her demon body even more shapely and beautiful than her human one.

She radiated power. Val could destroy the room, the house, the entire street, if she wanted to. Everyone would die, and only dust would be left. She laughed, stretching her bright arms, letting fire flow from her fingertips.

"I could bury you here, demigod, trap you forever. How would you stop me?"

Demitri pushed back the covers. He felt the familiar pull and twist of muscles as his body morphed, watched the world become black and white. Scents he'd ignored as a human assailed him—the people in rooms around them, the food they'd eaten, the sex he'd had with Val.

His tiger claws dug into the bed as he laid his ears back and snarled. Val stared at him in shock, then her sudden laughter rang to the ceiling.

"Oh, my, what a beauty you are." The demon flared once, then became Val the woman again. She climbed onto the bed, sinking her hands into his fur. "Why have you hidden your true self from me?"

Demitri let her stroke his head and back, but rumbled a warning. He could kill her quickly if he had to.

"How did you know I liked cats?" Val crooned. She lay down next to him and rested her face against his broad forehead. "You really do know how to tame me, don't you? My sweet Demitri, you don't have to hold me prisoner to get me to stay with you. I'll stay as long as you like."

She snuggled against him and went peacefully to sleep. Later, when full sunlight streamed through the shutters at the tiny window, Demitri morphed back to his human form and made love to her again, gently this time.

He'd made his decision. He wouldn't simply take her to Aphrodite. He'd watch over her, find out everything about her, give her a chance. She could do as she pleased, as long as he was with her.

So began the happiest weeks of his life. Demitri quickly discovered that he liked Valenarian. She had a quirky sense of humor, her laugh could warm him to his toes, and for some reason he could *talk* to her. Demitri conversed easily with his friends, but with Val he found himself opening up, telling her his deepest dreams and hopes and fears.

When she was with him, she was with him entirely. They walked together hand in hand; they sat on Demitri's rooftop late into the night watching the thick stars overhead. Sometimes they did nothing but lie on the bed together, holding each other; at other times they had sex that could start earthquakes. Val was skilled. She amazed Demitri with the things she could do, when Demitri had thought himself worldly and experienced.

Sometimes they'd go out into the countryside, where Demitri

would change to a tiger, and Val would ride on his back while he ran. He'd charge into the woods and lie down so Val toppled off, then he'd morph back into his human form and take her with tiger ferocity.

I don't need to give her to Aphrodite, he told himself. *As long as she's with me, I can keep her under control.* Aphrodite would kill Val, and as Demitri fell harder in love, he knew he couldn't let that happen.

Should he tell Val how he felt? He often started to, then Val would kiss him or do something flamingly erotic, and Demitri would remain silent. Valenarian didn't want love; she wanted excitement and sex. Demitri could give that to her and take everything she offered back. He wouldn't demand more.

He'd convinced himself that he could keep Val alive and with him forever—until the day he walked back into their room to find her on the bed astride a terrified man. She wasn't sexing him, but her hands were fiery claws that she'd started to bury in his chest.

The man stared at Demitri in wide-eyed hope. "Help me," he gasped.

"Val, let him go."

Val glared at Demitri, not moving he hands. Her hair was kinked into tight curls, her eyes midnight blue. "Adulterers must pay."

"I'm not," the man gibbered. "I looked, but my wife is dear to me. Please, I have children."

"*Val.*" Demitri stood poised, his tiger ready to tackle her. But he wanted her to make the choice, wanted her to spare the man of her own free will.

"I'm not interested in his pleadings," Val said. "I want to taste his blood." She dug her fingers deeper, and the man cried out. Demitri's heightened senses heard the man's pounding heartbeat, smelled his blood.

"Val, please stop."

"Let me have him, lover. Let me devour him. Share him with me."

Demitri grabbed Val and yanked her off him. She hissed and snarled, her body turning to demon under his hands.

"Run," Demitri advised the man.

The man leapt to his feet and fled out the door. People would see him running, his clothes in bloody shreds. They'd be coming.

Val's fire burned as she fought. Demitri had thought he could put her down fast, but in her rage she didn't care whether she hurt him. Demitri changed to his tiger and pinned her on the bed, claws biting into her chest.

"If this is what you want, lover . . . ," she said, stretching.

Demitri became human again, and so did she. "It's not what I want. We have to leave."

"Why?"

"They'll come for you. They'll drive us out."

"Who will?"

"The good people of Athens. They don't like to see their citizens mauled."

"Why do you care about what paltry humans want? We go where we please, do as we wish. They worship us and fear us. Let them come."

Demitri got to his feet and hauled her up. "No. We're leaving."

Val pouted. "Oh, well, I suppose I can punish adulterers as easily in Sparta or Persia, wherever you want. There are so many of them."

"You'll not punish anyone. That man hadn't even done anything."

She gave him a deprecating look. "Men all think about cheating on their wives and lovers. They should all die." She smiled a crazed smile. "Help me kill then, Demitri. Your tiger could hunt them down, and my demon can rip out their hearts."

A mad light burned in her eyes. Demitri looked at her, and his heart broke. He'd been a fool to think he could ever keep Val under control. She'd been letting him control her, behaving herself because she liked being with Demitri. But Val would get bored with their bliss, and she'd rampage again. She was already starting.

The pain of it tore at him. He'd allowed himself to get close to her, to fall in love with her. If he'd delivered her to Aphrodite right away, he'd have felt regret, but now it would hurt like nothing in his life ever had.

He pressed his hand against Val's and twined their fingers together. "I have a better idea. Why don't I take you to a place you're forbidden to go? A meadow so beautiful it will break your heart. We'll make love there, the best we'll ever have."

Her eyes flicked to a lighter blue. "You intrigue me. Where is this forbidden place?"

"Olympus."

Val smiled, her eyes sparkling. "Oh, lover, you are wonderful. A demon on the sacred mountain?" She wrapped her slim arms around Demitri's neck and kissed his lips. "Take me there, my love. You won't regret it."

~ ~ ~

DEMITRI woke in the hotel room in Luxor to find tears on his face. He threw back the covers and went to the window, opening it to let in the cool night air.

The dream made Demitri realize he was already tempted to make the same mistake he had in the past—to try to protect Valenarian despite the proof of her evil. If Valenarian was breaking free again, Demitri had to stop her.

He knew he was still in love with her—in love with the Val he'd laughed with and shared wine with, had kissed both playfully and passionately. But no one should die because Demitri was in love. Leon had been lucky that Valenarian had stopped at sex.

Demitri hadn't really wanted to watch them in Cairo—not at first—but he hadn't dared leave Val alone with a mortal. And then he hadn't been able to walk away. He'd burned with jealousy to see her with another man, and yet at the same time, it felt right that

Leon should be there. Demitri wasn't sure about that idea. He only knew he'd gotten hard watching them, and it had taken all his will-power not to walk in and join them.

Demitri left his room without dressing, walking down the empty hall to Val's door. He hadn't explained to Leon that he didn't need a key. He put his hand to the lock and whispered a word, and the door swung noiselessly open.

Val lay tangled in the sheets, her dark hair tumbling around her like strands of silk. She was heartbreakingly beautiful.

She slept quietly, her head cradled on her bent arm, her lips parted a little. Demitri wanted more than anything to climb in beside her, slide his arms around her, make love to her one last time.

Demitri watched her for a while, then he closed the door, locked it, and moved silently back to his own room.

~ ~ ~

VAL was dressed and ready by the time Leon softly knocked on her door. As she invited him in, she again regretted that she didn't remember being in bed with him in Cairo. He had a fine, hard body, his green eyes holding a warmth that she liked. He was rough and raw, so unlike Demitri, but he had a quiet sensuality that she appreciated.

His gaze raked her over as though he could see every inch of her body through her flowing clothes. "Ready for breakfast?"

Val nodded and joined him in the hall. "Did you sleep well?"

"Not really."

Demitri waited near the elevator, and they descended to break-fast together. Demitri kept close to Val like a bodyguard and wouldn't let her talk to anyone in passing.

As they ate breakfast, Val tried to start a conversation, but nei-ther man was interested. They spoke only to make a polite request for the salt or the coffeepot, if they spoke at all. It was as though three strangers shared a table.

Val was finishing her coffee when a smiling young woman

stopped at their table. "Excuse me," she said to Leon. "Are you Leon? Remy's brother?"

Both Leon and Demitri got to their feet, and Val stared in dismay. Val knew who she was, had pretty much been expecting her.

"I'm Felicia Mason," the woman said. "I work with Remy at the dig. I was meeting some of our sponsors here for breakfast, when I saw you in here, and thought you must be Leon. Do you know you look just like him?"

Leon agreed neutrally that all his brothers bore a great resemblance to one another. Demitri looked on, stone-faced, while Val ran her fingers around her coffee cup.

"Are you heading to the dig this morning?" Felicia asked after Leon made introductions to Val and Demitri. "I could give you a ride."

The woman was all that was bright and sunny. She was blond, with her hair caught in a practical ponytail. Slender from all the exercise she got on the digs, tanned from the sun. A pleasant face, hazel eyes that held intelligence, a winsome smile. The perfect woman to make Leon happy.

Val's heart burned in her chest. It was her task to bring these two people together, but never before had such a simple thing seemed so difficult.

She made herself stand. "I'd love to go back to the dig. It looked fascinating, and I'm sure Leon is anxious to start helping his brother."

Leon flicked her a surprised glance, but his stoic face betrayed nothing.

"We would be happy to," Demitri said in his deep voice.

"Sure," Leon said. They were back to being polite strangers.

"Great. Remy's already working. We start early, because of the heat."

Felicia talked in a friendly fashion as they headed for the west bank in her open Jeep. She pointed out monuments as they went, not seeming to notice that her companions rode in utter silence.

They made their way through bright green fields on the west

side of the river, until the cultivation ended abruptly and white desert began. Sweat trickled down Val's back to pool against her backside, and dust clogged her nostrils. Felicia, on the other hand, looked cool and calm, smiling under her sunglasses.

"Look who I found!" she called to Remy as they reached the dig.

Remy lay on his belly near an open hole, carefully brushing dust from something that lay within it. He climbed to his feet and grinned, cracking the sweat and dirt on his face.

"Welcome to hard labor," he said. "Leon, let me and Felicia show you around, while your friends have some cool drinks."

It was so impossibly cozy. Val felt the demon inside her stir with jealousy, Valenarian snarling to shove this bitch away and take her place at Leon's side.

Val seized Demitri's hand. "Cool drinks sound nice. I could use something very cold about now."

Remy called a student to lead them to the shade of the largest tent. Leon obviously did not want to let Val and Demitri out of his sight, but after seeing where they were heading, he finally turned and followed his brother and Felicia.

The grinning student gave Val and Demitri cold cans of soft drinks, then hurried away, saying a minion's work was never done. Val sat down and sipped the overly sweet drink. It was hot under the tent, but bearable with the sun kept at bay.

Demitri kept his gaze focused on the outcropping of rock where Remy and Felicia were talking and pointing while Leon looked on. Val sensed Demitri didn't want to be here with her but also knew he didn't want to leave her alone.

"Don't kill her," Demitri said, not taking his eyes from Leon.

Val jumped. "What? Who?"

"Felicia. I saw the way you looked at her, like you wanted to gouge her eyes out."

Val tucked her scarf more securely around her shoulders. "Don't be ridiculous. I don't kill women. Besides, she's my assignment. She and Leon are supposed to end up together."

Demitri's brow furrowed. "Are you sure?"

"I have dossiers on both of them. She's the perfect girl next door—lived in suburbs in some place called Michigan, was exceedingly good at her studies, went to college, fell in love with Egyptology, received a postdoc fellowship to come out here and work. Brainy, pretty, nice." She stopped. "Bitch."

"Are you always this pleased about your assignments?"

"I don't know. At least, I've never resented any before."

"Does this mean you're falling for Leon?" Demitri's tone was light, but he wouldn't look at her.

"How could I be? I only ever loved one man, and I doubt that will change." She gave him a significant look, then transferred her gaze to the bright desert.

She felt Demitri's stare. "If you mean you loved me, I don't believe you."

"You don't have to."

"Valenarian couldn't love," he said stubbornly.

"I adored you, Demitri. I always will love you, no matter what."

"Valenarian had to be stopped."

Val turned to him, her heart beating faster when she found his dark gaze directly on her. "I never blamed you. It was my fault for not controlling myself. We could have had something special, and I ruined it."

"We did have something special." His voice wrapped around her like sunshine.

"I know we did. I was just too stupid to acknowledge it."

"I wish . . ." Demitri trailed off. His eyes were haunted, the pain in them evident.

Val sighed. "Don't wish. It can never be. Just—when I'm gone, remember that I loved you."

Demitri closed his hand over hers. He bowed his head and kissed her palm, letting one tear trickle down his cheek.

The hot breeze stirred their hair and clothes. Outside Leon crouched at the base of a rock with his brother, learning about digging up the past. Felicia hung over them both, smiling and excited, a mortal woman untouched by darkness. *She* should at least find happiness, Val thought. Someone in this mess should.

~ ~ ~

Leon tried to concentrate on what Remy was telling him, but his attention repeatedly strayed to Val and Demitri under the tent. They sat side by side, seemingly resting, but Leon could feel the tension in them all the way over here.

Like hell he was going to let Demitri do anything to Val. If she did have a split personality, and one of those personalities was out of control, that wasn't her fault. She needed help, not Demitri's weird insistence that a goddess no one believed in anymore would judge Val and kill her.

No killing. Leon had seen enough of that. As a medic he'd cleaned off the bodies of young men who, first time away from home, had been shredded to bits by debris from bombs. Those boys hadn't done anything, didn't have evil thoughts or evil plans—they'd just been standing in the wrong place at the wrong time.

Why Leon had never been hurt in his two tours was beyond him. He'd accompanied platoons out, had patrolled the highway with them, had done everything from disinfecting insect bites to holding a man as he died. Even the chaplain couldn't tell Leon why he remained whole, though the man suggested that perhaps Leon hadn't filled God's purpose yet. At the time, Leon had thought that meant he still had to take care of his mother and brothers, but perhaps it meant he needed to come to Egypt and save Val.

Felicia said something, and Leon dragged his attention back to what Remy was trying to explain.

"When we remove the fill, we find things that got caught in it," Remy said, his Louisiana accent sounding both strange and familiar out here in the desert. "Beads, combs, little things people might have tossed out as unimportant. But they're important to us."

"Trash can tell you more about a civilization than treasures," Felicia put in.

Shit, these two finished each other's sentences. Leon glanced up to find Felicia's gaze resting on Remy's bent head, wistful hunger in her eyes.

Good. Baby brother needed someone, and this girl liked to dig in the dirt just like he did. They'd make a great couple.

"We keep the things we've already studied and cataloged in a storeroom at the dig house," Remy said, unfolding to his feet. Felicia casually looked away, pretending she wasn't interested in everything he did.

"Some of them are quite pretty," Felicia said. "Faience can be lovely."

"I'll show you," Remy said, then gave Leon a meaningful glance. "We can talk there."

"Bring your friends," Felicia said. "They'll enjoy seeing the artifacts."

Val would. Leon suddenly wanted to show her pretty things, wanted to watch her smile in delight. "Sure. I'll get her."

Remy grinned. "Leon has his eyes on that good-looking lady. He's ready to cut out her boyfriend."

"Ex-boyfriend," Leon said.

"See what I mean?"

Felicia smiled. She had straight, white teeth, courtesy of a Michigan orthodontist. "I can keep a secret. Although her boyfriend—sorry, ex-boyfriend—is pretty hot."

"Is he?" Remy looked over at the tent, the idea clearly new to him.

"Trust me. Some of the women out here haven't seen beefcake in a long time."

"Gee thanks, Felicia," Remy drawled.

"Archaeologists are always dirty and hunched over. They only clean up if they're being interviewed."

"That goes for the female archaeologists, too."

Felicia stuck her tongue out at him, and Leon had to look away. They were so sweet they were nauseating. His thoughts flashed to the future—Remy and Felicia coming to the bayous for Christmas, dragging their blond, sunny children behind them. The kids would romp around Uncle Leon's houseboat, play at being archaeologists, and be impossibly cute.

Leon's imagination put Val there with him, smiling at the children's antics and looking devastatingly beautiful as always. She'd bring them drinks from the kitchen, slip off her shoes as she walked out onto Leon's back porch.

Sure. Like that's ever gonna happen.

"Leon?" Remy waved his hand in front of Leon's face. "You awake?"

Leon straightened up and brushed off his jeans. "Yeah. I'm right behind you."

They collected Val and Demitri, and Remy led them all back to the dig house. The house was long and low, with bedrooms and a kitchen and living room opening to a central courtyard. One end of the U-shaped complex held two large rooms, one a lab with tables covered in instruments, from microscopes to computers. Through the lab was a storage room, the door to which Remy unlocked with a key on his crowded key ring.

The room was packed with shelves. Half the shelves were loaded with labeled boxes, the other half contained artifacts all laid out neatly. There were partially assembled pots, piles of potsherds, fragments of flat slabs covered with hieroglyphs. One shelf held beads of all shapes and sizes, another an assortment of tiny figures carved of stone and pottery. Val glanced over it all with interest, but Leon felt a bit dismayed. Some of this stuff was minuscule. It would be easy to smuggle out with no one knowing.

Remy's brother shut the door. "The missing things have all come from here."

Felicia nodded gravely, obviously in the know.

"You keep it locked," Leon said, looking at the door. "Who has the keys?"

"An inside job, you mean?" Remy shook his head. "The door is usually locked, but we let people in all the time. People working in the lab need to get in and out of here. It could be anyone."

"Are the things valuable?" Val asked, scanning the shelves.

"Not intrinsically," Remy said. "We've already photographed and recorded all the pieces that are in here, and they'll go to the Egyptian Museum in Cairo when we're done. The thief isn't going for the obvious stuff—our lab equipment and the computers. They specifically want the artifacts."

"Why?" Leon asked.

Felicia answered. "Collectors will pay a lot of money for antiquities, even small things like ushabtis and potsherds. It's illegal to take what we find out of Egypt, but people will pay a high price for these things and stay quiet about it."

Val peered at a long string of bright blue beads. "Some of it is beautiful. I love the jewelry."

"Faience," Felicia said. "It is pretty, even if it's only ceramic."

Demitri came to see what Val was looking at, then he tensed, his body stilling. Neither Felicia nor Remy seemed to notice, but Val looked at him sharply.

In front of them was a necklace of blue faience, the beads placed in order on a card, though whatever string had held them together must have long since dissolved into dust. At the bottom was the remains of a pendant. It looked like a flat charm with a woman etched into it, but the right half of the pendant was gone, the remaining edge ragged.

"Where did you find this?" Demitri asked, never taking his eyes from it.

Remy glanced at it over Demitri's shoulder. "In the fill from the tomb we're clearing. We never found the other part of the pendant. It might have broken off when the tomb was robbed, and the robbers dropped it. It might have come from another tomb entirely, maybe thrown away by the robbers because it was broken."

"No, this was broken deliberately, a woman split in half. It's a curse."

Felicia looked interested. "Are you sure? My specialty is Egyptian magic—spells and curses, rituals and things. I've never seen or heard of that one. I could research it."

Demitri shook his head but continued to gaze at the necklace. "It's not important."

The words were offhand, but Leon's senses sharpened. The necklace was important, very important, from the way Demitri's eyes had gone catlike, his slitted pupils widening. Demitri looked straight at Leon, then he closed his eyes and turned away.

~ ~ ~

LEON didn't get a chance to ask Demitri about the necklace. Demitri's driver came to fetch them back to the hotel in Luxor, and Demitri obviously didn't want to talk in front of the driver. Neither did Val. When they reached the hotel, Demitri sent for room service for Val, locked her in her room, gave Leon the key, then disappeared.

"Business," he said flatly when Leon shot him a questioning look. So much for that.

Leon showered off the limestone dust and sat down in his room to go over what Remy had told him about the layout of the archaeological site and who had the keys to the artifact storage room building.

Leon sketched it out, made a list of names, Felicia Mason included, and sat back to think. His conclusion was that anyone on Remy's archaeological team could be the thief, including the couple that kept the house. Terrific. He hoped Remy's faith in him wasn't misplaced.

Leon threw down his pencil and laced his hands behind his head. He needed to get real. Remy hadn't asked him to come all the way to Egypt because he thought Leon could help him hunt a thief. Remy had invited Leon because he thought Leon needed something to do. Leon had seen bad things, and Remy didn't want Leon sitting around in his houseboat outside Fontaine getting PTSD.

"Shit." Leon got up and stalked around his room. It was a large room, Demitri's friend having given them the best ones in the hotel. They had the entire floor to themselves—it had only three bedrooms and its own private pool and sauna.

Why the hell anyone would want to sit in a sauna when it was a hundred degrees outside, Leon didn't know. The pool sounded good, though. He changed into swim trunks he'd crammed into his duffel bag as an afterthought before he left home.

As he headed down the hall, he paused as he passed Val's door. She could swim with him. He started to get hard thinking about her stripped down for bathing; got even harder wondering whether she'd wear that gold chain around her waist into the water.

Leon made himself keep walking. If he let Val out, even to stay on the same floor, Demitri might take the key back from Leon. And Leon refused to leave Val at Demitri's mercy.

He swam alone in the small pool, liking stretching his muscles in the cool water. The shifter in him wanted him to change into some kind of animal that liked the water—a bear maybe, but he resisted. If someone on the staff came in and saw a grizzly bear frolicking in the pool, that would be just too damn hard to explain.

Leon dried himself off. What the hell, he'd give the sauna a try, too. He opened the door of the small enclosure, feeling a wash of hot air roll over his body. He stepped inside.

Demitri sat on a bench across from the door. His head was back, his eyes closed, and the big man wasn't wearing a stitch of clothing.

6

"HOLY shit," Leon spluttered. "I thought you had business to do."

Demitri open his eyes a crack. "I did. I finished."

"You want a towel?"

"No."

Leon debated swinging around and rushing out, leaving Demitri naked and alone with himself, but he refused to be intimidated. He was a medic. He knew what men looked like without their clothes.

He closed the door, shutting them into the stuffy, heated room. Leon sat on the bench on the adjacent wall, his knees nearly touching Demitri's.

"So tell me," Leon said as he leaned back. "Do all demigods grow them that big?"

"Very funny."

"Hey, if you don't want to use a towel, I'll make jokes. Talk about the elephant in the room."

"I'm sure your army friends liked your sense of humor."

"My army friends didn't keep their enormous cocks hanging out. I never in my life saw anything that big."

Demitri's gaze swiveled to him. "I don't much care what a mortal man thinks of my endowments."

"It's hard not to think about it, considering how much it's sticking out."

"You exaggerate."

"Not by much."

It didn't help that Demitri was hard. The long ridge of his penis lay over his abdomen, reaching almost to his navel. The man was in great shape, with sculpted muscles and flat abs. He had the kind of body Leon worked constantly to keep up, but Leon had never seen Demitri exercise.

"So," Leon asked, "was that erection caused by you thinking about Val?"

Demitri nodded. "I was remembering watching the two of you together."

Leon felt his own cock swiftly rise, but at least his was hidden by a towel. "Did we entertain you enough?"

"I was surprised by how much I liked watching her with you. I thought I'd be eaten up by jealousy, but I loved watching her find pleasure."

Leon's hot face flushed even more. "Are you always this blunt about sex?"

"If you choose to make comments about my penis, I will speak truthfully about sex."

"Yes, but you're talking about watching *me* have sex."

"With Val," Demitri said. "I liked watching her take you and shivering with it. I liked hearing her moan."

"I've got to be honest; I liked it, too."

"It's been a very long time since I touched her." Demitri's voice went soft. "Was she tight?"

Leon gave up. If Demitri could drop his inhibitions, so could Leon. It was almost a relief to.

"Damn fucking tight," Leon said. "And so wet. She was dripping with it."

Demitri made a noise in his throat. His cock extended a little farther, though Leon hadn't thought that possible. "Which way was best?" he asked.

"I liked taking her from behind. I could get in deep, and she clenched me hard. But I liked face-to-face best. I could kiss her, lick her nipples."

"She always tasted good."

"She still does."

"I'll never have her again," Demitri said, his voice hollow with regret. "But I can remember."

You can if you help her, Leon wanted to say, but he didn't want to spoil the moment. They were two men sharing a fantasy about a beautiful woman, and he wanted to keep on with it. If Val knew that they were talking about her, she'd probably roll her eyes. She was quite a lady.

"What was your best time with her?" Leon asked.

Demitri closed his eyes, considering. "On the roof of the house where I rented rooms in Athens. The stones would still be warm from the day's sunshine, even when the night was cool. Val would shed her clothes and stand over me, oh so beautiful. I sat up and drank her. She has the best pussy in the world."

"You've got that right."

"You're tenting."

Leon looked down at his lap. The towel had risen, his cock beneath pushing it upward.

To hell with it. Leon tossed the towel aside. He wasn't as big as Demitri, but he wasn't ashamed of what he had.

"I need release," Demitri said.

"Hey, you go for it, man. I won't look."

Demitri didn't move. He'd rested his elbows on the bench back, and his large hands dangled at his sides. "If my friends were here, they'd help me."

"Shit, what kind of friends do you have? Does Val know about these ladies?"

"Nico and Andreas. They're demigods, too. We've been friends for millennia."

Male friends. Leon remembered Val suggesting that Leon and Demitri sate themselves on each other. "So call them."

"They both married a few months ago. They went back to America to start families."

"Lucky them," Leon said, meaning it.

"I'm happy for them. They're both very much in love, and their ladies are beautiful."

"But it leaves you by your lonesome. I'm real sorry for you, even if I don't understand why men are gay."

"I'm not a man," Demitri reminded him. "And I'm not gay, as you call it. It is different in the world of gods and their offspring. We don't regard males having sex with males or females with females with the horror that many humans do. And it changes through the centuries—sometimes among humans it's taboo, at other times not."

"I was just never around it," Leon said. "Or if I was, the guy kept it to himself. I come from a small town, and some people didn't put up with it."

"I know. I learned all about you. Why are you not disgusted with me like the people in your small town would be?"

For one thing, Leon was enjoying sitting in here with this man, both of them naked, both of them talking about Val. Maybe having a woman in the equation took away his discomfort.

"I met a lot of people in the army. From all places, all races, all upbringings. I traveled around, learned different cultures, realized that people are pretty much the same, no matter how they grew up. Even if they like guys on guys."

"I like men on women. Or demigods on demigods."

"That's why when Val suggested you and I go for it, you said 'he's mortal,' like that made you sick."

"And she rightly pointed out you aren't mortal."

Leon's comeback died in his mouth. Demitri remained in his relaxed position, his eyes dark between half-closed lids. His voice had gone deeper, but not seductive. He was a man suggesting he and another man play together, but he might have been suggesting a swim or a game of one-on-one basketball.

"I've never in my life touched another man," Leon said. "I'm not looking to start now."

"Then we are both on our own."

"Looks like."

Demitri shrugged his large shoulders, then he reached down and closed his fist over his own cock.

~ ~ ~

VAL woke with a start. She lay still a moment, her breath quick, wondering what had awakened her. Moonlight streamed through the windows, curtains left open to catch the white light of the nearly full moon. She'd forgotten how intense light could be at night in Egypt.

Something hot prickled her skin. Val relaxed on her pillows and let it come. For a moment, she basked in the warmth of the feeling, then she sat up, realizing what she sensed. Sex. Somewhere close by, a man was releasing the sexual tension from his body. *Two men.*

Val went still, her blood thrumming and hot. She felt the demon stir inside, and hugged her knees to her chest.

She couldn't let it out. Valenarian was vicious—she might try to kill Leon. Val pictured Leon's tight body, his green eyes that had seen pain, a haunted man who was trying to be kind to the rest of the world. She remembered when he'd shifted back from the tiger, standing upright and naked, as beautiful as Demitri.

Move over and let me enjoy it, sweetie. Val felt her eyes changing, her body growing hot with the demon's fire.

No, please don't do this.

Wimp. Demitri is going to kill me anyway. At least let me go out enjoying myself.

I don't want to hurt them.

I can't hurt them. They're strong, powerful men, who aren't going to go down for the likes of me.

No, Val tried one last time.

Too late. Valenarian laughed, and Val lost her hold on reality.

She rose, pulled off the pajamas Valerie had donned, then shrugged on a silk robe. The door lock was easy to destroy with a small burst of demon fire. The door opened, and Valenarian was free.

She had no desire to rush out of the hotel and into the night. The pheromones of the shifters down the hall drew her like a magnet.

The pool room was really an enclosed area resting on the roof of the floors below, with awnings and plants to cool things down from the intense sun. At night, hidden lights illuminated the greenery, and moonlight reflected in the soft blue of the water.

On the other side of the pool were doors that led to dressing rooms and a small sauna. Val went unerringly to the door of the sauna, opened it, and looked in.

Her blood heated in delight. Leon and Demitri sat against adjacent walls, knees touching, each with a fist around his hard cock. Demitri had his eyes closed, his head bowed, and Leon stared up at the ceiling, his face relaxed.

Val paused to take in the delectable picture. Both men gleamed with sweat, Demitri's skin dark, Leon's lighter. Muscles rippled as they stroked themselves.

Demitri groaned softly. His cock was long and stiff; black hair curled at its base. Leon's was shorter but thicker, the wide rod

Valenarian now remembered penetrating her. Leon rubbed himself quickly, but Demitri's stroke was smooth and slow, practiced.

Val moved quietly toward them, not wanting to interrupt. She stopped in front of them and let her silk robe slide to the floor.

"Let me do that for you, lovers."

Demitri's eyes snapped open. The next instant Val found herself pinned against the opposite wall, Demitri's hand around her throat. He didn't squeeze—he'd never hurt her. She laughed.

Leon was on his feet, hands wrapping around Demitri's big arm. "Let her go."

"I thought you had the key," Demitri snapped at him.

"I do. It's in my room."

"Ordinary locks can't hold me," Valenarian purred. "You should know that."

Demitri's face hung close to hers. His eyes still held the frenzy of pleasuring cut short. "Fine, I'll add magic to it."

"Let me stay." Val pouted. She looked at Leon, who still clutched Demitri's arm. "If you're going to give me to Aphrodite, let me stay and play a little. One last fling."

"It's too dangerous."

"That's what Valerie tried to tell me. I don't know why you like her. She's so tame and worried."

"She doesn't slay people."

Val flicked a fingernail over Demitri's cheek. "Lover, I haven't slain anyone in thousands of years. You stopped me, remember?"

"Only because you've been sequestered for thousands of years."

"Please, Demitri. Do I have to beg?" She smiled. "Or would you enjoy that?"

"Stop it."

"The two of you are more than a match for a demon—a demi-god and a shape shifter, nice and strong." She let her nail trail down the side of Demitri's neck, then transferred her touch to Leon's muscular forearm. "You two can contain me. And both of you are going to go crazy if you don't release."

Demitri wanted her. She saw it in his eyes, in the tension in his body. She leaned to him and licked the hollow of his throat.

"One last time," she whispered into his skin. She felt his pulse pounding swiftly under her lips. "Leon is here to make sure I don't get out of hand."

She rose on tiptoe and kissed Demitri's mouth, then she turned her head and kissed Leon. Leon's eyes darkened with sudden passion.

"All right," Demitri said, his voice soft. "But it doesn't change what must happen."

"I know." Val shook out her hair, liking the way her silken curls felt on her skin. "I only want a chance to say good-bye, before boring Valerie takes over again."

Demitri traced her cheek. "I know."

"Command me, lover. Like you used to."

Demitri's hand tightened in her hair, and he pulled her forward for a hard kiss. "On your knees."

Val smiled as she lowered herself to the floor. She allowed no other man in the world to tell her what to do, but she loved it when Demitri mastered her.

She loved the long cock in front of her, too. Demitri's was perfect, a long, dark shaft that ended in a rigid knob, the tiny slit in the end beckoning her tongue. And joy of joys, another cock hung next to it: Leon's, because he wouldn't back up and let Demitri alone with her.

Val swirled her tongue around Demitri's tip then turned and did the same to Leon's. Leon took a half step back, sucking his breath in through his teeth.

"What do *you* want me to do?" she asked him.

"Suck."

Val grinned. "Stand facing Demitri. Put your hands on his shoulders."

Demitri knew what she wanted. He clasped Leon's shoulders and moved the man so that Val knelt between them.

"Closer," Val said.

Her heart hammered, her body so hot she thought she'd melt. Here she was, a big, bad vengeance demon, shaking and weak in front of two men. One was a demigod, true, but Leon was more or less mortal.

Leon's thighs tightened as he resisted. Demitri took one step closer to him, and Leon flinched as the tips of their penises touched.

What a beautiful gift. Val ran her gaze around the dark length of Demitri and up Leon's on her other side. Could a girl ask for anything more?

She traced a line across the double cock with her tongue. Demitri's tasted fiery and salty; Leon's taste was smoother. Val closed her eyes and enjoyed tasting where one cock ended and the other began.

"Damn." Leon's voice was slow and drawling. "You're gonna kill me."

Val smiled, feeling her power and liking it. She might be kneeling at their feet, but she could make them want her.

She separated the cocks with her tongue and rewarded Leon by sucking his into her mouth. He groaned and rocked his hips, and she took him faster.

Demitri gently bumped her cheek, his own cock wanting to tuck itself inside her mouth. She withdrew from Leon and closed her lips around Demitri.

Leon groaned. "Aw, don't stop."

Val suckled Demitri a moment, then changed back to Leon. His hand twisted her hair, but gently, not hurting.

She went back and forth, taking one, then the other. She had to open her lips wider for Leon but her throat more for Demitri. She hadn't had this much fun in centuries.

After a short time, Demitri's hand closed on her shoulder. "I can't take this anymore. Choose."

Val sat back on her heels and looked at the two delightful cocks stiff for her pleasure. She touched first Demitri's, then Leon's. Leon let out a soft swear word, and Demitri stood frozen, waiting.

"Demitri," she said. If she was going to have one last mouthful of come, she wanted it from the man she'd loved forever.

"That's not fair," Leon said. "Why's he better than me?"

She looked up at Demitri, and he looked down from his great height with his eyes golden like his tiger's. "Bring him off for me," she told Demitri. "I want both of you."

"What?" Leon broke off as Demitri reached over and wrapped his hand around Leon's cock. "Holy shit."

Val closed her mouth over Demitri at the same time Demitri started to stroke Leon.

~ ~ ~

"WAIT . . ." Leon's voice trailed off as Demitri's talented hand started to bring him to life. His brain didn't care whether the hand belonged to a man or a woman; it just wanted the pleasure.

Val knelt at his feet, her red lips firmly around Demitri's cock. She was beautiful, her dark lashes resting against her skin, her tightly curled hair tumbling down her back. She still wore the gold chain, which glinted against the sweet curve of her waist. Leon liked her breasts, firm little globes finished with dark red tips.

Watching her do Demitri got him more excited than he'd been in a long time. She knew how—suckling and then backing off and licking under Demitri's tip before taking him again.

At the same time, Demitri stroked Leon's hard cock. Demitri's hand was big and strong, powerful. Leon parted his legs so Demitri could reach farther, his own fists balling on his hips.

Never in a million years would Leon have figured he'd be standing in a sauna watching a woman suck off another man while that man gave Leon a hand job. He'd never thought he'd let another man touch him.

But he had to admit that a man would know what another man liked. Demitri flicked his thumb under Leon's tip at the same time

Val licked Demitri there. When Val took Demitri fully into her mouth, Demitri closed his big hand around Leon.

"Son of a bitch," Leon whispered. He rocked his hips a little, fucking Demitri's fist while Demitri fucked Val's mouth. Leon wanted to come, felt the buildup, the tingling rise that made him rock faster.

Not yet, not yet. Enjoy it. You'll get back to reality soon enough.

Val was so damn beautiful. She had her hands spread on Demitri's ass, sucking him for all she was worth. Demitri must be having one hell of a good time.

The big man's head was back, his eyes closed in rapture. His ponytail had come loose, and glistening black hair brushed his shoulders. Leon reached over and ran his hand through it.

Demitri opened his eyes halfway, a slow smile on his face. He sped up his assault on Leon's penis, while Leon let his arm come around the other man's back. He caressed Demitri's skin, liking how warm and smooth it was.

Demitri leaned to Leon, and before Leon could decide what he meant to do, Demitri slid his tongue into Leon's mouth.

Leon had never kissed another man, not even his brothers, and certainly not with tongue. He made himself stand still, unflinching, while Demitri explored his mouth.

A man's kiss. Women were softer, more questioning—*Do you like this?*

Demitri's kiss commanded, *You will like this, mortal man.*

Leon answered with his tongue and lips, liking the strange burn of whiskers against his mouth. *Only with this guy,* he told himself. *We're not going to pick out wallpaper together. Just damn good pleasure and sharing a fucking beautiful woman.*

Demitri kissed Leon harder, demanding acceptance. Leon kissed him back just as hard, refusing to surrender.

Then Demitri jerked his head back and groaned, his eyes closing. At the same time, he stroked Leon in short, quick pulls, and Leon felt his seed release.

"Fuck," he said, his fingers biting down on Demitri's shoulder in pure joy.

Valerie laughed. She caught Demitri's come on her tongue, then turned and tasted Leon's as it trickled out. "My lovers," she crooned.

Demitri pulled her to her feet. He wrapped his arms around her and kissed her. Val arched against him, her breasts tight against his chest.

"Hey," Leon said, kissing Val's cheek. "Share some of that with me."

Val broke from Demitri and kissed him. Demitri pulled her back to him almost right away, then he eased away from her and kissed Leon himself.

This was wild, the most sexual thing Leon had ever done. And there hadn't even been any true sex. Not yet anyway.

They shared kisses for a while longer, Leon and Val, Demitri and Val, Demitri and Leon. Tongues and lips, hands and bodies. It was fantastic.

Val gasped out loud, then she stumbled, her wide eyes going a shade of light blue. Demitri caught her before she fell.

"Are you all right?" Leon asked in concern.

"She's gone." Val put her hands to her face. "Valenarian is gone. Oh, Demitri, what have I done?"

Val gave them a wild look, and Leon couldn't hold back his disappointment. He'd wanted to fuck her until both he and Val screamed with it, but now she looked at them with frightened eyes.

Leon leaned over and retrieved her robe. He helped her slide it on, then tied the belt at her waist. "It's all right, baby," he said.

Demitri stroked her hair and kissed the top of her head. He looked subdued, almost sad. "Come," he said. "I'll take you back to your room."

7

DEMITRI ate breakfast with Val in her room, and hid his irritation when Leon insisted on joining them. Leon seemed uncomfortable, but Demitri ignored him. If the man couldn't handle mutual pleasuring, he could go to his brother's dig and bandage scraped knees.

What Val had given them was a beautiful gift. She knew she'd soon face the wrath of a goddess, but instead of taking her unhappiness out on Demitri and Leon, she'd given them pleasure. Great pleasure. *Something to remember me by,* she'd said. As though Demitri could ever forget her.

Leon might not be able to look Demitri in the eye, but the glances he gave Val were of a man falling for a woman. Trouble. Leon couldn't understand the danger a loose demon could cause, especially one as volatile as Valenarian. She'd only been gentle last night because she liked them.

"So what do we do today?" Leon asked as he scraped an American breakfast of steak, eggs, and potatoes around his plate. Demitri satisfied himself with bread and hummus, and Val demurely ate yogurt.

"I'm staying here," Val said. "Less risk."

Demitri put a hand on hers. "Are you sure? I'll be close to you if you want to go somewhere. I won't let her come back."

"And I'll be on the other side of you," Leon put in grimly. He'd returned to his belligerence, and Demitri knew he'd have to fight Leon tonight.

Val looked wistful. "Perhaps if I could see Karnak one last time . . ."

"Of course." Demitri started to squeeze her hand, but she snatched it away. "I'll take you there."

"And me," Leon said. Yes, he could become a problem. "Something I meant to ask you yesterday, Demitri. What is the deal with that necklace you were looking at? The one at my brother's excavation?"

Demitri recalled the long necklace of faience with the broken pendant. "It may mean nothing. It's a necklace made to curse someone, but it's a curse that can be undone."

Val's sad look was replaced with one of interest. "You said the pendant had been deliberately split?"

"It's a broken woman. The pendant was whole at first. In ancient times, a person would buy the pendant from a maker of magic objects. They'd give it as a gift to someone they wanted to curse, then break the pendant. The broken bit would be destroyed or hidden. If the cursed person could find the broken part and put the pendant back together, the curse would be lifted."

"What kind of curse?" Leon asked. "What was supposed to happen when the pendant broke?"

"Insanity. The broken woman means a broken mind. Someone who has been split in half inside, who might be mended if the two halves of the pendant are rejoined."

Leon looked at Val, and she raised her brows. "An interesting idea. But I wasn't cursed by an Egyptian buying a trinket from a magician. Aphrodite erased my personality, or tried to. She didn't quite succeed, obviously."

"It's worth a try," Demitri insisted. "If we find the second half of the pendant, the magic might work in reverse. Perhaps it could be used to make a broken woman whole again."

"Why would you want me to be whole? Don't you want Valenarian gone for good?"

"Because I think it's the key. You can't be Valenarian, because she's too deadly. As Valerie you can't control the demon, can't even remember what you do when the demon takes over. But if you can be both, in equal balance, maybe then you won't have to be destroyed."

"Then I say let's find the pendant," Leon said.

Demitri knew what the man was thinking. Leon didn't believe Aphrodite or Valenarian were real, but he'd go along with finding a "magic" cure for Val if it kept Demitri from talking about Val being judged and eradicated. Leon was protective of Val, which Demitri liked, even if he was protective for the wrong reasons.

"We don't have time," Val pointed out. "The full moon is tonight."

"We can look. We can also ask Aphrodite for the time to find it and try it. She doesn't necessarily want you dead, Val, she wants Valenarian stopped. She said she wanted you whole. If we can make the broken woman whole, maybe we can save you."

"I'm all for that," Leon said.

Val sighed. "Do I have room to argue? I can't say 'No, please, Demitri, don't try to save me.' I think it's futile, but I won't stop you from trying."

"I'm glad you have so much confidence in me," Demitri said dryly.

"I do in *you*, but not in Aphrodite. She can be arbitrary and odd."

"Like all the gods in the Greek pantheon," Demitri agreed. "They're arrogant and egotistical and enjoy making our lives hell."

Leon stared at them. "My very Catholic mother would be crossing herself about now. Maybe sprinkling holy water over the two of you."

"Her belief doesn't mean the gods aren't real," Demitri said. "They don't interfere in the lives of humans much anymore, but they squabble among themselves, and with the demigods they sired."

"Fine, just don't mention it around my mother."

"I'd love to meet her," Valerie said, turning her smile on Leon. "She must be very strong, having to raise four boys all on her own."

A fond light entered Leon's eyes. "She is. She never pushed us to do what she wanted us to; she just gave us the tools and sent us off. She's a good woman."

"You deserve a good woman, too," Val said softly. "One to take care of your children."

"I don't have any children."

"You know what I mean. To bear you strong sons and daughters."

Leon snorted. "I'm not thinking about getting married anytime soon. I'm too restless and messed up. Besides," he added, "I've already met the woman of my dreams."

"Felicia?"

Leon nearly choked on his coffee. "Felicia? The archaeologist woman making eyes at my brother?"

"You didn't find her attractive?"

Leon looked blank. "I didn't find her anything. She's obviously in love with Remy, except he's too stuck in his artifacts to see it."

"You think she's in love with him?" Val sounded baffled.

"Didn't you see her? She couldn't take her eyes off him."

"But she approached *you* yesterday in the restaurant. Came right to you."

"Because I look like Remy. I bet she thought I was him sitting there, which is why she rushed over. She only remembered he had a brother coming to visit when she realized I wasn't Remy."

"But that's not—" Val broke off and clamped her lips shut.

"That's not what?"

"Nothing. Never mind."

"What?" Leon peered at her. Val shook her head quickly and went back to eating her yogurt.

"I think you're crazy," Leon said. "But I guess you already know that."

"You're right," Val agreed. "Valenarian is mad. But Demitri is wrong about one thing." She licked her spoon. "What Valenarian did last night—that, I remember."

Demitri came alert. "You remember the sauna?"

"Oh, yes." Her eyes went a darker shade of blue. "I wasn't in control, I had no will, but I remember." She gave the yogurt spoon another thoughtful lick.

Leon flushed. "I remember, too."

Val glanced at Leon through lowered lashes. "Of course you do. And I remember what a very fine cock you have, and how nice it tasted. Thank you for giving me the memory."

Leon's face grew redder. "Sure."

"I think he's shy, Demitri."

"Not exactly," Leon said. "But I'd appreciate it if you wouldn't mention, outside of the three of us, that you saw me kiss a man."

"You liked it." Val smiled.

"Yeah, I did. Keep it to yourself."

Demitri remembered the fire of kissing Leon. Demitri had never touched a mortal male before, finding them too crude for his tastes, but Leon was different. Perhaps because Leon had some magic in him? Demitri didn't know. All he knew was that Leon's tongue was talented, and his cock had felt fine against Demitri's palm.

I don't have to live with him and buy him gifts, he told himself. *I enjoyed him, and it is over.*

Leon dug into his breakfast, concentrating on it to hide his embarrassment, not looking at Val or Demitri. Val finished her yogurt and drifted to the bathroom to ready herself for their outing to Karnak. The conversation about what happened in the sauna was finished. For now.

Demitri's hired driver took them the short distance to the temples at Karnak, crowded with tourists. Buses lined the road outside, and flocks of people of all races and nationalities followed tour guides like ducklings behind mother ducks.

Val looked about with nostalgic wistfulness as they walked past the small sphinxes to the entrance. "There was a canal here," she said, pointing to the paved courtyard. "It led to the Nile. I remember how, at the Festival of Opet, they'd bring out the statues of the gods and take them up the river to Luxor Temple. It was quite a celebration. Everyone in the country would come, and the pharaoh would honor the gods, especially Amun and Mut. There was food and drink, dancing and acrobats. Wonderful times."

"When was this?" Leon asked.

"About thirty-five hundred years ago."

Leon stared at her in disbelief, then looked away, clearly deciding this was part of Val's madness.

"Hatshepsut ruled then," Val went on. "A woman who had the courage and wherewithal to become pharaoh herself. I liked her. I didn't mind helping her rise to power."

She confirmed what Demitri had suspected, that Valenarian's hand had been in the oracle that declared that Hatshepsut would become a female pharaoh. When Hatshepsut died and Val left Egypt, the new pharaoh, Hatshepsut's nephew Tuthmosis, did his best to obliterate all traces of Hatshepsut from the records. No coincidence there, Demitri thought. Val's magic had departed.

Today, Val didn't seem to have a destination in mind as she wandered through Karnak. She looked around her as though seeing the halls and sanctuaries as they had been in the past. The huge papyrus columns that now held up nothing had supported a roof covered with pictures, the walls telling tales of the gods.

Val moved through the huge columns, Leon studying the hieroglyphs with interest but no understanding. Val eventually left the main temple and hiked across uneven, treacherous, weed-strewn ground to the north side of the complex. No tourists lingered here; they preferred the wonders of the pylons and obelisks in the main temple. Val stopped near a wall and a series of half-ruined gates that led in a straight line to an inner sanctuary.

"What's this place?" Leon looked at the brochure and map of Karnak he'd picked up. "The Temple of Ptah. Who's Ptah?"

"The father of all the gods," Val said. "Like Saturn, and Uranus of the Greek pantheon."

Leon looked doubtful. "I've heard of Isis. That's about all I know about Egyptian gods."

Val gave him a sorrowful look. "They're so forgotten now."

No other tourists seemed interested in the Temple of Ptah. The door to the inner temple was locked, but Demitri found an attendant to open it for them.

Val walked slowly, studying the walls and the black granite statue of Sekhmet, lost in her thoughts. Leon stayed near her protectively, and Demitri watched them both from the doorway.

"I would have thought you'd prefer the Hatshepsut monuments," Demitri said. "To remember your achievements."

Val shrugged. "Too many people tramping over things nowadays. They don't reverence things like the priests of old did. Hatshepsut was a god on earth, even if she had a mortal body, but no one believes that now."

"Do you remember everything Valenarian did back then?" Demitri asked in curiosity.

"I have all of Valenarian's memories—well, most of them. And all of Valerie's. Valenarian is right: Valerie is a dull woman."

"I don't think so," Leon said defensively. "I think you're just right."

He kissed her lightly on the lips. Val flinched, and Demitri held his breath, waiting for Valenarian to come out.

Nothing happened. Val smiled at Leon. "Thank you."

Demitri went to them and turned Val's face up to his for a kiss. She darted her tongue into his mouth, but the kiss remained sweet, no demon fire. Demitri kissed her again, then studied her eyes, which remained light blue.

Val stepped away from him, her look hopeful. "Perhaps we sated her yesterday," she said.

Leon flushed. "It was intense. I've never done a threesome before."

"You still haven't," Demitri said.

"Because we didn't have full sex? Doesn't matter. That was the closest I've ever come. I still don't know why I did that. I've always been a vanilla kind of boy."

Val smiled. "Valenarian is good at releasing inhibitions. But it doesn't matter. You'll forget all about me when I'm gone."

"No, I won't." Leon kissed her again. "I'll never forget you."

He would. Mortals who survived Valenarian always forgot her, for their own good.

"But you'll still have Demitri," she said.

Leon glanced at him. "Not without you."

"I agree," Demitri said.

Val grinned. "I don't know. You were enjoying each other's company when I walked in."

"We were horny," Leon said. "Nothing we could do about it."

"Kiss him now," Val said to Leon. "While you're not aroused."

Leon shook his head. "I was pretty wound up last night."

"Please. I want to see you."

Leon started to argue, but Demitri stepped between them. He looked into Leon's green cat's eyes, then caught him by the nape of the neck and gave him a deep kiss.

Leon started, then met Demitri's tongue with a flicker of his own. Leon's mouth was hot, with a salty taste that Demitri liked. The kiss turned rapid and bruising.

Val's laughter rang through the temple. "Don't hurt yourselves."

Demitri pulled Leon closer. He felt Leon's hand grip his ass, his answering kiss as hard as Demitri's. Andreas used to kiss like this—but then, Andreas was a were-leopard. Maybe all shifters were fierce kissers.

Leon pulled away, breathing hard. "Damn. I don't know why I liked that."

"I do." Val smiled at him, then slid her hand in his. "Demitri is hard to resist."

Leon slanted Demitri a wary glance. "Yeah, well. Like I said, don't you dare ever tell anyone I did that."

As they left the temple, the attendant closed and locked the door. He watched them go with a secret smile they didn't notice. "Not a soul," the small god Bes said.

~ ~ ~

VAL noticed that Leon had stopped arguing with Demitri. As they prepared for their midnight visit to Luxor Temple, Leon didn't say anything at all.

Val dressed in a gauzy white robe with a deep hood, and Demitri carried a similar robe, planning to wear it when they got there. Leon looked at them askance and stuck to his shirt and jeans.

Luxor Temple was not far from their hotel, and they walked together to it, Val pulling her hood over her head. The temple had officially closed at nine, though it was still floodlit, the columns and statues beautiful in the lights' yellow glow. Demitri confidently strolled past the row of sphinxes that led to the entrance. He moved like smoke, the security guards noticing nothing.

Leon followed, looking alert but asking no questions. He'd been very, very quiet since they began, and now he proved he could move like smoke, too.

They walked unimpeded through the courts, feet making almost no noise on the pavement. Like Karnak, this temple had been so different during Hatshepsut's time. It had been much smaller, with walls and columns painted with scenes to honor Amun and Mut. Later pharaohs had enlarged and embellished it with reliefs and paintings. The paintings showed the temple alive with royalty and acrobats, a bounty of food and wine, celebration and glory.

Now all was silent, the paintings faded. A cool wind blew through the open roof, the wide columns holding up nothing. In the inner hypostyle hall, a forest of rearing columns, Demitri stopped and opened an electric lantern.

"Here."

"Why didn't the guards see us?" Leon spoke in a low, murmuring voice, no hissing whispers.

"I have magic that will dampen sound and distract attention."

Val knelt next to Demitri and the light. "It was handy for muffling the sounds of sex. We used to be quite noisy."

"I'll bet." Leon looked skeptical but didn't argue. "What are you fixing to do?"

"Summon the goddess," Demitri said.

Leon looked up at the moonlight shimmering on the columns. "This is the sacred space you were talking about?"

Val answered. "The ancient pharaohs built this temple to the gods, to honor them, but this place was sacred even before that— to fertility gods and goddesses who made the sun rise and the crops grow. Aphrodite is a fertility goddess when all is said and done."

"Kind of all connected, in a roundabout way."

"Connected through sacred space, yes." Val could feel that connection here, the ancient power and bonds of the gods and their ties to the cycle of life. "Eons ago, there were only a few gods, one pantheon, if you can call it that, and the world was in harmony. When they each became enamored of their own peoples they split off, going elsewhere in the world, forming pantheons of their own."

"If that was true, it would knock a few world religions on their heads," Leon said. "Not to mention the theory of evolution."

"Only if you believe in them."

Demitri's mouth turned down. "It's time, Val."

Val nodded. The moon was directly overhead, round and full, and she heard the whispers of the gods as they moved through the columns. Some were stronger than others, some mere ghosts, but they still lived, watched, waited.

Demitri cupped Val's face in his warm hands. His dark gaze roved it, and he leaned down and brushed her lips with his. "I'm sorry, love."

Val brushed a lock of hair from his face. "I've always loved you, Demitri."

Demitri kissed the line of her hair, his breath warm. His arms slid around her. "I won't leave you. Whatever happens, I'll be with you."

"And me," Leon said grimly.

Val reached over and pressed her hand to Leon's cheek. His skin was warm to her ice-cold fingers. "Thank you."

"I won't let her hurt you," Demitri promised.

"It's all right." Val kissed Demitri one more time, then Leon, then she withdrew from them both. "I have to face this."

Demitri nodded, anger and pain in his eyes. He donned his robe and knelt next to her. Leon said nothing as he joined them.

Val leaned forward over her knees until her forehead touched the dirt floor. She stretched her hands behind her on the stones, palms upward. "Mistress," she murmured in a language so ancient it predated the writing on the walls around them. "Hear my supplication."

Wind whispered above them, sliding around the thick columns and their splayed tops. A night bird called over the river, and cars rumbled on the street behind the temple.

For a long time nothing happened. Leon moved restlessly, though Demitri sat utterly still. Val's hood partly obscured her vision, but she became aware of a growing brightness that wasn't the lantern.

Leon got to his feet. Demitri remained kneeling beside Val, his white robes making him look like a priest of old.

"What is *that*?" Leon demanded.

Val didn't dare lift her head. She took comfort in the sight of

Demitri's thigh near her, of the thick-soled combat boots Leon wore.

The brightness grew, and with it, heat. The entire hall lit up as though warm sunshine poured onto it. The paint on the columns reverted to its original clarity, and the crumbling stones under Val became solid.

"What the fuck?" Leon rasped.

Val raised her head and slowly sat up. The temple was whole and unblemished, the roof soaring overhead. The only sound outside was the rush of the river and wind in the reeds—no traffic, no people.

"It isn't real," Val told him. "This is the temple at the height of its greatness, but it's an illusion."

"She likes to make an entrance," Demitri rumbled.

Again they waited. The temple was enclosed now, no open view of the Nile and modern Luxor. One moment the three of them were alone in the cool, shadowy place, the next Aphrodite stood with them, clad in the same kind of gauzy white robes Val and Demitri wore.

The difference was, Val and Demitri had donned the thin robes over their clothes, while Aphrodite was blatantly naked beneath. The robes enhanced more than hid her firm breasts, slender waist, and curving hips. The thatch of hair between her legs was ebony black, like the hair on her head.

Leon flinched, but he didn't look away. Mortals could be overwhelmed by her beauty, even die from gazing upon her if she wished it, but Leon held his ground. Aphrodite smiled at Leon with sensual red lips. She liked being admired.

"Well?" Aphrodite said to Val. "I'm here. What do you want?"

8

VAL bent again in her posture of supplication. "Mistress, I confess to you that I broke my vows. I had carnal pleasures with the demigod Demitri and the human shape shifter Leon, in violation of my oath of celibacy. I allowed the demon Valenarian to escape her prison in my mind and take over my body. She seduced the shape shifter, whom I was assigned to join to another woman. I bring these two men as witnesses to my crimes."

Val closed her eyes, her speech finished.

"It wasn't her fault." Leon's harsh voice rang through the hall. "She didn't understand what she was doing."

Val looked up to see Aphrodite pin Leon with a deadly glare. "You would defend her?"

"Yeah, I would. Whatever weird thing you have in mind, I don't want you hurting her."

"You dare defy a goddess, mortal man?"

"I protect Val."

Leon still didn't believe, Val could see. Aphrodite looked him up and down, her lip curled.

"Demitri? Why don't you control this mortal?"

"Because I agree with him. It wasn't Val's fault. She did everything she could to suppress the demon, and if Valenarian emerged, it was because she broke your magic."

Aphrodite's eyes burned red. She was still breathtakingly beautiful, but now she was terrifying. "Are you saying it was *my* fault?"

"You knew this would happen," Demitri said. "You knew she was unstable, yet you sent her here and put temptation in her way."

Aphrodite raised her hand and let fly a bolt of light. Val screamed. Leon lunged across the empty space and knocked Demitri out of the way. The bolt burst stones in the wall behind Demitri with a sharp explosion.

Aphrodite lowered her hand. "Your mortal defends you. Interesting. Very well, then, he shall share your fate."

Val stepped in front of both men, but they closed in behind her, hulking warmth at her back. "They don't deserve to be punished for what I did. Demitri tried to stop me, and Leon was innocent, unaware of what I was."

Aphrodite scowled. "But Demitri didn't succeed, the shifter *did* discover what you were, and they both still let you seduce them in the hotel yesterday evening. How wonderful to enjoy two beautiful men at once."

"I will go readily to my fate if you let them go back to their lives," Val said.

She wasn't afraid. As she'd told Leon, she'd simply cease to be. She feared more that Valenarian would hurt or kill Demitri and Leon if she remained out of control. Valenarian had great strength, and she'd been holding back.

"It isn't that simple, Val dear." The red left Aphrodite's eyes, and her voice returned to normal tones. "I don't want to kill you, I want to save you, but that path will be very, very difficult."

"Save me?" Val glanced at Demitri.

"Yes, dear. I've grown fond of you, and Demitri's heartbreak is more than I can bear. I *am* the Goddess of Love, you know."

"What does that have to do with how dangerous the demon is?" Val demanded. "I can't control her anymore. I never could."

"But that is exactly what you must do. You must learn to control Valenarian, integrate her into the being that is Valerie, my priestess."

"Integrate her? How?"

"That is up to you."

Val stared at her. "Why would you want me to do this?"

"I don't, necessarily. I like you when you're obedient and sweet Valerie." Aphrodite sighed, a sound like a soft summer breeze. "The male gods, you see, especially Apollo and Zeus, have issued me a challenge. They want you dead."

"But I've never hurt them, or anyone under their protection."

Aphrodite sighed again. "They aren't fond of female vengeance demons who like to murder promiscuous men. They fear you, dear. They have issued a challenge. Either you change Valenarian's destruction into goodness, integrate her personality and Valerie's, or you die. And not a nice clean death, either. They propose something horrible and godlike."

Val's heart beat in fear. The Greek gods were good at terrible punishments, like Prometheus having his liver pecked out every day.

Sweat beaded her lip. "How am I supposed to achieve this? I can barely keep Valenarian under control as it is—she can take over without me even knowing it."

Aphrodite gestured to Demitri and Leon. "You have your two men to help you."

"Leon is supposed to fall in love with Felicia."

"No, he isn't. That was a little invention of mine, an excuse to send you to Egypt. Felicia Mason and Remy Dupree are the match. Do try to push them together while you're here, will you?"

"If Leon and Demitri help me, and I don't succeed, what happens to them?"

"They share your fate."

Val balled her fists. "Then I don't want their help."

"I'm afraid you can't succeed without it. It's another part of the test, forcing Valenarian to need the help of male creatures. A delicious irony, they think."

"But Demitri and Leon are innocent. They're only here because of your interference—you're the one who made Demitri capture me in the first place, all those centuries ago."

"Demitri is Apollo's son," Aphrodite said. "Apollo is willing to risk him to stop Valenarian."

"How very fair-minded of him," Val said in a hard voice. "What about Leon?"

"His own fault for welcoming you into his bed instead of throwing you out."

"He wouldn't have been able to fight Valenarian."

"He didn't know that."

Leon put his hand on Valerie's shoulder. "Hey, Val, I don't mind, no matter what she says. If I can help you, I will."

Val swung to him. "You have no idea what you're promising."

"She's right about that," Demitri said to Leon. "No idea at all. This is god business, and mortals have no place here."

"I keep telling you, I'm not a normal human being."

Demitri ignored him. "Let Leon go and help his brother," he said to Aphrodite. "He doesn't need this."

Aphrodite shook her head. "It's not up to me—Apollo and my father have already decided. My role is to keep watch and report the results. You have until the new moon, fourteen days."

Fourteen days. Two weeks. Half an eyeblink to Valenarian, who'd lived thousands of years. Half an eyeblink that would determine the fate of the two men beside her.

"I haven't the faintest idea where to start," Val protested. "Or how."

Aphrodite adjusted the filmy drape across her bosom. "You have been given a clue already."

"The broken pendant," Demitri said.

"Very good, dear boy. If, when you find the missing bit, the two halves fuse together, then you have been successful. If they remain broken, then you will know you failed."

"What if we can't find the other piece?" Leon asked. "It could be anywhere."

The goddess shrugged. "That, too, will indicate your failure. I'd start looking right away, were I you. Now, I really must be going."

"If you could wait one more minute," Leon said, his voice angry. "How is this a challenge to *you*? Seems like we'll be doing all the work and suffering all the consequences."

"Because I'll *worry* about Val," Aphrodite said. "I'll likely not sleep, and I'll get bags under my eyes." She delicately touched her face. "That would be a disaster."

"Yeah, I can see that."

"I'm glad you understand how important it is that you succeed." Aphrodite's body started to brighten, the light growing in intensity. "By the way, Val, I release you from your oath of celibacy. Temptation will be much more difficult to resist if you don't have the oath to hide behind."

Val gasped as she felt something ripped from her. "Wait . . ."

"Now, I really must go. Don't fail me, Val. There's a good girl."

The light grew until it burned like a bright star. Val screwed up her eyes against it; then, suddenly, the light went out. They were standing in the ruined temple, its walls and roof gone again. Late-night traffic flowed past on the streets outside, in twenty-first-century Luxor.

~ ~ ~

LEON woke in his bed alone the next morning. He barely remembered the walk back to the hotel from the temple, moving quietly through the dark. He'd felt half-asleep and numb, trying to piece together what had happened.

He remembered the goddess, though, the terrible beauty of her and the weight of her power. Years ago he might have dismissed the encounter as theatrical lighting and picture projection. But he'd spent enough time in this part of the world that he knew the mysterious didn't always have ordinary explanations. In the ancient ruins of Egypt, it was easy to remember that the old gods were powerful, that people had worshipped them for thousands of years.

He also knew that it didn't matter what he believed. Val was in trouble, and Leon would help her. However weird the task was, he was not a man who walked out on his friends.

Leon showered and descended the staircase to the main floor. He found Val and Demitri eating breakfast in the high-ceilinged dining room. He felt out of place in all this opulence, but he slid into the empty chair the waiter held out for him. Last year he'd been eating rations heated in his helmet; he couldn't quite get used to tables laid with exquisite china and seven different kinds of forks.

Val said nothing. She ate her small meal in silence, and when Leon finally got her to look up, he saw terror in her light blue eyes. He reached over and covered her hand with his. Leon was used to taking care of people: his brothers, his mom, the guys he patched up in his platoon. He'd take care of Val, too.

Demitri suggested they take rooms in a hotel on the west bank for a while. His friend would let them keep the bulk of their things in their rooms here, but they might need to be closer to the dig to look for the missing piece of the necklace. Leon agreed, wanting to get started helping his brother as well, though he wondered how the hell Demitri afforded to rent two sets of hotel rooms. Leon had some money stashed away for himself, but it wouldn't last forever, and he'd never be able to pay Demitri back. Another thing to bug him.

The three of them didn't say much as they split to pack. Leon quickly threw things into his duffel bag and met the other two in the lobby. They took a taxi to the ferry landing, Demitri deciding to dismiss the driver he'd hired. They wouldn't need him in the west valley.

Once across the Nile, Demitri found another taxi that took them to a small hotel near the ticket office for the west bank's monuments. Inside the suite Demitri had booked for them Leon stared out the window at the towering statues that stood like sentinels, marking the way into the valley of the dead.

"They make me think of Shelley," Demitri said beside him. The tall man had his hands behind his back, his dark gaze steady as he took in the statues.

Leon had no idea what he was talking about. "Who?"

"His poem, 'Ozymandias.'" Demitri gestured out the window. "The Colossi of Memnon were part of a temple bigger than Karnak, a monument to the greatness of the pharaoh Amenophis. But later pharaohs looted what they wanted of the gold and silver adornments, and the Nile washed away the rest. The statues are all that remain, a monument to futility." Demitri stood silently a moment, then went on in a sonorous voice. "'"Look on my works, ye mighty, and despair!"' . . . Round the decay of that colossal wreck, boundless and bare, the lone and level sands stretch far away.'"

"Don't be maudlin," Val said from the sofa. She lay with her head propped on a cushion, her long legs crossed at her ankles. "Amenophis is happy in his afterlife, where I imagine he's built a temple twice that size. He's probably frolicking with his darling Tiy and has three times as many concubines as he did when he was alive. And anyway, Shelley was writing about Ramses."

Leon didn't know enough about history to follow what they were talking about, but he moved to the sofa and sat down. He took Val's feet in his lap and began to rub them.

"How're you doing?"

"Fine," Val said, her voice tense. "Fine for a woman who doesn't know when she'll turn into a sex-crazed demon. Aphrodite just had to lift that oath, didn't she?"

"Why's that bad? One less thing to worry about, right?"

Val gave him a tired smile. "She was right; I hid behind my vows. It's easier to deny yourself something when you take an oath—it makes your decisions black and white, life or death. *Do I do this? No, I took a vow.* It's so much easier to make a concrete promise than simply try to be good in general."

Leon thought about how comforting it could be to follow orders in the army. He knew what he had to do every day because the company commander made the decision and it came down the channels through his platoon sergeant. Leon had in turn relayed the orders to those beneath him. No indecision about *what* they were going to do, just thinking on how they were going to do it to the best of their ability. And how hard they were going to party when the mission was done.

At home, away from the army's discipline, Leon had found himself rudderless. Waking up every morning not knowing what he'd do that day had been terrifying at first. What if he made the wrong decision, or worse, what if he harmed someone with that wrong decision? It had taken him a long time to find and get used to a new routine.

"I guess I get it," he said.

Val squeezed his hand. "I'm so glad I met you."

"Likewise."

"But I dragged you into my problems, and you might be killed because of it."

"Maybe, but I know what I need to do now." Leon ran his thumb over the back of her hand. He was going to save Val, no matter what. If she decided afterward that she wanted Demitri and not Leon, he'd bow out. A lady like Val belonged with a rich guy like Demitri anyway.

He looked at Demitri, wondering why his heart gave a strange twinge. Leon realized he didn't want to bow out or shrug this off. Val had touched something in him, and he wanted time to explore it.

Demitri wanted to go to Remy's excavation site before the day got too hot. Val didn't seem interested, but Leon agreed with Demitri that she shouldn't be left alone, so they all went.

Unlike the quiet of their hotel suite, the Valley of the Queens was bustling. Tour buses belched forth hordes of passengers who lined up to look upon the wonders of the painted tombs. Remy's dig was a bit off the beaten path, but more adventurous and interested tourists ventured to take photos of the holes Remy's team had dug in the base of the cliffs.

"Ready to start?" Remy looked happy to have his face and hands grimy, his knees plastered with white dust. "Your friends going to be all right?" He glanced to where Demitri and Val, pristinely dressed, had gone back to the tent where they'd sat before.

"They're used to Egypt," Leon said. If all the shit they spouted about Val living here in the time of the pharaohs was true, they were more used to it than Remy and his archaeologists would ever be.

Remy took Leon to where members of his team were sifting through rubble that was being cleared from the tomb. Remy's team was a mixture of American and Egyptian students of archaeology plus local men who were experts at digging up artifacts. Remy explained that while Leon wasn't waiting to bandage people up, he'd help out looking through the fill for potsherds and other tiny artifacts.

Felicia showed him what to look for, and stressed that even the tiniest bits could be important clues to the puzzle of ancient life. The limestone felt almost silky beneath Leon's fingers as he picked through it, hoping Remy's faith in his ability to find artifacts in this dirt wasn't misplaced. Remy left Leon to it, but Felicia, in charge of this part of the team, remained. The woman was damn enthusiastic about sifting through dust.

While Leon worked, he casually mentioned the necklace with

the broken pendant. "It was pretty," Leon said. "I'd love to get something like that as a gift for my mom."

"You can't take real artifacts out of Egypt," Felicia told him. "But you can buy reproductions in all the souvenir shops. I'll tell you which are the best dealers. Your friend Val can help you pick something out."

"Where did that necklace come from? You think you'll find any more?"

Leon had always been good at guileless inquiry. All he had to do was mention his mom and let his hard face look interested, and people told him everything he wanted to know.

"We might. We aren't sure if the necklace was meant to be in the tomb at all. It might have been taken from another tomb and dropped by robbers. I looked it up, by the way. I couldn't find any references in the databases or in any articles to a curse that used a pendant like that. Why did your friend think it was used for magic?"

"I don't know. I'm not really up on Egyptian stuff like he is. If you find another one, will it give you a clue?"

"Maybe. But necklaces of faience were pretty common, not worth a lot. This one was broken, so someone might have simply thrown it out."

Leon agreed it was an interesting mystery, then they went on with their work. It was dull, but Leon discovered that he wasn't bad at it. Life in the army was a lot of routine, and you did it until you got the job done. He could see that excavating was much the same.

He didn't find any treasure, but he did come across a couple of small beads, which made Felicia very happy. When Leon finished, he discovered that Val and Demitri had left the tent, to go back to the dig house, someone told him.

But when he arrived at the dig house with Remy, Demitri and Val weren't there, either, and according to the housekeeper and her husband, they never had been there. Leon stepped back outside, scanning the desert. The tired team streamed in along the path to the site, laughing and talking, eager for food and drink.

Leon saw no one else against the stark hills and broken terrain, no silhouettes against the darkening blue sky. Val and Demitri had vanished.

9

"L ET go of me," Valenarian said fiercely. Demitri hung on to her, pulling her around an outcropping that hid them from the site and the dig house. They'd been quietly sipping bottled water in the tent when Val suddenly turned to him and said, "I'm bored, lover. Let's find some nice, deserted tomb and screw until we scream."

"I shouldn't have brought you out here," Demitri growled at her now. He addressed her in ancient Athenian, the language he and Val had spoken to each other when they first met.

Val looked back at him with her dark demon's eyes. "But you couldn't leave me alone at the hotel, either, could you? I might devour a delicious man." She curled her tongue sensually.

"Control this. You can."

"Why should I? You like Valenarian better than that mealy-mouthed Valerie. Would you like me to go down on you right here in the dust? Like old times?"

Demitri *would* like it, that was the trouble. He'd loved everything Val had done to him, everything they'd shared. He'd loved it too much.

Val wet her lips, making them red and moist. "What did you do without me all these centuries, Demitri? Really, I want to know how you survived."

"I had lovers."

"None like me, I'll bet."

"No, none of them were evil incarnate."

"I'm not quite evil incarnate." She draped her arms around his neck. Her body was hot with the desert heat and her own latent power. "I did a job, that's all. Performed an important function."

"Until you went insane with it."

"Well, perhaps I did go a little overboard. But I'm a good girl now. Do you believe me?"

"I wish I could."

Her body rubbing against his drove him crazy. Demitri pinned Val against the rock wall, holding her wrists over her head.

She laughed. "Just like old times. What are you going to do to me?"

"What I *want* to do is fuck you with my hands and tongue and then my cock, but I'm not going to."

"Oh, you're no fun."

"Because that's what Valenarian wants. Sex hard, rough, and fast, with a little kink to it."

"Keep talking dirty, lover. It makes me wet."

Demitri pushed his face close to hers. Val's breath was hot on his lips, her breasts tight against his own chest. "Which is why I'm not going to do it. I'm not going to do it because you want it so much."

"Tease." Val extended her claws a little, pressed them into his neck. "Do you know what I do to men who tease me?"

"I'm not a man. You can't best me with strength."

"That's why I've always bested you with seduction."

"Not anymore." Demitri let his voice go soft as he brushed his lips across hers. "You're getting it when I say you are, and you're getting what I say you'll get."

Her breath tangled with his. "That sounds like fun."

"It won't be fun. It will be hell, and you'll do anything I say until I've tamed you."

"I don't want to be tamed. Aphrodite tried to tame me, but as you can see, it hasn't worked."

"You must have had some of Valerie in you already. Aphrodite didn't paste a new personality on top of you; she brought out what you had suppressed."

"Oh, please."

"I'm afraid it's true, my love."

Val tugged him closer, opened her mouth over his. He allowed one burning kiss, then he lifted his head. "No, sweetheart."

Val seized his obviously aroused cock through his pants. "You want me, lover."

"I do want you." Demitri kissed the line of her hair and drew his tongue down her cheek. "I want it bad. But I'm not going to let you have it."

"You will."

Demitri smiled, grimly determined. "I won't." He yanked Val's hands from him and stepped away, right into Leon.

"So, what are y'all doing?" Leon asked. He voice was a soft drawl, his green eyes glittering with anger.

Demitri switched abruptly back to English. "Is there a way to get her out of here that's not through the site?"

Leon looked past him to Val, and his eyes widened. "Is she . . . ?"

Val laughed. "Of course, darling. Demitri doesn't want anyone to see me, in case I decide to seduce and kill your brother's colleagues."

"I can't argue with him for that," Leon said.

"As if I'm interested in them. I have all I can handle right here." She arched against Demitri.

"We need to get her back to the hotel," Demitri said.

"I can see that."

"Don't worry, I'll go quietly." Val stepped out of Demitri's embrace and wound her arms around Leon's neck. "If Demitri won't fuck me, maybe you will."

Leon's eyes flickered yellow, his arousal obvious. He sucked in a breath and pulled Val's hands away.

"There's a path that leads around the other ridge to the entrance of the valley. It's a long way, but it circles around the dig house."

"Lead the way."

Demitri held Val's arm as Leon took them along the dusty path in the light of the setting sun. The sky flushed golden and red, the blue softening as the sun slid westward. Once twilight set in, the desert cooled quickly.

Val walked close to Demitri, not speaking, but when he looked down at her, she sent him a wicked smile. Tightening his grip only made her smile increase. If she wasn't looking at Demitri, she let her gaze run over Leon walking ahead of them.

"You have a gorgeous ass, Leon," she said. "Demitri thinks so, too."

Leon glanced once over his shoulder, obviously uncomfortable, but he continued to lead the way in silence.

The hotel was a mile from the entrance to the Valley of the Queens, and they walked to it rather than bother with a taxi. Once upstairs, Val smiled at them both and sank to the sofa, her eyes dark, her hair in tight red black ringlets.

"Val, will you be all right while I shower?" Leon asked, wiping sweat and dust from his face.

"Go on, lover. I'll keep Demitri company."

Leon threw Demitri a dark look and went into the bathroom.

Demitri stood in front of Val and folded his arms. "Let Valerie come back."

"I don't think so." Val lounged against the cushions, her arm over her head, returning to the dialect of ancient Athens. "Not for a while."

"You might regret that."

"Why? What can you possibly do to me?"

"Stand up."

Val yawned. "What for?"

Demitri reached down and yanked her to her feet. Val laughed as she fell against him. "All right, lover." She squeezed his ass.

Demitri seized her wrists in an iron grip. "If you're going to touch, it has to be nice."

"You never liked it nice before, Demitri. As I recall, you preferred it so very rough."

"I like it both ways," Demitri said, his voice low. "But you only know one way, don't you? You don't know what it's like to be tender."

"I can be tender." She stroked her thumb over his wrist then stroked again with one claw, nearly drawing blood.

Demitri didn't flinch. "Do you see? You can't do this without hurting, and liking it. I'm going to teach you how wonderful it is to be gentle."

"Wussy, you mean."

"That proves you don't understand. Undress for me."

She looked startled, then her smile came back. "*You* don't understand, Demitri. You pretend to be in so much control, but you can't control yourself at all. You burn."

"That doesn't matter. Undress."

"If that's what you want."

She stripped slowly, unbuttoning her tunic, sliding it over her head to reveal her delicate, lacy bra. She slipped out of her long pants, her panties a thin black slash across her skin. A lacy garter belt was another band of black, and silk garters clasped sheer black stockings.

She was breathtakingly erotic. She was right about Demitri having difficulty controlling himself. His erection was tight, his blood hot. But he'd hold it in. He had fourteen days to save Val, and if he had to be horny and unfulfilled to save her, so be it.

"Keep going. Take off every single stitch."

Val's lips curved seductively. She unsnapped the garters and rolled off her stockings, then pulled off the bra. Her breasts were firm globes, white, whereas her neck and arms were tanned. As a priestess Val had kept herself covered.

Instead of stripping off her panties, Val raised her arms to her sides and began a slow belly dance. Her hips undulated, accented by the curve of the panties. Then she raised her arms above her head and slid her torso from side to side, breasts gently moving.

Demitri caught her in his arms. He kissed her, loving the feel of her bare flesh beneath his hands. He pushed her panties down over her hips, briefly cupping her buttocks before he let her go.

Val tried to continue the kiss, but Demitri pressed her away. He laced his fingers through hers. "Slowly."

"You don't want to be slow." Her eyes burned dark blue, and her nipples were hard little points. "Neither do I."

"I don't care."

Valerie tried to yank away. "I'll find Leon. He's happy to take it fast."

The shower was still pattering in the bathroom. "Leave Leon be for now."

"He was very good." Valerie subsided, but her look was wicked. "He fucked me hard and kept going until he couldn't do any more."

"Are you trying to make me jealous or turn me on?"

She smiled sweetly. "Both."

"Hearing that you were willing to screw a man until he dropped dead of it doesn't do it for me."

"Bullshit."

"Leon was lucky he had a shifter's stamina. It wasn't nice of you to drag him into this."

"You're glad I did," Val said. "You like him, too, don't you?"

Demitri did. "That's another reason why I want to save you, because it will save him, too."

"Aw, how sweet."

Demitri tightened his clasp on her hands. "He doesn't deserve to die because of you. And I have a feeling you don't want him to."

"Well, no. He is cute."

Demitri leaned closer. "You care what happens to him. I'm going to find the core of that care and drag it out of you."

Her eyes flickered. "How do you plan to do that?"

"Carefully. It might hurt."

"Mmm, now you're talking."

"You won't like it."

"Bet me."

She smelled good, like a warm flower. Demitri nuzzled her hair, let his lips drift across her face, but pulled back when she tried to catch him with a kiss.

Val pouted when he pulled away, but she let him hold her hands. He traced circles on her wrists with his thumbs, watched her gaze focus on that.

"I love your skin," Demitri whispered. "The feel of it."

He looked down at her breasts, firm and high as they'd been all these centuries, Valenarian forever young.

Val wanted to rage at his slowness, but she wouldn't let herself. Her need for him boiled through her, at levels he couldn't begin to understand.

She held herself still while he ran his thumbs over her wrists, trying not to betray the fires sliding through her body. Feeling his still-clothed body against her naked one was incredibly erotic. Her nipples were tight peaks, tightening even more under his gaze. She wanted to yank his head down to them, bury her breast in his mouth. He'd suckle and suckle, hands gripping her.

I want him.

"You're a bastard," she whispered.

Demitri lowered his head so his lips were an inch from hers. "I'll save you, no matter what it takes."

He kissed her. Val relaxed under his lips, snaked her tongue into his mouth. She clamped her hands down on his and turned the kiss hard.

"No." Demitri pulled back and deliberately broke his hold. "Slowly."

"I can't."

"You can."

Tears of rage pricked her eyes. "I can't, Demitri. It's not what I am. Either fuck me or leave me alone."

He stepped away from her. "I'm not going to do either."

The loss of his heat was like a physical blow. Here she was, standing stark naked in the middle of a hotel room, her clothes strewn about her feet, and he didn't want her. She burned for him, needed him. Her quim was hot and wet. She made a noise of frustration and sank her own fingers into it.

She had one second of pleasure before Demitri jerked her hand out again. "No."

"Damn you."

"Wait."

The shower went off in the bathroom, and Val's heartbeat sped. He wanted her to wait until Leon was with them. Her skin warmed. Oh, yes, Demitri was good.

In a few seconds, Leon walked out with a towel around his waist. Water droplets beaded his shoulders, and his hair was slick and wet. Golden brown hair brushed his chest and narrowed to a point above his navel. He had a nice navel, a firm indent in his taut belly.

Leon took in naked Val and clothed Demitri. "What the hell?"

Demitri switched to English and signaled Leon closer. "Val, I want you to touch him. Just his chest, just lightly. Slowly."

Val swallowed. "I want him. I want him to take me and you to watch."

"Too bad. Touch him. That's all."

Val sauntered to Leon. Leon held his ground, his green eyes steady on her. He didn't drop the towel, but she saw his arousal outlined behind it.

She curved her hands into claws, and Leon took a step back.

"No, Val," Demitri said quietly. "Fingertips only. Touch him."

This would be a challenge. Val sheathed her claws and pressed her fingertips to Leon's skin, feeling his heart flutter beneath her touch. She drew her hand down, loving the silkiness of the damp hair on his chest.

She reached his navel, drew her finger around it. She longed to kneel and thrust her tongue into it, like she had when she'd climbed into bed with him in Cairo. She drew her tongue across her lips, reminding him.

Leon remained motionless, his chest rising. "This is hurting me, too, babe," he said softly.

"But you'll sacrifice yourself to save me?" she purred.

"Something like that."

"Keep touching him," Demitri said.

"His ass?" Val suggested hopefully.

"His arms."

"Can't blame a girl for trying."

Leon waited. Val brushed fingertips over his forearms, liking how his muscles moved at her touch. The hair on them was wiry and shone like gold, kissed by the sun.

Val moved her hands up the insides of his arms to his biceps. He was corded with muscles, such delicious strength. She remembered how he'd held her when they'd made love, tempering himself to not hurt her.

Val skimmed her fingers up and down his arms, enjoying the heat of his skin. Demitri had something here. Touching was marvelous.

"Now his face."

Val took her fingers over his shoulders, up his strong neck and brushing along his jaw. He'd shaved in the shower, his skin smooth except for the tiny band of golden whiskers he'd missed. The small burn of those made her heart skip.

She brushed his chin, then his lips, then traced his cheekbones. Forehead next and around the eyes, then his lips again. Leon's lips were narrow and smooth, light red brown, perfect for kissing. She started to rise to them.

"No," Demitri said harshly. "Touch only."

Val lowered herself to the floor, scowling. "You're no fun."

"Leon, take off the towel."

A muscle moved in Leon's jaw. He loosened the small scrap of terry cloth and let it drop to the floor.

Oh, yes. His thighs were hard, like a runner's, and a thatch of dark brown curled between them. His penis was erect and fully extended, pointing directly at her.

"Mmm, it wants me."

Leon lightly stroked its underside. "It does, *chere.*"

Val couldn't stop herself. His cock was too beautiful. She closed her hand around it, stroking from base to tip. Leon groaned.

Demitri was at her side faster than she thought he could move. He yanked her hand away and held her wrist. "I didn't give you permission."

"Lover, I see hard cock pointing at me, I grab it."

"Not anymore, you don't." Demitri released her and nodded at Leon. "She does that again, you spank her."

Beads of sweat dotted Leon's forehead. "Shit, who are you punishing? Her or me?"

"Me," Val said. "You can always go find someone else to fuck."

"No, *chere.* I'm staying right here."

Val's heart warmed the slightest bit, then she told herself not to be stupid. Of course Leon would stay. Valenarian's lure was magical, a seduction no man could resist. Only Demitri had ever resisted.

"Touch his thighs, his abdomen," Demitri said. "Everything but his cock, balls, and ass."

Val heaved an exaggerated sigh. "Oh, all right."

She didn't say that she was finding touching non-erogenous zones not to be bad at all. Val put her hands on either side of Leon's navel then drew her fingers down the muscles of his stomach. She circled through the hair at the base of his abdomen, then moved her hands to his thighs.

"Spread your legs," she commanded.

Leon moved his feet apart, as he had for Demitri when they'd played together in the sauna. Under Demitri's close scrutiny, Val slid her fingers to his inner thighs, drawing her fingertips along the crease between thigh and torso.

Leon clenched his fists. Val sank to her knees as she circled her fingers along the same path, ending up almost, but not quite, touching his scrotum.

"Do you like that?" Val asked him.

"Being tortured?" Leon rasped. "Sure."

Val traced the path again, but this time drew her fingers down his legs. She smoothed the skin behind his knees and moved to his ankles, then used the backs of her fingers to make the return journey.

When she reached his inner thighs again, she couldn't resist palming his balls, then running her hand on the underside of Leon's cock. She laughed when Demitri grabbed her wrists.

"Too late, lover. I already did it."

Demitri dragged Val to her feet. "I warned you."

Leon took a breath. "You want me to?"

"Yes," Demitri said. "On the couch."

Leon moved to the sofa and sat down, his legs spread delectably. Val's heart beat in excitement as Demitri pushed her over Leon's left thigh, her bare ass in the air. She nearly screamed when Leon rested his warm hand on her buttock.

"How many?" Leon said, his voice strained.

"Ten. For now."

"All right." His voice held tense anticipation.

Val clenched her fists, waiting, then let out a squeal when the first stinging slap landed on her backside.

"One." Leon counted in his beautiful, flowing accent. "Two."

He kept spanking her, not very hard, the sting minimal. But Val was so aroused, and the combined pheromones of Leon and Demitri were so heady, that a climax swamped her.

She screamed and squirmed as Leon kept on with the count. He said "Ten," and she was completely gone.

Val bucked and rocked, her face in the cushions of the sofa, Leon's hard thigh rubbing her clit just right. She heard Demitri's voice, gentle now.

"Let her ride it out."

Leon kept his hand on her backside, the other stroking her hair as she pleasured herself. She dug harder into him, her demon claws extending and ripping into the sofa.

"Goddess," she panted. She sat up, her body tender and raw, and flung her arms around Leon's neck. "Thank you. Thank you." She kissed his throat, having no desire to bite. She simply wanted to hang on to him, to have him hold her.

"You all right?" Leon asked, eyes worried.

"Fine. Wonderful." Val kissed him, her quim hot, relaxed with her release.

"You see," Demitri said softly behind her. "It is possible. You came and loved it without hurting anyone. You barely touched him."

Val collapsed against Leon, feeling an overwhelming need to sleep. "Make him shut up," she murmured, and Leon grinned.

10

THERE'S a problem," Leon said when Demitri walked out of the bedroom again.

Demitri had carried Val off and to put her to bed while Leon remained on the sofa, his body throbbing with the excitement of what he'd just done. His hand stung from the spanking, but it had been so pleasurable watching Val squirm in joy. Her ass had been sweet cherry red when he finished, and he'd wanted to screw her so bad it had been physical agony to hold back.

"What problem?" Demitri asked him.

"I still have this fucking big hard-on." Leon scraped his hands through his damp hair. "You made her touch me, you had me spank her and let her cream all over me. What are you going to do for me?"

"What do you want? A woman?"

"Screw you. I want Val." Leon sighed. "Don't worry, I'll leave her alone. I know it's important. I guess I'll have to make do with my talented hand again."

"You don't have to." Demitri's warm gaze was palpable.

Leon was way out of his depth and he knew it. He remembered what he'd let Demitri do in the sauna, remembered kissing the man, and kissing him again in the temple of Ptah at Karnak. But Val had been there. It had been a show for Val.

"I'm not gay," Leon repeated.

"I know. But we're both shifters."

"I'm not fucking you when we're both tigers. Forget it."

Demitri gave him a ghost of a smile. "I'm not suggesting that. But maybe shifting will help rid us of our frustration." He ran his hand down the seam of his fly. "I also have, as you say, a fucking big hard-on."

He had a point. The energy of the change might release the tension in a different way than a sexual one. It was worth a try.

Leon was already naked, so he simply stood up and willed the change to come. The tiger came surprisingly quickly. He remembered the sensation of it from their encounter in Cairo, except this time, he wasn't angry or challenging. In a short time, Leon landed on all four paws and waited to see what Demitri would do.

Demitri's eyes were already golden yellow, already slitted like a cat's. The man ran strong hands across Leon's back then straightened up and stripped himself down. His naked body gleamed with sweat, his huge cock standing straight out.

Leon's tiger brain didn't much notice or care about Demitri's nakedness. He butted the man's sinewy legs with his head. Demitri rubbed Leon behind the ears, then he stepped away to make his change.

As before, Demitri's body brightened as his god-energy filled him. Fur rippled itself across his skin, the tiger stripes solidifying as Demitri morphed. He head-butted Leon in greeting, and Leon turned and swiped Demitri with his tongue.

What seemed wrong or constrained when they were human didn't seem unnatural when Leon was in animal shape. He licked Demitri across the nose, and Demitri put a huge paw on Leon's neck.

Both cats went down to the carpet, not in a dominance contest this time, but in play. Leon rolled over while he let Demitri bat him with a sheathed paw, then Leon righted himself and tugged Demitri's ear with gentle teeth.

Demitri licked Leon again, holding him with his paw while he carefully and thoroughly groomed his face. Leon let him, then licked the underside of Demitri's jaw.

They rolled closer to each other, licking, nibbling, stroking. Leon felt his sexual tension ease and his affection rise. This was nothing he hadn't done with his brothers when they'd shifted to bobcats as kids and piled themselves on their long-suffering mother's best carpet.

He and his brothers had often groomed one another as wildcats, a sign of acceptance and affection. The grooming sessions would turn to rougher games, he and his brothers romping and playing like overgrown kittens.

Leon half rose to his feet and tackled Demitri. Demitri growled as he rolled over, and Leon landed on top of him. A table rocked and crashed to the floor, the lamp smashing. Both cats stopped, waiting to see if anyone heard, but Val didn't wake, and no one came hurrying to the door.

Demitri huffed, his lips rolling, then he tackled Leon. They wrestled back and forth, not using teeth or claws but plenty of muscle. Demitri was good at swiping, but Leon was excellent at getting the other cat in a headlock. When Demitri broke away, he bounded off into his bedroom, and Leon followed.

The bed creaked when first one big cat than another jumped on it, and Demitri lay down right away. Leon landed next to him with a foreleg around Demitri's neck. Demitri resumed the grooming, and Leon followed suit, feeling the pleasant lassitude of sleep coming over him.

He stretched out, his back to Demitri and let his eyes drift closed. He loved sleeping in an animal form—when animals felt safe, they gave over to sleep without tension. Only baby humans could sleep like that.

Leon drifted off, feeling the stillness of the night, the bright moon floating outside the windows. Demitri yawned, canines sharp, his eyes closing. Leon felt Demitri lay his great head on Leon's back, then the sound of a soft tiger snore.

When Leon woke again, the sun slanted through the windows. He was still a tiger, still stretched out across the mattress, which had sunk some in the middle. Leon yawned, mouth opening so wide that his ears touched in the back. He settled back down, finding himself looking straight into Demitri's open eyes. Demitri started licking Leon's face, and Leon returned the greeting.

As though they'd choreographed it, each man slid back to his human form at the same time. Leon and Demitri lay on their stomachs, side by side, both naked. In the unworried state Leon always found himself in after shifting, he licked Demitri's human face. He liked the taste of the man's unshaven whiskers, the salt of his skin.

Leon met Demitri's tongue as Demitri licked him back. The licks turned into kisses, full-mouthed, warm and slow. Leon slid his arm around Demitri's back and settled in.

They kissed for a long time. The erection Leon had conquered last night by becoming a tiger returned hard and strong.

I'm getting turned on by another man. The thought seemed dim and far away, the shifter in him simply enjoying sensations.

Demitri stroked Leon's hair then his hand moved down Leon's back to cup his buttocks. Leon tightened his arm around Demitri's middle and went on kissing him.

The hotel phone on the nightstand rang, the shrill peal cutting through the tranquility of the morning. Demitri didn't reach for it. He stopped, nose to nose with Leon, as though wondering what Leon would do.

The sharp peal of the phone cut through some of the fog in Leon's brain. Instinct made him wanted to spring away in shock, but he made himself lie still and press a light kiss to Demitri's lips.

The phone stopped. "Damn," Leon whispered.

"They'll call back if it's important."

"No, I meant, damn, I don't hate this."

Demitri traced his cheek. "I don't hate this, either."

"I've always liked women. Even when I went weeks at a time without seeing a woman, I didn't want a man. All us men talked about women. Breasts. Pussy."

Demitri's touch was soothing. "The shifters within us connected. Maybe that's why."

"Maybe." Leon shrugged. "All I know is, I wouldn't mind kissing you again."

For answer, Demitri slanted his lips across Leon's. Leon answered the kiss, loving the feel of Demitri's strong tongue inside his mouth.

The bedroom door opened. Leon rolled over and saw Val standing in the doorway, her eyes wide. They were light blue eyes, and she averted them. Valerie, the good girl, had returned.

"I knew there was some benefit to letting you help me," she said, her cheeks red. "I seriously hate to interrupt, but your brother called, Leon."

Leon rolled to his feet, looked for his clothes, and realized he'd only worn a towel last night, which he'd dropped in the living room. Demitri propped himself up on his elbow, not seeming to mind.

"He wants you to come to the dig house," Val went on. "He and Felicia discovered that more things had gone missing this morning. He hopes you can help him take a look around."

~ ~ ~

VALERIE had recovered herself by the time they arrived at the site and found a worried Remy in the dig house. She wandered the aisles in the storage room, straightening things here and there. Behind her,

Demitri and Leon listened to Remy pour out his troubles, but Val couldn't concentrate on what he said. She kept picturing how she'd walked into Demitri's bedroom that morning, Valerie once more, to see two naked men kissing each other on Demitri's bed.

Two bare backs, one pale, one deeply tanned, two firm backsides, four tightly muscled legs intertwined. She'd stopped, arrested by the beauty of the picture. They'd been nose to nose, Demitri's hand in Leon's hair, mouths devouring each other. They hadn't kissed for her benefit. They hadn't even known she was there.

Thinking on it even now made the space between her legs hot. She wanted to watch Demitri and Leon kiss some more, wanted to watch them touch each other, wanted to watch Demitri rise up to enter Leon, while Leon watched him with warm eyes.

Val made a longing noise in her throat, and the others broke off to stare at her.

"Don't mind me," she said, fanning herself with one hand. "I'm just shocked by the theft. Go on, Remy."

"That faience necklace you were so interested in is gone," Remy said. "Plus a couple of fragments of pottery and a few ushabtis—those are the things that look like little dolls. The thief didn't take anything we haven't found hundreds of, but it's bad that they're missing. I'm the team leader. If I can't control what goes on at the dig, I'll be replaced. My reputation will be tarnished, my career over."

Felecia, standing next to Remy, bit her lip. "We'll find them, Remy."

Remy gave Val and Demitri a worried look. "Please, don't breathe a word of this. If we can find the thief or find the things before anyone knows, then maybe we can keep it quiet. I don't need this kind of trouble on my first dig."

Leon studied the room. "You said the door was locked, but you let people in whenever they need to find something?"

Remy nodded. "I have a key, Felicia does, and Habib, the postdoc who's my Egyptian equivalent. I don't think he's doing this, because it's his career at stake as well as mine, plus he's adamant about antiquities staying in Egypt."

"Doesn't hurt to talk to him, though," Leon said. "He might be very adamant, maybe thinks stealing them is the best way to protect them."

Remy looked doubtful. "He's intense, but he is a stickler for rules, not the kind to break them, even for a good cause."

"Maybe he lent the key to someone, and that person had it duplicated."

"Could be." Remy looked glum. "This bites."

"What about you?" Leon asked Felicia. "Did you lend your key to anyone?"

Felicia pulled a key ring out of her pocket and showed it to him. "I have it on me at all times, and I haven't given it to anyone. If someone needs to get into the storage room, I let them in, then lock it up when they're done."

"Do you watch them every minute they're in here?"

Felicia flushed. "Not really."

"Someone using the room could easily pocket an artifact. Everything you describe that's missing is small, even the necklace."

Val felt a pang of despair. They needed the necklace to complete their task—what happened if they couldn't find it?

"I'm sorry, Remy," Felicia said. "I never thought of that."

"You can't breathe over everyone's shoulder all the time," Remy snapped. "I don't watch them when I'm in here, either. There's too much to do and not enough people to do it."

"You said the pieces aren't valuable?" Val asked. Nothing in this room was silver or gold or precious stones. It all looked brown and drab to her.

"That's the thing, not really. We find tons of the stuff. We've recorded every one including photographing it in the exact location we found it, but the artifacts are commonplace. Nothing out of the ordinary, nothing we don't already know about. They don't contribute much to archaeological knowledge."

"I think what Val means is, are they valuable to someone who doesn't know anything about archaeology? Could someone sell them to collectors or tourists?"

"Would it be lucrative?" Val asked. "Selling these bits to a European or American or Japanese traveler who wanted to take home a real artifact?"

Remy didn't look happy. "Probably. Not a fortune, but they wouldn't do too bad out of it."

"Well then, all we have to do is find the person offering these things to tourists," Val concluded. "I suppose a dealer in illegal antiquities would likely approach foreign tourists near the hotels or the shops in Luxor? We can wander around there and see if anyone offers us something."

"I can't. Everyone knows me, or they know I'm with the dig. They'd just hide the stuff." Remy looked hopefully at Leon.

Leon shook his head. "They wouldn't believe I could afford an illegal souvenir, and they'd be right. My friends, on the other hand . . ."

Val smiled. "I am excellent at going undercover." She lifted her gauzy scarf and drew it over her mouth. "I can be a rich tourist looking for something exciting to take home to my friends. I'll make sure they know that money is no object. Demitri is rolling in it."

"Thank you, I'd be happy to volunteer," Demitri said in a dry voice.

"I'll pose as your wife, and you'll have given me a *huge* roll of cash for my little expenses." She held out her hand, and Demitri raised a brow at her.

"That's nice of you, but too risky," Remy said. "I can't let you endanger yourselves. The thief might fight to keep from getting caught."

Leon gave him a look. "I wouldn't worry. Demitri and Val are good at taking care of themselves."

"Are you sure?"

"Real sure."

Remy looked like he wanted to argue, but he sighed, resigned. "You do what you have to do. I can't tell you how grateful I am for the help."

"I can keep an eye on things here, too," Leon said. "We'll find the guy, Remy."

"I appreciate this, big brother. Truly." Remy's eyes held affection and admiration. Val found it touching. Would Valenarian? Perhaps she would.

Leon and Remy left to look around the outside of the building and in the lab. Felicia lingered, pretending to straighten things on a shelf.

Demitri gestured for Val to follow with him, but Val whispered, "I'm going to stay behind a minute."

Demitri gave her a stern look, and Val shook her head. "Valenarian never hurt women. She'll be safe, and I want to talk to her about the other thing I'm supposed to be doing."

Demitri hesitated, then he gave her a nod. "I'll be right outside. Waiting. Don't take too long, or I'll be back to drag you out."

"You worry too much." Val rose on tiptoe to kiss his cheek, and Demitri finally departed.

Val dusted off her tunic and wandered to where Felicia was straightening the shelves, her work-roughened hands trembling.

"This must be distressing for you," Val said in her most sympathetic voice. She perched on the end of an empty table next to the clipboard that held a list of the artifacts on the shelves. "I'm sure Remy doesn't blame you."

"I'm sure he does." Felicia jerked a box off a shelf, looked inside, and replaced it. "I have a key to this room. It's my responsibility."

"He seemed certain you had nothing to do with it."

"Yes, but he's afraid this will jeopardize his career, and he's right. Committees are always looking for reasons to pull funding. And in a research profession, if you can't get grant funding, you're sunk."

"You're worried for him."

"Of course I am. He's a brilliant archaeologist. He worked his way up from nothing—he and his brothers were raised in a backwater Louisiana town, and their family had no money at all. Remy pulled himself up by his own bootstraps."

Felicia's voice rang with admiration, her flushed face almost pretty.

"You're a good friend to care like that."

Felicia's voice was stiff. "We're friends, yes."

"Nothing more than that?"

"Of course not. Remy is very appropriate. He'd never take advantage of a work situation."

Val smiled gently. "No matter how much you might want him to?"

Felicia looked at her in outrage, her face bright red. She started to splutter something, then she deflated. "Damn it, does it show that much?"

"Don't worry, my dear. I'm an expert at reading the signs. Doesn't Remy see what's right under his nose?"

Felicia leaned on the edge of the table and folded her arms. "Remy hired me for my brains. We've known each other since we started grad school. He read my dissertation and invited me to apply for a position on his team. He respects my theories, he said."

"My, how sexy of him." Val studied Felicia, her blond hair, even teeth, hazel eyes, plain but well-shaped face. "We'll just have to make him see more than your theories."

Felicia gave a short laugh. "I've never been the gorgeous girl with beautiful eyes and big boobs. Men like me because I'm safe."

"Ah, *safe*. The kiss of death."

"I don't think Remy has a girlfriend waiting for him in Louisiana," Felicia said glumly. "He never mentions one, anyway, so that can't be why he . . ."

"Never notices you?" Val finished. "But there's hope. If he was repulsed by you, he'd make sure he talked about a girlfriend every chance he got, to broadcast that he was unavailable."

"Or maybe he just doesn't like to talk about his personal life."

"If he's anything like Leon, he's not ashamed of his past. You know all about his life on the bayous, whatever bayous are. If he had a girlfriend, or someone he was in love with back home, he'd have mentioned her."

"Possibly."

"Definitely. My guess is that he's enamored with his work and takes you for granted. Men should never be allowed to take women for granted."

Felicia laughed again. "I don't think he sees me as a woman. I'm a sexless archaeologist. A mobile brain and a pair of hands to help sort and log in pottery."

"Well, we'll just have to change that."

"Why should you want to help me? You're beautiful, and you have that gorgeous Demitri following you around. Leon, too."

How wonderful it would be if they were following her around because they couldn't resist her. Val couldn't explain to Felicia that the two men followed her because they didn't trust her.

"I want to help you because I'm an expert at bringing people together," she said. "Call it my raison d'être."

Felicia's look turned wistful. "I was never a girly-girl, doing my nails and styling my hair. I was more interested in ancient languages and tombs full of hieroglyphs."

"There's no reason you can't be both brainy and beautiful. We'll go shopping in Luxor, and I'll transform you. I'll be your . . . What's that story about the girl who meets a prince while riding a pumpkin? Or was it a pomegranate?"

"'Cinderella.' You mean you'll be my fairy godmother."

Val grinned. "Your fairy goddess-mother, is more like it."

Felicia looked dubious. "I don't have a lot of money for clothes."

Val ran her gaze over Felicia's khaki working shorts, white socks and sneakers, and mannish button-up shirt. "We'll work something out. And don't worry about the expense. I didn't lie when I said Demitri was filthy rich."

"And he just gives you money?" Felicia sounded both envious and disapproving.

"Demitri and I have a long and complicated relationship. Money is the least of our worries."

"What does Demitri do? For a living, I mean."

Val made an indifferent gesture. "He owns things. Hotels and the like. I admit that when I'm with him I'm not thinking about what he does in his professional capacity."

"I wish I could be that comfortable around men."

"What you need to learn is how to make men *un*comfortable around you. When you want them to be."

Felicia looked thoughtful. "I've never tried that before. It might be fun."

"It is. I promise."

The two women shared a very feminine smile, then Val hopped off the table. Felicia put away the clipboard, and they left the building together.

Demitri lounged outside, watching a string of tourist-laden donkeys trot past. Val slipped her hand under Demitri's arm and gave Felicia a broad wink. Felicia gave a very un-academic giggle, and Demitri scowled in suspicion.

11

VAL looked better today, Demitri thought as he escorted her through the streets of Luxor that afternoon. With the white scarf draped loosely over her hair and her round sunglasses, she looked a little bit like a 1930s Hollywood star. She wouldn't understand what that meant, but she was elegantly beautiful and utterly composed.

He wandered with her around the less reputable shops Remy had told them about, making it known that a wealthy couple was interested in real antiquities, never mind the bloody rules and regulations. Val played it well, acting the spoiled and slightly vacant wife with aplomb.

"There is a problem with this method," Val said as she sat down at a restaurant table and removed her sunglasses. She spoke again in the ancient language, the lilting syllables lovely on her tongue. "We're likely to attract *every* person willing to smuggle out antiquities, and who knows—the police might get word of it, too."

"Leon might have success on his end," Demitri replied in the same language. "He's a good listener."

"True, he doesn't talk much. That must come from him being a soldier."

"Soldiers have been much the same over the centuries, haven't they?"

"Oh, they're different deep down inside," Val said. "But they live knowing that each minute might mean their death. I suppose that could make one quiet, and careful of to whom one talked."

"He talked to you." Demitri sipped the coffee the waiter had brought, enjoying watching Val drink hers. She held the cup delicately, her red lips just touching the rim before she swallowed. He wanted to lick away the drop that lingered on her lips.

Val shrugged. "I'm a servant of the Goddess of Love. People open up to me."

"Did Felicia?"

"Yes, but not about the missing objects." She smiled sweetly. "It was girl talk."

"I wish you had picked her brain about the key. I'd like to clear up this distraction so we can focus on saving you."

"But the thief took the necklace, too. I'd say that was more than just a distraction."

Demitri traced the rim of his cup. "The thief didn't take the necklace. I did."

She blinked. "You did?"

"I thought it would be safer with me instead of available for someone to steal."

"But what will happen to Leon's brother when it never turns up again? It was the best piece in their collection of scraps."

"When we finish with it, I'll return it. Or make certain it gets returned if I can't do it myself."

"Because you might be hanging from your thumbs over an escarpment." Val clenched her cup. "Demitri, why did you agree to do this? You could have let me go easily, but if you fail—if I fail—you die. I don't want that."

"We won't fail."

"Valenarian is a demon. The definition of *demon* is evil spirit. You can't ever trust her."

"No, but I can trust you." Demitri leaned forward and clasped her fingers loosely in his. "I also trust Aphrodite. She wants you to live. If she didn't, she'd have killed you long, long ago, when she found us in the meadow on Mount Olympus."

Val flushed. "I remember that day."

"You think I don't? It's the day I betrayed you."

"You had to. Valenarian had to be stopped."

Demitri closed his other hand around hers, capturing her. "I wanted to keep you with me forever. I was arrogant enough to think I could control you. I loved you so much."

Val's eyes were moist. "You loved me?"

"With my heart and soul, body and mind. I was insane with it."

"And now?"

He withdrew his hands. "I'm still arrogant enough to think I can tame you."

"Not me. Valenarian."

"Both of you. All of you." He lowered his voice, though they were speaking a language no one had heard on earth in thousands of years. "I want to have you *and* Valenarian. I want Valenarian in my bed at night, to fuck as I like, and I want Valerie to hold hands with in a café. I want you both in the same woman. I'd do anything to have that."

"What about Leon?"

Demitri sat back. "He's mortal. Even if he is a shifter, he was born mortal and will age and die as mortals do."

"This makes you sad."

"I don't like growing attached to mortals. It's too difficult to let them go."

Val smiled wistfully. "I'm growing attached to him, too."

"As Val or as Valenarian?"

"Both. If I hadn't liked him so much when I talked to him that night, Valenarian would never have come out." Her smile grew wider, and she licked her lips. "I'm glad she did."

Demitri tensed, but Val's softer smile returned. Valerie was still with him.

"You do like him," she said, and she winked. "I know what I saw when I came into your bedroom this morning. Why didn't you wake me up to let me watch?"

Demitri remembered the warmth of lying beside Leon, kissing him. "Don't worry, we didn't do anything that would satisfy your voyeuristic appetite. We slept together, as tigers. Slept only."

Her smile widened. "I see. That's why you were kissing him so hard."

Demitri refused to be embarrassed. "It seemed natural."

"I noticed he wasn't reluctant to touch you. You must have just shifted back."

"In his human form, Leon does have the inhibitions of a mortal human of this century. He has difficulty violating his cultural taboos."

"Don't analyze him, Demitri. Simply teach him how wonderful it is to ignore those taboos." Dimples appeared in her cheeks. "And please let me watch."

Demitri flushed. "You really are sex-crazed, aren't you?"

"Only when it involves you." Val traced the broad backs of his fingers. "And a hot man like Leon. I like this. The three of us, I mean. I like you both, and I like you sharing me with him, and him with me."

"You, Valerie?"

"What do you think, lover?"

Demitri's hand tightened on hers. "Don't do that to me."

Her eyes twinkled. "Why not? Will you spank me like you made Leon do last night?"

Demitri peered at her. Was it a good sign that he suddenly

wasn't sure which side of Val he was dealing with? "Is that what Valerie wants?"

Val's smile faded. "I'm not certain what I want. What if I can't do this, Demitri?"

"I'll make sure you can do it." He dabbed his lips with his napkin and set it on the table. "Let's go back to the hotel here. I have an idea."

"What idea?"

"I'll have to show you."

The fact that Val contained her curiosity as they rose and left the restaurant confirmed that Demitri was dealing with Valerie. Valenarian would have tried to wheedle his plans out of him, argued if she didn't like them.

Valerie walked obediently at his side, and said nothing as they passed the Old Winter Palace Hotel and entered the one they'd stayed in two nights ago. They ascended to their floor in silence.

"What are we doing here?" Val asked as they passed the sauna where they'd had interesting three-way play.

Demitri unlocked his bedroom, towed her in, and shut the door. The beds were made and ready for them, his suits still hanging neatly in the open closet.

Demitri slid his hands around Val's waist and kissed her deeply. Val gasped, then sank into the kiss, her eyes closing.

Demitri glided his tongue behind her teeth. He put his thumbs to the corners of her mouth, encouraging her to open to him. She groaned low in her throat.

He eased back. "I want Valerie. Not Valenarian. Do you hear me?"

"You don't like Valerie."

"Why do you say that?"

"I don't care what you said in the restaurant. You loved what I was, not what I became."

Demitri cupped her shoulders. "You became calm and safe, no longer dangerous."

"And dull." Val smiled. "You loved the spark in Valenarian, the woman who would do anything. You couldn't control me, and you didn't really want to. Valerie will do anything you say, and you don't like that."

"You're wrong. I want to help you."

"You don't want me to die, but for Valenarian's sake, not mine. When this is over, if we win, you'll be happy when we go our separate ways."

He frowned. "I never said that."

"I think that's why you want Leon with us, why you aren't jealous of him and me. You can hand me off to him when we're done, knowing he'll make me happy. You won't have to feel guilty."

His anger stirred. "You're dreaming. I want you, Val."

"You're trying to tame me, Demitri, but you like it rough, and so does Valenarian. That's why you couldn't tame her before—you didn't want to."

"Damn it, Val, I still love you."

She held his face between her hands. "I'm not stupid, Demitri, or blind. When she comes out and I recede, there's a sparkle in your eyes that's not there now. You want *her*. She challenges you, and you love that."

He shook his head, his heart beating hard. "I want you to live. I want to be with *you*. I told you."

"You want her."

"No."

She dropped her hands and stepped back. "Then make love to me right now. That's why you brought me up here, isn't it? Make love to me in a way that won't release her."

"That's what I had in mind."

"I don't think you can do it."

Demitri clenched his jaw. "You underestimate me. And you're wrong."

Val unwound her scarf and dropped it onto the table next to her sunglasses. Her eyes were clear blue, her hair sleek and long. He held his breath as she began unbuttoning her blouse.

Her breasts were beautiful, creamy and untouched by the sun. Her black lace bra pushed them into soft cleavage.

Val let the blouse drop and unhooked the bra. As it fell, she ran her hands through her long hair and spilled it through her fingers.

Demitri's cock tightened as Val cupped her hands around her breasts. "As a priestess of Aphrodite, I was celibate," she said. "But I still needed to release. We all did. The priestesses would gather when we had spare time, and we'd dance for each other. We'd do stripteases sometimes, pretend we were doing them for the men we wanted. And we touched ourselves. We couldn't have each other, because we were celibate, but we were allowed to release ourselves. We taught each other many techniques."

Demitri felt his eyes change. The world suddenly became more clear, the scent of Val sharp in his nostrils.

Val ran her fingers down her bare abdomen and unhooked and unzipped her pants. The flowing garment dropped easily to the ground, leaving her standing in nothing but lace panties.

She slid her fingers inside the panties, her head dropping back as she touched her clit. Demitri's gaze fixed on the black lace, watching her finger move back and forth beneath it.

Don't change. The tiger rose in him, and Demitri clenched his fists, willing himself to stay in human shape. Val withdrew her fingers. Her fingertips glittered with moisture. She put them into her mouth and sucked them clean.

Demitri groaned. Val slipped her fingers back inside her panties, playing some more. This time when she withdrew, he caught her hand, wanting to taste her.

"No, don't touch me." She moved from his grasp then ran her tongue up her glistening fingers. "This is Valerie, playing for you."

Demitri swallowed, and he let her go.

She slid her hand back into her panties again, her nipples tightening as she played. Her tongue wound its way around her lips, making them red and moist as her hips moved with the joy of it. At last she began to jerk, her thighs squeezing together as though she wanted to pull her lover deep inside herself.

Demitri shed his coat and shirt, unable to stay away from her. He tossed the clothes aside and wrapped his arms around her.

She didn't try to pull away this time. But she was Valerie, her eyes light blue and lovely. He kissed her, plunging his tongue into her mouth as she wriggled against him.

Demitri's hand went to his waistband, and he quickly got rid of the rest of his clothes. He lifted Val with his hands on her buttocks, and she wrapped her legs around him. Demitri backed her into the wall, leaned her against it, and slid his cock inside her.

Val screamed. Demitri rocked her on him, the position not letting him thrust as well as he would have liked, but it didn't matter. He was wound up and wild, the tiger in him wanting to let loose. He held it back and simply rode her. In her ecstasy, she squeezed his sheath hard, harder, until he came.

Demitri felt his seed shoot deep into her, and they both shouted, laughing. Demitri's legs weakened, and he collapsed to the floor, cushioning her fall onto him.

They lay on the carpet, Val smiling and Demitri still laughing. Demitri rolled her over, and held her, kissing her face and throat.

They wound down together. Val ran her fingers through his hair, and Demitri touched little kisses to her lips. Then silence, lassitude, lovely calm, drifting toward sleep.

The calm was shattered by the chirp of Demitri's cell phone. Stifling a curse, he dragged his pants to him and slid his phone out of its holder.

"Hello," he said, his voice bleary.

"Shit." Leon's voice buzzed on the other end, echoing in the way of cell phones. "You're having sex, aren't you?"

"Not anymore."

"I thought you were supposed to be flushing out thieves."

Demitri sat up, drawing a hand through his hair. Val propped herself up beside him, smiling sleepily. "We laid the groundwork. We'll go back out this evening and see if we get any bites."

"I found a few things here I need to tell you about. Not on the phone."

Demitri's curiosity stirred. "We'll be back tonight."

Leon hesitated, then he drew a breath. "There's something else I need to say to you." Demitri waited, and Leon hesitated again.

"Is someone there with you?" Demitri asked.

"Hang on. Not anymore." Leon drew another breath. "I never thought these words would come out of my mouth, but thinking of you there, with Val . . ."

"What?"

Leon lowered his voice, as though putting his mouth closer to the phone. "I want to suck your fucking huge cock."

Demitri's pulse sped, an agreeable excitement washing through him. "Really? Well, I want you to suck until my come rides down your throat."

"Fuck," Leon said.

Val draped her bare body over Demitri's. "Mmm, are you talking dirty? Let me hear, lover."

Demitri looked down at her. Her eyes had gone dark, her smile wide and feral. "Damn it," he whispered.

"What's wrong?"

"I'll call you back," Demitri said.

He clicked off the phone. Val plucked it from his hand and threw it aside before she dragged him down to her and wrapped her legs around his waist.

~ ~ ~

FELICIA looked up from her after-dinner coffee as Remy slid into the seat opposite her. The archaeology team usually went their separate ways for dinner but often fetched up at the same little restaurant for *kofta* and coffee.

Remy looked so glum that Felicia's heart twinged. He had the greenest eyes. So did his brother, but Leon had a hard face and a forbidding air that made you want to take three steps back. Remy she wanted to cuddle, running fingers through his tousled sand-colored hair.

"Are you all right?" she asked him. She pushed the sugar at him, knowing he liked to dump a lot of it into his coffee.

"I wish I knew." Remy stirred to dissolve the sugar mounded in his cup. "I feel better with Leon helping me out, but I'm asking him to find a needle in a haystack. And I feel bad dragging his friends into it. He really didn't need to involve them."

"What do you think of them?" Felicia said "them," but she knew she really meant Valerie, a woman beautiful in a way Felicia would never be.

Remy shrugged. "They're rich. Demitri was nice to put up Leon in his hotel in Cairo. My mom would say he has real Southern hospitality."

"They're interesting, aren't they? I've never met anyone like them."

Remy wrapped strong fingers around his cup. "I guess. I didn't really pay attention to them, but if they can help me keep my job, I'll embrace them with open arms."

Felicia relaxed the slightest bit. Remy had his head in the ancient past—if someone wasn't from the Nineteenth Dynasty, he barely saw them.

"Any theories as to who is stealing the artifacts?" she asked.

"Not really. I trust the members of my team, so it's got to be someone from the outside. Someone got hold of a key somehow and is stealing to sell to unscrupulous tourists."

"At least the things aren't important historically," Felicia pointed out. "Just things every dig finds dozens of."

"That's just it." Remy frowned. "Why doesn't the thief go after things that would bring him more money on the market? It's like he knows what things we won't miss too much."

"They took the necklace."

"True, but that's still not much more valuable than anything else. It's only faience. Still, it's the principle of the thing, and if anyone finds out, it will be bad for me."

Felicia daringly reached over and touched his fingers. Remy's hands were work-worn, cracked by sun and wind. His skin was tanned, his forearms dusted with gold hair. He was a solid man, born to work hard, with a brain that fortunately had been nurtured.

"We'll find out what happened," she said, trying to sound reassuring.

Remy sighed and lifted his coffee cup. "I hope you're right."

Felicia's hand slid away. Remy hadn't even noticed her touch.

She swallowed her hurt and frustration and drank her coffee. She couldn't afford much, but she determined then and there to let Valerie help her pull Remy's attention from 1250 BCE to the twenty-first-century woman who wanted him.

~ ~ ~

VAL woke to find herself facedown on a bed beside Demitri. Her hair tangled around her, and she was hugging the pillow like it was a lifeline. Valenarian the demon had gone, and Valerie gazed at Demitri. He slept with his back to her, his delectable body bare.

He slept hard. Demigods might be immortal—only gods could take their life—but they needed to eat and sleep like human beings. Demitri could push himself past the endurance of mortals, but he eventually had to replenish.

Val slipped out of bed and stood up. The living room of the suite was bright as day, though the windows revealed dark night outside.

Val padded out of the bedroom on bare feet. Aphrodite was stretched across the sofa in ancient Egyptian dress: a translucent sheath pinned at one shoulder, a heavy gold collar around her neck, and gold cuffs on her wrists. She let her black tresses spill around her, and she was nibbling on grapes.

"Hello, Val, dear," she said without looking up. "We need to talk."

12

VALERIE faced her goddess after having lain with a man, having done the things she'd done with Demitri. As a priestess, she should feel shame, guilt, remorse, but Val felt none of these. Demitri was beautiful, she loved him, and she wasn't ashamed of lying with him.

"Talk about what?" she asked Aphrodite.

"This and that."

"I'll get dressed." Val started to turn away, but Aphrodite pointed at the bedroom door, and it closed with a soft click.

"No need, Val darling. I know what a woman's body looks like, and yours is very pretty. If you're cold, your scarf is there."

Val refrained from covering herself, knowing Aphrodite would take it as a sign of weakness. Right now, Val wanted to appear strong.

"What do we need to talk about?" she repeated.

"You, dear." Aphrodite patted the sofa beside her. "Come. Sit. Have a grape."

Val perched herself on the sliver of sofa next to Aphrodite's foot. Val didn't reach for the fruit, not trusting where it came from. Eating food from Mount Olympus or some other sacred place could carry unknown consequences.

"I obtained them at the market at the end of the road," Aphrodite said, as though reading her thoughts.

"You bought them?" Val couldn't imagine Aphrodite marching into a market and actually purchasing something with mundane money.

"I persuaded the merchant to let me have them. He will have peace and prosperity for a year for his generosity."

Val didn't answer. She'd worked for Aphrodite for several thousand years and still feared her a bit. Goddesses did things for a variety of reasons, not all of them beneficial. They were short-tempered and easily offended, and their vengeance for the smallest transgression could be dire.

"Do eat, Val. You're too thin."

Val obediently took a grape and ate it, putting the seeds in a small bowl already filled with a collection of them. The grape was sweet and good.

"I am looking forward to having you back in my fold, my dear. You are so pretty and obedient. A joy, really."

Val nearly choked on the grape. "You want me to go back to being your priestess?"

"Of course I do. Why do you think I persuaded the gods to let me try to cure you?"

Val coughed, her eyes streaming. "I thought, if I conquered Valenarian, Demitri and I could . . ."

"You can spend time with him, of course, but no, you will come back to me. I thought you might misinterpret that, so I wanted to pop along and make sure you understood."

Val stared at her, stunned. She had somehow assumed that if they won, she would stay with Demitri. And Leon. Demitri was growing fond of Leon, it was obvious. The three of them together would be unconventional by human standards, but demigods could follow different conventions.

"Then I will have to lose him again," Val said softly. "No matter what happens."

"I believe you'll find that when you drive the demon out of you, you won't want to stay with him," Aphrodite said, sounding complacent. "You'll be my obedient servant, living for your work. That's the way I see it, anyway."

Val looked at the floor so Aphrodite wouldn't see her eyes flood with tears. She'd have to say good-bye to both of them. In fourteen days—thirteen now.

Hurt twisted her heart. She thought of Demitri lying in bed in the next room, his handsome face relaxed in sleep. She loved him. She'd always loved him. And she was falling in love with Leon as well.

"You expect me to let them go."

Aphrodite eyed her keenly. "Yes, I do. I want you to love *me*. I saved your life, after all, when all the other gods wanted to kill you."

"Why should you? You're not even of my pantheon. I'm Egyptian."

"I know that. But where were Isis and Mut and Sekhmet when you needed them? The Egyptian goddesses left this plane long ago and care not what happens on it. The pharaohs who worshipped them have vanished, and people now care nothing for them. The old gods keep their distance. The Greek gods are much stronger and have always been more connected to this world. Do not schoolchildren in the places called England and America still read of the Greeks and their gods?"

"I have no idea," Val said.

"They do. Poets such as Homer and Virgil kept us alive. The Egyptians lost their stories until the archaeologists of the last hundred years dug them up again. And still not many people know them."

Val curled her fingers on the sofa, wishing Aphrodite would stop babbling about which pantheon was better. In Val's opinion, all gods were cruel and capricious. Aphrodite was giving her a typical goddess-like choice: defeat Valenarian and say good-bye to Demitri and Leon forever, or let Valenarian win and watch the men she loved die lingering deaths.

Val wanted to withdraw into herself and weep until she had no more tears. She suddenly hated Aphrodite, who sat there nibbling grapes while Val's world was crumbling around her.

Aphrodite rose, smiling. "I'm glad I could clear things up, dear. Before you are finished here, of course, your shifter's brother needs to pair up with the washed-out Felicia. You can also pair Demitri and your shifter. Two couples to live happily ever after. That should console you."

Val got to her feet, folding her arms over her chest. "Matchmaker to the end?" she asked in a dry voice.

"Of course. I wish you good luck."

Someone knocked on the door. Val glanced at it just as Aphrodite began to fade.

The knock sounded again, a muffled voice saying something about room service. Val cursed, grabbed her clothes, and tugged them on as she went to the door. Aphrodite's light had faded all the way as Val opened the door a crack.

"Oh no," she groaned. "Not another one."

An Egyptian waiter stood outside the door holding a tray covered with silver dishes, a bewildered expression on his face.

"Come in," Val said, throwing open the door and gesturing toward the table. "But I warn you, I've had it up to here with gods today, so be careful what you say."

The man glided into the room and set the tray on the table. "Compliments of Mr. Karim, the owner of this hotel. He is a friend to Mr. Demitri, yes?"

"Yes. I know it's you, Bes. Stop pretending."

The man straightened up, letting his godlike aura shine through his disguise. He looked completely different from the carpet shop owner in Cairo and the man who'd showed them the erotic paintings in the west valley, but his brown eyes were the same.

"I came to tell you that not all gods are against you, Valenarian. I want to help you, like I helped the friends of Demitri—Nikolaus and Andreas and their ladies."

"How can you?" Val asked. "If you were eavesdropping, you heard what she said. I have to be healed, or they'll die. But to save them, I'll have to leave them."

"Perhaps." Bes tried to look wise, but he only looked worried. "I will help you, child of Egypt. Not all the gods of old Egypt are gone."

Val softened. She didn't believe for a minute that Bes, the small god who protected the home from scorpions and snakes, could prevail over Aphrodite, daughter of Zeus, but it was nice to know he cared. "Thank you. Is this really from the kitchen? Come to think of it, I'm famished. But I warn you, if you brought any grapes, I'll throw them out the window."

~ ~ ~

WHEN Demitri woke, he found Val curled beside him, head cradled on her bent arm. He had no doubt that Valenarian had receded— Val's hair was soft and straight, her breathing peaceful and even.

Demitri got carefully out of bed so as not to disturb her. He showered and shaved, then redressed and went out to the front room.

The remains of a meal lay on the table, with a bowl of tabbouleh still carefully covered and a wrapped flatbread next to it. He smiled at Val's thoughtfulness. After he ate, he pulled out his cell phone and called Leon.

A sleepy answer came to him. "Hello?"

"Sorry, I didn't mean to wake you. Are you at the hotel over there?"

"No, I'm camping out at the dig house. Hang on." There was a long pause, and just when Demitri thought he'd lost the connection, Leon came back on. "I'm outside where I can talk. No one's up yet."

"Watch out for snakes."

"It's too cold for snakes." Leon's voice held amusement. "Way too cold for scorpions, too, so don't bother trying to scare me."

"But the snakes might want to curl up in bed next to your nice, warm body."

"Thank you, I got all the snake stories from Remy already. Plus I grew up with water moccasins and coral snakes. Do you want to hear what I found out, or what?"

"Sorry. Go ahead."

"I talked to the Egyptian guy, Habib, who also has a key to the storage building. He says the key hasn't left his key ring, which is always in his pocket. He looked amazed when I suggested borrowing it. He says it's in his trust and he lends it to no one. He lets people in and out of the storage room, but he watches them closely, according to several other people I asked about him."

"Habib might be the thief himself."

"I don't think so. If he was, I'd think he'd try to claim someone stole his key. He told me pretty blatantly that people on the American team were careless with their keys, but not him. He's also very big on keeping Egyptian artifacts in Egypt, like Remy told us. He gave me a fifteen-minute lecture on the subject. So unless he's a terrific actor, I don't think he's the guy."

Demitri digested all this. "You know we might run out of time to investigate. If I have to choose between saving Val and helping your brother, you know I have to choose Val."

"I know. I'm trying my damndest to do both."

Demitri explained in a low voice that he'd taken the pendant necklace from Remy's storage room. Leon wasn't happy, but he understood.

"Have you found any clues to the whereabouts of the pendant's other half?" Demitri asked him.

"No. Felicia says she's trying to figure out how it got into their tomb—she thinks it was brought from another tomb by robbers several thousand years ago. If we can figure out where it came from in the first place, we might find the other piece."

"It took archaeologists almost a hundred years of searching to find the tomb of Tutankhamun."

"Thanks, Demitri, that's real encouraging."

"Sorry. I'm . . ."

"Worried. I know."

"Scared," Demitri said. "I'm not ashamed to admit it. I love her. I'll do anything to keep her alive."

"I hear you. I might not have known her as long as you have, but I want to help her, too. For many reasons." Leon paused. "How is she?"

Demitri knew what he meant. "Sleeping. She's fine."

Leon knew what Demitri meant as well. "You might as well stay there for the night. I want to watch here anyway, see if I can catch someone in the act."

"I hope so. Good luck."

Another pause, then Leon went on slowly, "About what I said to you before . . ."

Demitri smiled into the phone. "About wanting to suck my fucking huge cock?"

"Yeah."

"Have you changed your mind?"

"No. I don't know why I wanted to say that. I've never said stuff like that to a guy."

"So you keep telling me."

"I always chased hot ladies. Hell, I think all ladies are beautiful. Tits and ass, that's what I dream about."

"That hasn't changed. I see how you look at Val."

"And why doesn't that bug you? If you love her so much, why are you letting me touch her? She screwed me the night she met me, and you watched."

Demitri leaned his elbows on the table, picturing Leon on the other end of the phone. The night air would ruffle his short hair, and he'd frown, green eyes troubled as he asked Demitri questions difficult for both of them.

"I don't know," Demitri said. "It seemed right, somehow. I was more worried about her hurting you than anything else."

"Why should you care about a Cajun boy out on his own?"

"Maybe because you had such a sweet, tight body?" Demitri said, his blood heating. "And a cock my hands wanted to reach for?"

Leon's voice went low, as though he fought the words he needed to say. "You have a great ass. I want to fuck your ass every time I see it."

"I could arrange that."

"I want to stick my tongue down your throat," Leon said. "Then I want to bend you over and fuck you until you scream."

Demitri gripped the phone tighter. "And then what?"

"I'll fuck you until I come in your beautiful ass. Then I'll have you turn around, and I'll suck your cock until you come, too."

Demitri slid one hand to his trousers, where his hardness pressed the zipper. He massaged himself, the tingle feeling good.

"What do you want to do to me?" Leon asked. "Tell me. I can take it."

Demitri didn't have to think for long. "I want you to lie down on a bed. I want to pull up your shirt and tongue your nipples. You'll like that. Then I want to lick down to your crotch and use my mouth to make you hard. We'll be face-to-face so I can come up and kiss you anytime I want."

He let himself dissolve into the fantasy, Leon lying bare on a bed, Demitri over him, licking, kissing, suckling. Leon with his hand tucked behind his head, smiling his rare smile as he watched Demitri work on him. Val would be there, too, nibbling her finger as she watched, eyes shining.

"Then what?" Leon said, his voice raw. "Come on, don't leave me hanging."

"I'll spread your legs and ease my cock inside you. I'll lift your hips so I can go in deep, and I'll watch your face while you take me."

"Sounds good."

"You've never been taken by a man. It will be a slow process. I'll have to get you ready, play with you a *lot*, start with my fingers, use lots of lube. But eventually, you'll take my cock."

"I'm looking forward to it."

"Before that I might warm you up with my tongue. You'll climb over me, and you can suck my cock while I lie back and stick my tongue in your ass."

"Oh yeah?"

"Think about it. My tongue all wet and strong, probing you."

"Fuck." The word was low, strained.

"What's the matter?" Demitri asked him. "You must have talked about tongue sex before."

"Not with a man."

"We'll have Val with us. She'll watch me playing with you, and she'll slide her hand into her pussy, showing us how wet we're making her. She'll likely want to stroke your cock while I'm licking your ass."

"Damn it, I think I'm going to come right now."

Demitri chuckled. "Enjoy yourself," he said, then he started to close the phone.

"You asshole—" Leon's voice cut off as the phone snapped shut.

Demitri chuckled again, then broke off with a soft groan. Leon wasn't the only one who'd gotten worked up at their exchange. Demitri tossed the phone aside, unfastened his trousers, and caught his own aching cock in his hand.

~ ~ ~

ON the other side of the phone, Leon hung up, swearing. He walked swiftly down the path toward the excavation site, letting the night air cool his hot skin. His cock throbbed, but he didn't want to open up and yank himself out here in the open.

His swearing gave way to laughter. He threw his head back, looking up at the sky blazing with stars. Back home, he didn't always see such a full sky. Haze, humidity, clouds, or light pollution obscured the stars, but in the deserts they were thick.

Leon laughed again. He'd just had phone sex with a man, and he'd liked it. He'd felt good and giddy and as excited as he'd been with his first girl at fifteen. He'd spilled his seed pretty fast with her, and it was all he could do not to spill it now.

When Leon met up with Demitri again, when they had time alone . . . Damn, what they'd do.

The sound of rock clicking on rock brought Leon swiftly out of his thoughts. He stepped silently into deeper shadow, standing so still he might be a shadow himself.

A small figure in an Egyptian galabiya darted along the path toward the dig house, his movements silent and furtive. Leon blessed the thief for striking, a good distraction to get rid of his pesky hard-on.

He let the thief get most of the way to the storage room before he moved from the shadow and silently followed.

~ ~ ~

I won't let her take me back, Valenarian snapped.

Val had spent all morning having an argument inside her own head. It unnerved her that she couldn't control the voice, and outwardly she was very quiet as she and Demitri once again wandered the streets of Luxor, waiting for someone to offer them stolen antiquities.

I can't let Demitri and Leon die, Valerie returned.

They won't die. I'll take them somewhere she'll never find them.

Where? Val asked herself tartly. *She's a goddess, daughter and sister of gods who want me dead. They can go anywhere, be anywhere. We can't hide from gods.*

No? Gods are too powerful to be smart. We can deceive them. They are trapped in their ancient thoughts, unaware of how the world has changed. There are places beyond their ken, where they've never been heard of.

Oh, sure. We can live on a glacier or in the depths of a South American rain forest. Sounds like paradise. I'm sure Leon and Demitri will rush to join us.

Not quite, Valenarian said. *There are primal forces in the world more ancient than they are. I will guide those forces, and we will be free together.*

By primal, you mean demon. I left all that behind. I won't embrace it again.

You might have tried to leave it, my weak-willed friend, but the demon hasn't left you. I am not going back to a life of obedience and celibacy. I'm sick of prayer and meditation while I'm dying for a good fuck.

Go away. Please. I can't afford to be distracted by you.

Valenarian laughed, even while her voice faded. *You can take the girl out of the demon . . .*

She was gone. Demitri looked at her, eyes narrowing in concern. Val tried to give him a reassuring smile, but Demitri watched her carefully as they crossed a street and entered yet another souvenir shop.

~ ~ ~

"I drew a blank," Leon said at the dig house. "Sorry, Remy."

After breakfast, once the team had headed to the site, Remy met Leon alone. Even Felicia had taken off, apologetically saying she needed to finish tracing a frieze in the tomb before it became too exposed.

"Whoever it was didn't try to get into the lab," Leon told his brother. "He walked around the compound then headed back into the hills. I lost him in the dark."

"It's all right." Remy looked downcast, but Leon's little brother always tried to make everyone feel better. "Could be he had nothing to do with it."

"Anything missing today?"

"Nope." Remy led the way down through the lab and into the storage room. "I took stock last night before I turned in, and everything's still here."

"Weird that they don't go for the computers if they're looking for money."

Remy shrugged. "Whoever it is has targeted his buyers and knows we'll be more likely to cover up the theft than go to the police. Which I'll have to do if we come up with nothing. Then I'll have to come up with a reason we didn't go to the police in the first place."

"Remy." Leon put a hand on his brother's shoulder. "I'm sorry, man. I'm doing my best. We'll catch him. Or her."

Remy gave him a startled look. "Her?"

"It might have been a woman I saw last night. I could only see someone in a galabiya, a light-colored smudge in the dark. A woman could put on one of those and run through the night, and I wouldn't know the difference at a distance. Galabiyas are pretty shapeless."

"Most of the women here are foreign. Not Egyptian I mean, except for a couple of specialists from Cairo. I can't believe they'd steal anything. They've worked far too hard for their jobs to jeopardize them."

Leon studied his younger brother, his worried look and furrowed brow, the tension in his shoulders. "How long has it been since you had a run?"

Remy glanced furtively around them, but the room was as empty of people as when they came in. "You mean shifted?"

"Yeah. What'd you think I meant?"

"Not much opportunity, is there?"

"You can't deny the shift, little brother. We have to release the energy. Just like when you haven't had sex in a while, you go a little nuts." Leon peered at Remy again. "How long has it been for that?"

Remy laughed. "Too long. Everyone lives on top of each other in a dig house. No privacy. And if anything goes on, everyone knows about it. It's worse than living in a small town."

"Aw damn, and here I thought you'd gotten away from all that."

"Archaeology is a small world, and gossip is everyone's favorite hobby. Besides, there isn't much opportunity for sex when we're all exhausted and covered with dirt."

His voice was light, but Leon saw the tiredness in his eyes. The worry of the thefts on top of being team leader for the first time was draining him.

"What about Felicia?" Leon asked.

"Felicia?" Remy looked at Leon in genuine surprise. "I like her, but she's only got one thing on her mind. Conservation of tomb decorations, especially those pertaining to magic. If she's not copying and tracing pictures and friezes, she's not happy. I don't even think she knows she and I are different genders."

Leon wondered how Remy could be so blind, but he decided to leave the matchmaking to Val. "Tonight, come out with me, and we'll go for a run," he said. "We'll keep watch on the storage unit, and who knows? Maybe as wild cats, we'll sniff out the thief."

13

WHEN Demitri and Val returned to the hotel in Luxor for lunch, Demitri's friend Karim gave him a sealed envelope. "A well-dressed German asked the manager to make sure you got this," he said. "I thought I'd deliver it myself."

Demitri thanked him. Karim looked curious but would never pry, a trait that made him easy to be friends with. Demitri found a note, in German, asking to meet him inside the Old Winter Palace Hotel. Alone.

"Might be our thief," he said, showing the note to Val.

Val raised her brows. "A far cry from an archaeology student wishing to make extra money."

"This man might be the fence, who can lead us to the thief. I should meet him." He hesitated.

"I'll be fine. I planned to take Felicia shopping, anyway. She called me and said she had a free afternoon today. She's going to meet me here."

"You might be safer locked in your room."

"Aphrodite wants me to shove Felicia and Remy together, which I'd do even if she didn't insist. I like this part of my job, Demitri. I'll make sure Valenarian doesn't take over."

Val spoke glibly and hid her worry. Valenarian's voice had been strong this morning, stronger than it had ever been. Val sometimes heard the demon's voice faintly, but usually Valenarian either took over completely or vanished. Never had Val felt a duel existence inside her.

"All right." Demitri reluctantly rose, pressing a kiss to the top of her head. "Meet me back up in the suite at four. If you're late, I'll take the town apart to find you."

"I'll be fine," Val repeated.

She met Felicia as the young woman entered the hotel lobby looking for her. Felicia wore a plain shirt and pants, and she'd washed up from the dig, but that's was the extent of her effort.

"Come with me," Val said, tucking her hand under Felicia's arm. "We'll make you beautiful."

"I'd like to see that," Felicia laughed.

Val decided to ignore Valenarian and enjoy herself that afternoon. She took Felicia to a dressmaker, and they entered a private, cushioned, closed-off room that was feminine and comfortable.

A beautiful Egyptian woman sat down next to Felicia and looked her over while an assistant ran back and forth to bring out assorted dresses, shirts and slacks, tunics, and jewelry.

"I don't know what to get," Felicia said, bewilderment in her eyes. "And I know I can't afford it."

"But Demitri can," Val assured her.

"He won't want you buying clothes for me."

"Don't be ridiculous. He wants me to spend the money on whatever I wish, and today, I wish to spend it on you."

"I'll pay you back."

"No, you will not." Valenarian snapped forth in that moment, her rage mounting. Stupid, vapid girl. Couldn't she see that Val was trying to help her?

Val gasped and Valenarian was gone. The shop owner and Felicia looked at her in concern.

"I'm fine," Val said, fanning herself. "I'm warm, that's all."

The shop owner called to her assistant who instantly returned with cool drinks and a cloth for Val's head. Val accepted graciously, too shaken to protest she didn't need them.

Felicia bent over the clothing, probably fearing she'd cause Val a seizure if she argued any longer. After a time, Val sat up and helped her, realizing that Felicia didn't have any clothes sense whatsoever.

At the end of the afternoon, they'd draped Felicia in a light yellow tunic covered with deeper yellow roses, black slacks, and sandals with low heels. Val draped Felicia with gold jewelry, holding up a hand mirror so she could see how lovely the ornaments made her. Felicia laughed as the earrings tinkled in her ears and bangles whispered on her wrists.

Felicia put up another protest at the makeup, but finally let the assistant dab on eye shadow and eyeliner, powder and blush, and a little light lipstick. When Felicia finally viewed herself in the shop's full-length mirror, her eyes widened. "I'm pretty."

"Of course you are. Remy can't ignore you now."

"Yes, he could. I doubt he'd notice a belly dancer if she started dancing in his lap."

"Hmm," Val said, and she abruptly lost control to Valenarian again. "Do you have any dancing costumes?" she asked the shop assistant. "Real ones, I mean. Not the glittery shit tourists buy."

The shop owner blinked, but her assistant nodded and hurried out, returning with her arms full of velvet and silk. Felicia gaped at the tiny jacket, the skirt that was simply an embroidered band with swaths of silk that would cover nothing. Minuscule mirrors had been sewn among the embroidery, making the costume shimmer whichever way it moved.

"Good lord," Felicia said. "I can't wear that."

Valenarian took the costume in delight. "But I can." She ducked behind a curtain, where she enjoyed herself closing the jacket over her full breasts and clasping the embroidered band around her hips. She emerged and spun around, laughing as the lovely costume flared.

"You see?" she said to Felicia. "A good dancing costume makes you look provocative without revealing anything essential." She raised her arms and began to move her hips and legs in a dance that hadn't been done in a thousand years.

The shop owner clasped her hands in delight. "You are very skilled, madam."

Val laughed. It felt good to break free, to throw off her shackles. She went through the movements of the old dance, which had been created at a time when dancers were trained to entertain the women of the harem, not the men. This modern shop looked much like a seraglio of old, with silk hangings, carpets, wooden screens, and an audience of women drinking coffee and smiling as they watched her.

Val changed from a classic belly dance to one much older, from thousands of years ago but still Egyptian. The dancers on tomb walls might have been painted in stiff and angular poses, but the true dance was soft and flowing, erotic and beautiful.

Val flashed to the past, when she'd danced this same dance for Demitri. She could see him through the haze of memory, lying on his back in a grove, smiling lazily as he watched her dance for him.

Her body moved in the same way it had then, bangles clinking softly on her wrists and ankles. Demitri had worn nothing but a thin linen tunic, one that bared half his torso. Dark hair dusted his chest, and his long legs were tanned by the sun.

She loved how he admired her. Demitri loved her body, but she knew in her heart he didn't love *her*. He was enchanted with Valenarian and loved to sex her, but he'd never love a demon. On the other hand, Valenarian had lost her heart to him, to a demigod who could kill her without effort. Demitri was the only man she'd never been able to tame, and she loved him with all her heart.

In that grove, Demitri had risen and caught her hands as she danced. He pulled her down to the ground with him, pressing kisses to her flesh.

He pushed her dress from her body and made love to her, his eyes liquid dark and sinful. "Do you like what I do to you?" he whispered to her. "Do you like how I make you feel?"

"Yes," she moaned, then she screamed it. "*Yes.*"

"You're mine, Val. You belong to me. No one else."

"Yes," she sobbed.

"Say it."

"I belong to you, Demitri. Only you. Forever."

In that grove, she'd believed it and thought he did, too. Demitri laughed at her, then he rolled to his feet and changed to his tiger. He wanted to play.

Val let him chase her through the groves on the edge of the river, sun dappling her skin through the trees. She almost let him catch her, then turned the tables by leaping onto his back and holding tight while he ran like a streak of light.

She loved him so much. Those days had been the happiest of her life, and she hadn't known it. She and Demitri had played and made love or walked quietly together, slept together under the stars or curled up inside Demitri's rooms for warmth. Being with Demitri had made Val feel special and complete. She belonged to him, and she'd thought he belonged to her.

She whirled in place and the silk-hung shop came back to her, the women watching her dance. Val stopped, tears streaming down her face. Felicia paused in her applause.

"Are you all right, Val?"

Val sank to her knees, burying her face in her hands. Valerie was going to let Valenarian die or drag her back to bondage at the hands of the Goddess of Love. A cruel fate for a woman who had trapped herself by falling hopelessly in love.

Felicia came to her, slender hands touching Val's shoulders. "What's the matter?"

Valenarian looked up at her so fiercely that Felicia took a step back. "They're not worth it. He'll pretend to fall in love with you, but in the end, he'll betray you."

"Who will? Remy?"

"Men! They're all treacherous. They'll cut out your heart and leave you to bleed."

Felicia sank to one knee, her expression sympathetic. "Did that happen to you, Val? Did Demitri do something like that to you?"

Val glared at her, then she burst into tears. She was going to lose Demitri and Leon and everything about life that she loved. One way or another, it was being ripped from her.

Felicia rubbed her shoulders, her look distressed. Good Lord, the woman cared that a demoness was kneeling half-naked in an Egyptian shop, crying her heart out. Valenarian flung her arms around the mortal girl and wept until she had no tears left.

~ ~ ~

"I couldn't control her." Val sat numbly in the living room of the suite, sipping the coffee Demitri had handed her. Dark smudges stained her face beneath her swollen eyes.

"What were you doing?"

"Dancing." Val sighed, warming her hands on the cup. "I danced like I danced for you in the olive groves in Greece."

Demitri well remembered. He'd lain in the grass while Val moved her body in flowing undulations. He remembered how beautiful she'd been with her eyes lined with kohl, her fingers painted with henna, her gold jewelry tinkling like music. She'd moved her wrists and ankles in sinuous motion, smiling her sensual smile.

In later centuries men claimed that Cleopatra was the most beautiful woman who'd ever lived, but Demitri knew differently. Cleopatra could make people believe she was beautiful, but she had nothing on Val. Even the famous Nefertiti and the even more lovely Nefertari paled in comparison with Val.

"Why were you dancing?" he asked her.

"I don't know," Val snapped. "I wanted to. *She* wanted to.

Demitri, you need to figure out how to tame her quickly. I don't think I'll be able to contain her much longer."

"I'll try to find Leon. I have some ideas."

"What kind of ideas?"

"You'll see." Demitri stopped talking. Nothing was working—Leon couldn't both help control Valenarian and help his brother. They needed to find the second piece of the necklace.

Valerie wiped her eyes. "What about the German man who wanted to meet you at the Winter Palace?"

Demitri shook his head, feeling renewed disappointment. "He tried to sell me emeralds, not broken pottery pieces. He was too high-dollar for what we were looking for. Strangely he ran into an officer from Interpol right after he left me."

Val tried to smile. "That wasn't so strange, I'm thinking."

"He was a smuggler, in it for the excitement."

Demitri had been angry at the well-dressed, arrogant business-man stealing from a country that was challenged to keep its population fed and clothed. Demitri hadn't even had to use magic to alert Interpol—he'd only had to signal his friends at the Winter Palace Hotel, and they'd done his bidding.

Demitri couldn't get Leon on his cell phone. Wherever the man was as the sun went down, Demitri hoped everything was all right with him.

~ ~ ~

Two lions ran across the darkened desert where no lion had run for hundreds of years. Leon kept pace with Remy, who obviously hadn't done this in far too long. Remy's tension flowed away from him as his powerful body stretched low across the desert floor.

As Leon ran, he felt the worries of the past few weeks rippling from him as well. He realized that before he came to Egypt he'd been drifting, uncertain, numb from his experiences. He'd had no direction, no purpose, no meaning to his life.

And then he'd seen Val across the hotel lobby, looking beautiful, charming, seductive. He'd followed her and didn't regret that for a minute. Not long after that, Demitri had walked into his life and confused Leon like he'd never been confused before.

He and Remy reached a rocky outcropping, and Remy stopped, panting in the cool night breeze. Leon stretched and shook himself, feeling his full mane against his sides. He hadn't chosen to be a lion in a long time.

Remy let out a roar that echoed across the cliffs, then his body shifted, and he became human once more. Leon yawned, loving how it felt to open his mouth wide until he felt like he could swallow his own face. Then his teeth clacked together and his balance shifted as he rose on two human legs.

The two brothers faced each other, Leon a little larger than Remy, Remy wiry and tanned from working on his digs. Leon folded his arms and leaned against a rock, his shifter brain not minding being naked in the desert lit by bright moon and stars.

"Watch out for snakes."

"Fuck snakes," Leon said, still thinking like a lion.

"Cobras," Remy said. "They can kill you very fast, lion or human."

"No kidding. Remember all the snakes in the creek behind Mom's house? Remember when we tried to fish for them that summer?"

"And Mom tanned our hides?" Remy winced. "I remember."

"I miss that life," Leon said softly. "We had it so good."

"We couldn't stay kids forever."

"No, I guess not."

The moon glinted in Remy's eyes, which were slowly turning to his human green. "You've never really talked since you got home," Remy said. "About the stuff you saw in Afghanistan."

"No."

"I didn't like to ask." But he was asking now.

"I really am all right, Remy. It was bad sometimes, people doing their best to kill each other and us, villages barely hanging on while other people got stinking rich smuggling out the opium. I tried to be nice, you know? Let people know I really wanted to help them. But so many were so burned out they didn't want to trust, or hope. I hated that."

Remy looked at him in surprise. "I was thinking more about the fear of getting blown up or shot."

"Well, yeah, that, too." Leon gave him a tight smile. "But you can't think about that all the time, or it will drive you crazy. You have to be careful and smart, not paranoid. Paranoid will get you just as killed."

"And here I am complaining because I can't have a ham and Swiss on rye until I get back home." Remy's words were light, but he wouldn't look at Leon.

"Hey, little brother, guilt is the very last thing you should feel. Joining up was my choice. I wanted a quick way to get money back to Mom and you. Now you're a bad-ass archaeologist, on your way to being a professor. In the long run, you'll be able to help Mom way better than I will. I don't even know what I'm doing out here."

"Helping me out. For free."

"Because you're my little brother, and Duprees take care of each other." Leon looked off into the moonlit desert. "I'll learn how to take care of myself some day."

"What about Val?"

"I don't think that's going anywhere. She's the lady of my dreams, but she loves Demitri. However this ends up, she'll go with him."

"It's not like you to give up."

"I'm not giving up." Leon straightened. "I'm just thinking about what will make *her* happy, not me."

"You do that too often, Leon."

Leon frowned. "Do what?"

"Make all your decisions based on what will make everyone else happy. Someday you have to make yourself happy. Just you, no matter what anyone else thinks."

Leon didn't answer. If he ever figured out what made him happy, he might go for it. But he had no idea. The whole world rolled away at his feet, and he didn't have a clue how to be happy in it.

He reached for the lion inside him, ready to run back to the dig.

"Hang on." Remy was staring at something at the base of the outcropping.

"What? Snake?"

"No." Remy crouched down, disregarding his own warning about snakes by putting his hand into a small hole. "I wonder . . ."

Leon crouched over him. "What is it?"

"It can't be. This area was mapped."

"What the hell are you talking about?"

"Look at this. It might be the entrance to a tomb. These chips of limestone—they could have been washed here by a flash flood, or they could be leftover from people hollowing out the rock. I wish I had more light."

Leon grabbed Remy and hauled him to his feet. "You're stark naked in the middle of nowhere. Mark it and we can come back later."

Remy brushed dirt from his knees, but his gaze was remote. "Do you know what this could mean?"

"That you found a hole and some rocks?"

Remy's smile dazzled him. "It could mean my career. Even with the theft from the dig. No one has found anything out here. It's too remote. Or so we thought."

Leon wanted to laugh. Remy looked like he did when he was seven and discovered a secret stash of candy he'd hidden at Halloween and forgotten about until March. "All right, Indiana Jones, let's go before we set off all the booby traps. We can come back and get the treasure later."

Remy looked at him like he was crazy. "What are you talking about? The Egyptians didn't leave booby traps." He piled a few stones together and looked around, memorizing the landscape. "I'll bring Felicia out here. She'll love this."

"You really know how to wow the ladies."

"She'll think this is much better than some rich guy giving her diamonds. Felicia's obsessed with archaeology, not afraid to get her hands dirty."

"So you like her?"

"You sound like we're in high school. There's nothing wrong with Felicia. She's a great addition to my team."

Leon rolled his eyes as he turned to look again for the lion within him. "So glad romance isn't dead," he muttered; then he became the big cat and words disappeared.

~ ~ ~

LEON left Remy poring over maps in his lab and answered the seven messages on his cell phone. "Get to the hotel in Luxor as soon as you can," was Demitri's first message. The last one was, "Leon, damn it, I need you."

Leon tried to call back, got nothing, and left in a hurry for Luxor.

14

I heard you were looking for me." Felicia paused in the doorway to the lab. She wore her new clothes, the tunic moving and flowing as she walked. Her hair curled softly, her face was lightly made up, and earrings tinkled in her ears. For the first time in her life, she felt pretty.

Remy hunched over a table, staring at a map. Occasionally he'd look away and make a note, then he'd go back to glaring at the map. "We went *that* way, I know we did. Why isn't it there?"

"Remy?"

Remy jumped a foot and swung around, pencil clamped between his fingers. "What? Oh, it's you. Come here and look at this."

He turned his back, registering nothing more than her standing in the doorway. Swallowing frustration, Felicia crossed to the table.

Remy didn't even look up. "Have you been out here?" He pointed with the pencil's eraser to a remote wadi off to the north and west of the Valley of Kings.

"I don't think so. Remy, I'd like to ask you something."

Remy's eyes sparkled as he looked up, but he obviously wasn't seeing her. "We need to go out there."

Felicia's heart beat faster. The scenario she'd gone over since standing in the shop and viewing her new clothes went as follows: Remy would look up from whatever archaeological fascination held his attention, look her over in astonishment and growing delight, then abandon what he was doing and smile at her. *At* her, not through her. He'd realize she was a woman, not just a colleague. He'd ask her out to dinner, ideally at one of the nice hotels in Luxor. Then they'd decide it was too late to cross the river back to the dig house. They'd stay the night in the hotel.

They'd start with kisses when he said good night to her, then end up in bed, where they'd slowly and thoroughly make love. In the morning, Remy would tell her he couldn't believe he'd never noticed that he loved her. They'd have breakfast in bed and maybe make love again before heading back to the dig and resuming their work. They'd still be partners and friends, but they'd let themselves fall more deeply in love. They'd be partners for life.

Stupid, romantic ideas. Felicia chided herself. *I let Val make me think I could be beautiful. What a waste of time.*

Beyond the hurt in her pounding heart, she focused on what Remy had just said: *We need to go out there.*

"Why?"

Remy's face lit up in near rapture. "Felicia, I might have discovered a tomb." He whispered it, his voice trembling.

His words were like a cold slap through her uncertainty. "A tomb? Are you sure?"

"I don't know. I'd like a better look."

Felicia peered at the map again. "Are you sure this was the place? It's a long way from the river."

"Very sure. There was an outcropping and a series of wadis. This map isn't detailed enough, but I can find it again."

"What were you doing out there? That's miles away."

"I was with my brother. We were, um, hiking." He waved that away. "It doesn't matter. There might be an entrance. I need to see. Come with me."

Felicia nodded automatically. Of course she'd come. She'd follow him to hell and back. "Have you told anyone?"

"No. Just you. It might be nothing."

Remy was holding his excitement in check with great effort. Felicia knew as well as he did that he might have stumbled upon nothing. The odds weren't in their favor. But then again, there was the story of KV 5. Everyone had thought it a minor tomb of only a few rooms. Then the excavators cleared a small doorway and discovered it led to a maze of corridors and the largest tomb ever discovered in the Valley of Kings. It had lain hidden from some of the best archaeologists in the world because no one had bothered to open one door.

Felicia tried without success to stifle her eagerness. "We should check it out, just in case."

Remy grabbed a flashlight. "Exactly." He looked her up and down and frowned. "You might want to change clothes, though. You'll ruin those."

~ ~ ~

Leon reached the hotel and knocked on the door of the suite. Demitri opened the door just wide enough to grab Leon and drag him inside.

Val lay on the couch, worry on her face, but other than that, Leon saw nothing wrong.

"Hey," he said to both of them. "Why'd you need me?"

"Take off your clothes," Demitri said.

"It's nice to see you, too. My brother and I had a good talk this evening, cleared up some stuff. What have y'all been up to?"

"You need to let Val make love to you, without Valenarian taking over," Demitri said, ignoring him. "We need to teach her that sex can be slow and sweet. Loving."

"So why aren't you at it?"

Val answered, her voice soft with fear. "Because I can't control her with Demitri. She remembers and wants him."

"So I get to be the sex slave?"

"We don't have much choice," Demitri said. "Valenarian loves her sexual power. Being celibate, Valerie never had the chance to make sex not about power. My idea is that we teach her about feeling rather than control, surrender instead of domination."

Leon drew in a breath, his blood warming. "I'm willing to give it a try."

"Do you know how to give massages?" Demitri asked him.

Leon fixed his gaze on Val, her beautiful face pleading. "I'll learn."

"Good," Demitri said. "Now, take your clothes off."

Leon skimmed his T-shirt off over his head. "What are you going to do?"

"Teach, watch, and enjoy."

Demitri's dark eyes were filled with anticipation. He was hard, Leon could tell, the shifter in Leon sensing the high pheromone concentration in the room.

Valerie's gaze was just as intense as Leon unzipped his jeans and shoved them down, then pulled off his socks as he stood in his tight briefs.

"Stop," Demitri said. "Val, touch him."

Val nodded and stood up. Unlike when Demitri had told Valenarian to touch Leon the other night, she looked more like a woman about to attempt a dangerous surveillance than one about to touch a ready and willing man. Valenarian then had been eager and unable to hold back. Valerie now looked afraid to let go.

Leon held his breath as Val stopped in front of him. She lifted her hands and spread her fingers, then very gently touched his chest.

Fire ran from her fingertips to heat his body. Leon stood still, arms at his sides. Val skimmed her fingertips across the curled hair on his chest and lightly traced his nipples. Leon sucked in his breath but remained still.

He was aware of Demitri standing a few feet behind Val, still clothed, his dark eyes fixed on the two of them.

He's loving this, Leon thought. *He's getting off on watching the woman he loves touch the man he wants to screw.*

And I don't hate it.

Val flicked her nail over his nipple again, a fine, tingling sensation. Then she drew her touch down to his abdomen, tracing the outline of his navel. She studied the skin as she touched it, trailing fire all the way.

She brushed his lower abdomen, dipping her fingers a fraction of an inch into the waistband.

"No." Demitri's command was sharp. "Not yet."

Val hesitated, as though she wanted to tell Demitri to fuck off, then she nodded, and continued her touching on Leon's back.

"You have scars," she murmured, tracing them. Irregular scars crisscrossed and puckered his right shoulder blade.

"From a few years ago. A bomb went off, and I got cut by debris."

"Oh dear. I'm sorry."

Leon didn't mind the scars. He'd gotten off lightly. If he'd been standing three feet closer to the car, he'd have died.

"I'm glad you survived," Demitri said.

"You and me both."

Val traced the scars again, and then he felt her tongue on them. He closed his eyes, his cock so stiff it ached.

Val kept her touch light and undemanding. She pressed harder with the pads of her fingers, but it was nothing like the erotic grappling she'd engaged in the night she'd jumped into Leon's bed.

She drew her fingers down to the small of his back, then knelt to touch the backs of his thighs and his legs. She touched everything but his underwear, even skimming her fingertips over his toes.

"You're doing well," Demitri said. "Keep it controlled, and take off his underwear."

Val obediently hooked her fingers in the elastic waistband and pulled down Leon's briefs.

"Who's going to keep *me* controlled?" Leon said.

"Me," Demitri answered. "Stand still and take it."

In the army, Leon had been in situations where he'd had to stand at attention no matter what was going on. Rain, a captain yelling at him, a bird shitting on him. Didn't matter, attention was attention.

He'd never had to do it while a beautiful woman relieved him of his underwear and ran her fingers all over his body. And never while a man he'd kissed watched intently, calling the shots.

None of my friends would believe it. And I'm never going to tell them.

Val was still on her knees behind him, and she cupped her palms over his ass. Fingers spread his cheeks, sinking in a little as she felt him.

Leon dragged in a breath as she traced the path with her tongue. Fingers moved between his ass, and her tongue followed.

"Son of a bitch," he murmured.

Demitri's eyes burned black. Leon looked at him, and found the man gazing at him with naked hunger.

Val, still kneeling behind him, slid her hand between his legs and touched his balls. Damn, he was going to die of this. Leon's heart pumped, and he spread his feet apart so she could reach whatever she wanted.

Leon felt Val press her cheek into his ass, resting there while she moved her hands around his hips and closed her fist on his cock.

It felt good. Not as fantastic as her mouth, or himself inside her pussy, but Leon was so wound up, her touch was like fire.

Val the celibate might not have had sex in a long time, but she had technique. She stroked his cock with talented fingers, running her touch around his tip, tickling the underside, pulling it through her closed hand.

Demitri's breath came faster as he watched, his body utterly still. Leon was going to come. He felt it build, and he wanted it to. He wanted to come all over Val's beautiful fingers, and he wanted Demitri to see him do it.

"Val," Demitri said softly. "Stop."

"Oh, you gotta be kidding me," Leon rasped.

"Val."

Val made a soft sound of disappointment, but she let go of Leon's cock. Cool air touched it, making his immediate need fade a little, but leaving him frustrated and needing release.

"You're a bastard," Leon told Demitri.

"This is to help Val."

"It's not like I'm enjoying it or anything," Leon countered.

Val remained on the floor, kneeling, waiting for Demitri to tell her what to do. Leon wondered how she could be so calm. He held himself back, not wanting to screw this up, but wanting to scream at Demitri to let him fuck her.

Demitri turned away to retrieve something from the table. Leon wasn't sure what it was—he saw leather straps and buckles. Some kind of harness, Leon decided.

"You going to make her wear that?" Leon asked. He wasn't sure how that made him feel. He wasn't into Dom/sub stuff, but at the same time, thinking of Val wrapped in leather, kneeling for his pleasure, made him even more excited.

"No," Demitri said. "It's for you."

"What?"

"Demitri," Val said. She knelt next to Leon, her hands clenching and unclenching. "How can you be so cruel to me?"

"Cruel to *you*? He wants me to strap on a harness."

"He wants me to control myself. To control Valenarian."

"And this will help?"

Demitri laced the harness around Leon's torso and began buck-ling it. The straps were thin, not meant to hide anything. Demitri's closeness made Leon growl low in his throat and wonder anew what was happening to him.

The harness looped around Leon's thighs, leaving a large gap for his cock. Another strap went around his throat, and Demitri clipped a leash to it.

Demitri started to hand the leash to Val, hesitated, then pulled Leon forward with it and kissed him on the mouth. Val made a noise of longing.

Leon could barely breathe. He felt his muscles constricting with excitement, his body ready to go over the top. Demitri stepped back and handed the leather strap to Val.

"Make him do what you want," he said.

Leon's toes curled into the carpet as Val looked up at him, a smile on her face. She tugged the leash and towed Leon a few inches until the end of his cock bumped her mouth. She kissed it.

Sorry, Remy, I can't make it back to the dig tomorrow. I'm tied up with my new girlfriend. And her boyfriend.

No, he'd never be able to explain that.

Val ran her tongue around his tip. Leon flinched, sucked in his breath. She played with him a little like that, pushing him with her tongue, nipping and licking.

When she started to suckle, Leon squeezed his eyes shut, his hands balling into fists. He felt a tug of the leash, and he couldn't hold himself back any longer. He threw back his head and gritted his teeth as his come shot out of him and into Val's mouth. Her hands gripped his thighs hard as she drank him, her mouth work-ing him.

"Damn," he whispered, his hips rocking. "Damn, damn, damn."

When he finally opened his eyes, panting and sweating, Val had knelt back, a smile on her face. She licked her lips.

"I liked that," she said, sounding surprised.

"Valenarian does," Demitri said.

"I'm not Valenarian."

Leon hauled Val to her feet. He kissed her, not minding his own taste on her lips. She wound her arms around his neck, still holding the leash.

Demitri came up behind her. He put his arms around her, turned her head from Leon and kissed her, then gently moved her aside. "Take off your clothes and wait on the sofa."

Val smiled at him and glided away. Leon started to follow, but Demitri held him back with the leash. "Not yet."

"Why not?"

"I want her to take her own time getting ready." He looked Leon up and down. "Now, about what we said on the phone."

Val looked up eagerly. "What did you say on the phone? Tell me, please."

"Patience."

Val finished unbuttoning her tunic and let it fall, then unhooked her bra. Leon's spent cock stiffened quickly. Her breasts were beautiful, firm like apples, the tips dark. What he'd talked about with Demitri had been raw and primal; Val was the softer side of their triangle.

"How long do I have to wait?" she asked, sliding out of her pants. She stood in nothing but her black lace panties, hands on her hips.

"As long as I say, my love," Demitri said. "We're doing this to teach you to control yourself."

"It's not fair for you two to have fun without me."

"We'd never do that," Demitri said, his voice low. "It's the three of us together."

"You had phone sex," she said accusingly, one hip curved in her sexy stance.

"Not so. We simply talked about what we wanted to do when next we all met."

"It was the weirdest thing I ever did," Leon said.

"But it felt good." Demitri turned his full attention on Leon. "It felt good to say what you really wanted to say, to be as wild as you wanted to be."

"Yeah, it did." Leon paused. "I think I wanted to say even more."

"You will grow used to it."

"Maybe."

"You will." Demitri gave him a long look, then nodded once and turned back to Val. Leon realized Demitri had brought him here not only to help teach Val, but to teach him, Leon.

He's teaching me to let go of my taboos. That there's so much more to the world than what I know.

Demitri looked pointedly at Val's underwear. "Off."

She smiled, her look so sly, Leon for a moment feared that Valenarian had emerged. But Val's eyes remained a serene light blue as she turned away. Sliding her hips back and forth like a belly dancer, she slid the panties down and off.

"Lie facedown on the sofa."

Val walked to it and eased herself down without question, arranging a pillow under her head. Demitri tugged on Leon's tether. "I want you to massage her. Rub her back and shoulders, nothing more."

Leon wanted to lower himself on top of her, kiss her, enter her, ride her. He made himself walk to the sofa, every muscle tense, and rest one hand on her back.

"I have oil." Demitri picked up a bottle and drizzled over Leon's hand oil that smelled of spices.

"Mmm," Val said. "Nice."

It smelled expensive to Leon, but then, Demitri was a bazillionaire. He owned a hotel, had a private jet, could afford suites, meals, clothes, and jewelry for Val. Could help strays like Leon, and never blink an eye. To Leon, who'd grown up in near-poverty Demitri seemed to come from a dream world.

The fact that such an untouchable man—demigod, whatever—would care about a demon woman like Val and a simple shifter like Leon also seemed unbelievable. But Leon was a realist. If Demitri wanted to make sure Leon had the best sexual experience of his life, Leon wasn't going to argue. If they failed to help Val against the gods, Leon might die. If they succeeded, he doubted either Val or Demitri would want Leon in their lives much longer. Leon would grow old and die; they wouldn't.

He shoved such thoughts away and rubbed his hands together, coating them in oil. He laid them on Val's back, and she hummed and turned her head, eyes closing in delight.

Leon glided his palms over her shoulders, kneading and rubbing, then trailed his hand down her back to her ass. Demitri poured oil on his own hands and joined in.

15

VAL thought she'd go crazy with delight. Four hands, two beautiful men, lovely scented oil on her body.

She could tell which hands belonged to which man, even with her eyes closed. Leon's hands were callused, his touch unpracticed but enthusiastic. Demitri's hands were well kept but strong. He knew how to massage, how to find and loosen the muscles in Val's body.

Leon dipped his hand between her buttocks, fleetingly touching Val's anal star. She licked her lips. She hadn't been fucked there since she'd been Valenarian. Wouldn't it be wonderful to take Demitri's full cock, or Leon's? Had Leon made love like that before?

Let me out, Valenarian pleaded longingly. *I haven't had this in so very long.*

No. You have to stay hidden, or we'll both die.

Bitch. You have no idea how to appreciate what you have. I want this.

No, Val thought in a panic. *No, not now.*

"Harder, lover," Valenarian said, looking out through Val's eyes. "Pin me down, Demitri. Then make Leon fuck my ass."

Leon froze in place, but Demitri closed his hand around Val's neck. "Not you. Let Valerie come back."

"Screw you. She's a bore. I want you both inside me. Double penetration."

Demitri's grip tightened. "Bring her back, or you get nothing."

"What will you do if I don't?" Valenarian looked up at Demitri, her smile wide. "Have Leon spank me again? Or strap me in the harness and whip me? Not much of a threat if I love it, is it?"

"I can do a hell of a lot more to you than that, and you know it."

"Oh, the dangerous Demitri emerges. You know you want me this way, lover. You don't want her. You never did. You love Valenarian, and you want to fuck me until we both can't walk. Then you'll make Leon do both of us."

"I want Valerie back." Demitri's voice was low but hard. *"Now."*

Valenarian wasn't a complete fool. Demitri was dangerous when he was pushed, and she'd pushed him. She let out a heavy sigh of disappointment, then Valerie gasped as Valenarian vanished.

"Demitri," she said worriedly.

Demitri's touch relaxed. "It's all right. You see? You're controlling her."

"No, she left because she decided to. It was her choice, not mine."

"You will get used to how it feels to send her away, and then you'll be able to do it at will." His fingers became soothing, massaging, and Leon started again as well. "I'll teach you, love."

"I know it's true," Val said. "You do love her, not me."

Demitri said nothing, and Val's heart ached.

"I don't," Leon broke in. "I like you just as you are, *Valerie*. Sweet and nice, but oh so sexy."

Val tried a smile. "I bet you say that to all the women with demons inside them."

Leon chuckled softly. "You betcha, babe."

Demitri patted her ass. "You wanted penetration. Leon's going to provide it."

Val's heart beat faster. She automatically drew her knees under her, raising her hips, her quim parting.

"Not like that." Demitri gave her a little spank. "Leon on that chair; Val, you on him."

Leon pulled the straight-backed chair from the desk as Demitri indicated. It was carved teak, a lovely antique. Leon sat down on it and opened his arms, his cock standing in a stiff point. The leather straps of the harness enhanced his already gorgeous body.

Val put her hands on Leon's shoulders and swung her leg over his lap. She lowered to him, slowly impaling herself on him. Leon closed his eyes.

He was huge and she was wet, and he slid easily inside her. Valerie couldn't remember her encounter with Leon in his hotel room in Cairo, and she was sorry for that. He must screw like a god.

I remember, Valenarian whispered. *Let me show you.*

"No," Val said out loud.

Leon opened his eyes, watching her, his hips rocking as he started to make love.

He's mortal, and he's mine, Valenarian said. *I had him first.*

"No!" Val clenched every muscle in her body, trying to drive out the demon's voice.

Demitri came up behind Leon and put his hands on Leon's shoulders. He leaned down and pressed his cheek against Leon's. "Hold her in, Val."

"I can't. She's too strong."

"You can. Do it."

Val ground her teeth, riding Leon and wrestling Valenarian at the same time. Demitri was cruel; this was too hard.

Give in, sweetheart. I'm way too strong. Let me punish Demitri as he deserves.

He's trying to help me, she thought desperately.

Bullshit. He's trying to destroy us. He wants to make us his tame animals, to add to the string of demigods and women he's seduced over the centuries. Look how quickly he's tamed Leon.

He hasn't tamed Leon at all, Val protested.

Leon never lusted after another man in his life, until now. Why is that, do you suppose? Because Demitri wanted him, and Demitri gets whoever he wants.

No.

You don't suppose Demitri was celibate all those years you didn't see him, do you? He had so many lovers. So many, while he forgot all about us.

Val's ire cut through her fear. *How the hell would you know? You were locked in the temple with me.*

Poor innocent. He had lovers before he met us, and he had them after we were gone. He's not a man to go to bed alone.

"Demitri," Val gasped. "Make her stop."

"You have to do that," Demitri answered. "You have the strength. It's your choice."

"You don't understand."

"Yes, I do." Demitri's voice was hard.

Valenarian shoved the struggling Valerie aside. She grabbed the leash around Leon's neck and pulled it tight. "No, *you* don't understand, lover. I'm stronger than she'll ever be."

Leon coughed and grabbed Val's wrist. The movement drove his cock wonderfully inside her, but Val eased her hold. "I'm sorry, baby. I didn't mean to hurt you. Unless you want me to."

"Fuck you."

Valenarian closed her eyes and rocked her head back. "You are. Deep."

"Let Valerie come back," Demitri said sternly.

Valenarian laughed. She bounced on Leon's lap, his cock so high inside her she wanted to scream. "Leon loves me. Go away, Demitri."

Leon sank his fingers into her buttocks, far gone in sex. Demitri watched them both with sin-dark eyes. Valenarian loved him, as much as she fought him. She loved him watching her with Leon, loved his scent and warmth so close. She laced her hand through Demitri's hair, pulled him down to her, and kissed him.

He kissed her back, as excited as she was. He wanted to control, and Valenarian didn't want to let him. It was a delicious fight, with Leon between them as a buffer. Judging by the way Leon was fucking her with all his might, he obviously didn't mind.

Demitri went on kissing her, his tongue plowing through her mouth. She felt Leon's lips on her cheek, fleeting. She wrenched her mouth from Demitri and started to kiss Leon.

Leon came. He threw his head back, an animal-like growl escaping from his mouth. Demitri kissed him, then Val leaned forward to kiss Leon's face, her breasts crushed against his chest.

Leon started to laugh as Demitri and Val rained kisses on him. "Christ, let me breathe."

Val drew back reluctantly, and Demitri rose, his eyes tiger-yellow, his pupils vertical slits. Leon continued to laugh. "Damn. I'm sorry I didn't meet you two a long time ago."

Valenarian sat back, Leon still inside her. She felt the insipid Valerie trying to push her out. The poor ninny never got to have any fun, but Valenarian didn't care.

"You stole my life, you bitch," she said out loud. "And now you're trying to steal my lovers."

"Not so," Demitri said. "If you become one, like Aphrodite wants you to, you can have it all."

Valenarian clenched her fists. "Aphrodite's lying to you. I get nothing. My reward for doing what Aphrodite wants is eternal servitude. To her, back in her temple. She said so. It's that or death."

Both men stared at her, Leon breathing hard from his climax. "That's not what she told us," Leon said.

"Don't you get it?" Val leaned into Leon's warmth, not wanting to let him go. "She lied. She's using you. She gets what *she* wants, not what will make us happy."

Leon stroked her hair. "You don't need to worry about that, baby. I'll take care of you."

"No," Val said, tears leaking from her eyes. "You'll die."

"She's right," Demitri said, his voice soft. "If we go against the wishes of the gods, we die."

"So you're going to give up?" Leon asked him incredulously.

"I didn't say that. What I want is Val alive and safe. What happens to me doesn't matter."

"What about Leon?" Val asked. Valenarian felt tired and broken, despite the climax she'd just had. She tried to hold on, but she was so tired. Tears slid down her face. "Does Leon get to die, too?"

"No. I'll make sure Leon is safe." Demitri kissed Leon's cheek, his eyes sad. "Whatever it takes."

~ ~ ~

REMY steered the Jeep around the next ridge, the headlights cutting swaths through the darkness. Normally he'd be nervous to be this far away from civilization at night, but the thought of the undiscovered tomb drove him on.

Felicia clung to the seat next to him as they rocked along the rutted road. She clutched the map in one hand and held a big flashlight in the other.

"You sure it was this far?" she asked. "A long way to come hiking with your brother. You two must walk fast."

"We used to run all over the bayous when we were kids. All day and all night."

"That's a little different from walking miles in the desert with no water."

"Maybe."

Remy stared around him, trying to get his bearings. The Jeep road took him at an angle from where he wanted to go, heading too far south. The problem was, things looked different to his human eyes than they had to his lion's eyes.

Why'd we pick lions? he asked himself irritably. Lions weren't night hunters, and their eyes didn't register things like a tiger's or leopard's would. But they'd wanted the strength and speed, and the moon had been so bright. It had been a lion kind of night.

Remy pulled off the road, took the map from Felicia, and tried to figure it out. "We need to go out there." He pointed.

"There's no road."

"No kidding. It will have to be on foot."

"Remy." Felicia's face under the moonlight looked soft, almost delicate. "If we get lost out here, we'll die of exposure. We didn't bring near enough water to do any hiking. Why don't we provision and come back out tomorrow?"

"It will be too hot during the day, and I might not be able to find it again."

"But you will in the middle of the night?"

Remy set the map back in Felicia's lap and gripped the steering wheel. "You can go back to the dig house if you want. Take the Jeep and leave me. If I'm not back by morning, you know where to start looking."

"Are you crazy?" Felicia fixed her flashlight on his face. "Leave you out in the middle of the desert by yourself? Did you have heat stroke today or something?"

Remy climbed out of the Jeep and scanned the terrain. He needed to go around the ridge to the flat land below. Beyond that, he was sure, lay the outcropping. As a lion, though, he'd not so much *seen* his way as smelled and heard and felt it. His human form could be limiting sometimes.

"I'll be all right," he said. "I know how to survive in the desert. I can't get to this place with the Jeep. It has to be on foot."

"Then I'm coming with you." Felicia climbed down and started rummaging for the canteens of water. "We can mark our trail from the Jeep so we can find our way back." She took a piece of bright orange tape from a bag of supplies and tied it around a rock next to the Jeep.

Remy sighed. "All right, you're right. We'll both go back, and I'll come out tomorrow." When he could slip away alone. He wished now he'd left Felicia behind, but he hadn't realized how difficult the site would be to find.

"Forget it." Felicia pulled out another bag of supplies and handed it to him. "We're this far, you think you know where it is, and we'll be careful. I want to find it, too."

Remy slung the pack over his shoulder. "I usually admire your persistence, but I'm not so sure tonight."

"First you're excited to bring me out here, and now you don't want me to go with you. You say you'll explore alone tonight, then you say you'll come back tomorrow. Whatever it was you found, I think it scrambled your brains."

"Yeah, I think it did, too."

Felicia held up the map. "Well, which way?"

Remy studied it, looked at the horizon, and pointed north and west. "This way." He started down the small slope from the Jeep, heading for the ridgeline. Felicia followed, stopping after ten feet to leave another orange strip on another rock.

~ ~ ~

DEMITRI carried Val into the bedroom and laid her on the bed, covering her with a sheet. Valenarian had retreated, and it was just Valerie, half-asleep with tears on her face.

Demitri kissed a tear away, smoothing back her red-streaked hair. Guilt churned inside him, because he knew Val was right. He loved Valenarian, always had. The woman Aphrodite had made her become hadn't been his girl, his love, and he'd stayed far away from her.

"She all right?" Leon asked when Demitri came out. The man was on his feet, unbuckling the harness.

"She's fine. Did I say you could take that off?"

Leon's hands stopped. "I figured we were done."

Demitri came to him and wrapped the leash around his fist. "We're not done by a long shot. I remember you telling me over the phone something you wanted to do."

Excitement skimmed through Leon. "You mean like I want to fuck your sweet ass?"

"Like that, yes."

"Are you always so proper?" Leon said. They stood nose to nose, Leon's green eyes on level with Demitri's dark ones. "Do you act like you have a stick up your ass because there's a real one there?"

Demitri unfastened his pants and let them fall. "Want to check?"

Leon's eyes flickered. He stood back and let Demitri pull off his underwear and socks, then Demitri leaned over the end of the sofa, his butt in the air. "What do you think?" Demitri asked him. "Anything there?"

He jerked when he felt Leon's fingertips softly brush over his ass.

"Doesn't look like it," Leon said.

"Look closer. The oil is on the table."

Leon picked up the lubricating oil Demitri had used on Val and spread some on his finger. "Want me to get a condom?" he asked.

"I'm a demigod. You can't give me a disease. And I can't give you anything—if I don't want to."

"Man, you're reassuring."

Leon set down the oil and lightly touched Demitri again.

"Slide your finger in," Demitri said softly. "Play with me a little. Get me ready for you."

It took Leon a while to become comfortable touching Demitri's ass, but finally Demitri felt the pressure of his finger. His large, hard finger. It felt good.

"Are you sure you've never done this before?" Demitri rasped.

"Not with a man."

"You don't have to be as gentle with me. Be tender with Val, but with me, you can do what you want. You can't hurt me."

Demitri felt the tension in Leon's whole body. His finger moved inside, making everything slick and open. A second finger joined the first.

"That's it." Demitri's voice went low, excitement warming him. "Keep doing that."

Leon stood closer, his thighs touching Demitri's. The heat of Leon's body loosened Demitri even more.

"I was right," Leon said. "You are tight-assed."

"But getting better by the second."

"Yeah, I can feel that."

When Leon eased out his fingers out to add more lube, Demitri arranged the sofa cushions so he could lean on them.

"I can take you now. Do it."

"You sure?" Leon asked.

"Of course, I'm sure. Your cock is stiff, and I'm lubed and ready. Fuck me."

Leon dragged in a breath. "Damn, I hope no one ever finds out I did this."

"Who am I going to tell besides Val?"

"You know a lot of people."

Demitri looked over his shoulder. Leon was ready, his eyes dark, his cock fully extended. "Your secret is safe with me, Leon. I promise you. Now do it. Please. I want you."

Leon nodded, his eyes shifting from human to cat and back again. He braced his hands on Demitri's hips, positioned his cock on Demitri's needy opening, and slid inside.

~ ~ ~

REMY stopped again, scanning the outcroppings around him while Felicia tied yet another strip of orange tape to another rock. He blew out his breath. He didn't recognize any of this. They had enough water to go maybe a few more miles before they'd have to turn back.

"This is no good," he said, his Cajun vowels deepening. All his years studying in northern schools, of hanging out with damn Yankees, hadn't quite erased his accent. "I got so close, you know?"

"We can try again tomorrow," Felicia said soothingly.

Remy knew that wouldn't be any good, either. He could drive out here early tomorrow morning, follow Felicia's little orange markers, and still never find the place he and Leon had stumbled upon. His sense of direction wasn't as good in his human form.

"Felicia," he said.

She looked up. He considered Felicia his colleague and one of his best friends, a woman who had believed in him, this Southern boy a long way from home. She'd stood by him back in Chicago when others didn't.

She'd looked prettier than usual when she'd come into the collection room today, all soft colors with her hair down. That must have been the difference he sensed—she'd let her hair wisp about her face instead of scraping it back into a severe ponytail.

"What?" Felicia wrapped up her orange tape, waiting for him to finish.

"I have to tell you something." The secret was supposed to stay in Remy's family forever; no one must know that they were different. No one. That's what their grandfather said, what their father said. Remy had always wondered how Leon had handled it in Afghanistan. Leon's animal instincts must have let him scramble out of the way moments before that car bomb had exploded.

"Remy, you keep starting to say something, then stopping."

Remy looked at Felicia. Her eyes were brown and soft, and he'd always liked them. He wanted to touch her face, to soothe away her worried expression.

"Felicia, I have to ask you to swear you will never, ever reveal to anyone what I'm about to do. It's life and death—not just for me, but for my whole family."

He had her full attention now. "What is it?"

Remy knew if he didn't get on with it, he'd chicken out. Then he'd blow his chance at finding his tomb, making his name, having Felicia's brown eyes glow with admiration. He had to trust her.

Remy started unbuttoning his shirt. He shucked it to the ground, then took off his boots and socks and started on his jeans.

"What are you doing?" Felicia asked, eyes wide.

"Sorry. This is going to be weird."

"Weirder than you stripping in the middle of the desert?"

Remy deposited his pants on his spread-out shirt and pulled off his underwear. Naked, he straightened up and closed his eyes, shutting out Felicia's shocked expression. He stilled his mind and called to the lion he'd been earlier tonight, the beast who'd reveled in running through the land of its ancestors.

Felicia screamed. Remy's hands changed to paws, his legs curving as his back elongated. He landed on all fours as a mane sprouted around his head.

Felicia stared at him in terror. "Remy?" she whispered.

He couldn't communicate in human words in his changed state. Remy slowly went to her and butted her legs with his head. He walked around her, rubbing his shoulder, flank, and tail against her as he passed.

She gasped a laugh. "Shit, I don't believe this." Daringly she put her hand on Remy's head, sinking fingers into his warm mane. "How did you do that?"

He couldn't tell her, of course. He closed his eyes as she started petting him, crooning at him like she would at a tabby cat.

Remy made himself back away. He shook himself then turned toward the outcroppings and sniffed the air, letting his lion senses stretch. His hearing and sense of smell had sharpened, and his paws remembered the feel of the earth.

After a few minutes, he spied the exact shape of the outcropping he was looking for. Of course. He started to bound toward it, then pulled himself up. Felicia would never keep up with the lion he'd become, and he couldn't leave her out here alone.

Remy circled back to her, then without warning, playfully dove between her legs. Before she could shriek, he rose with her squarely on his back.

Felicia overbalanced, dug into his mane, and held on. "Oh wait, the water."

Remy walked to it and picked up the pack in his mouth, holding it high. He turned and started trotting across the desert to his discovery with Felicia clinging desperately to his back.

16

"Damn," Leon groaned. This was too good. Val had been sweet and tight, squeezing him as he drove into her, but Demitri clamped his cock like a vise.

Demitri's broad, muscular back gleamed with sweat and oil. Leon slid inside him to the hilt, his hands splayed on Demitri's hips.

"What do I do?" Leon asked. "How do you like it?"

"Just fuck me," Demitri grated. "Do what feels good."

The crack in his voice, his slip in control, spurred Leon on. He started to pump, slowly at first, then as his mind blanked, he moved faster.

Demitri bucked against him, growling and groaning. Leon threw his head back. The noises coming out of his own mouth surprised him, but then, everything about this encounter had surprised him. The beautiful Val, the strange quest to help her, and most of all Leon falling in love with a big dark-eyed man who could turn into a tiger.

"What am I going to do?" he murmured, his thoughts disjointed. Fire burned where he joined Demitri, this sexing like nothing he'd ever experienced.

"Come on," Demitri said over his shoulder. Demitri's face was drawn with passion, his eyes dark and heavy. "Come on, lover."

He sounded like Valenarian, but without the frantic edge she had in her voice. Leon started to laugh. "I'm fucking as fast as I can."

Leon closed his eyes again, surrendering to the feeling. There was no sound in the room but flesh against flesh, the gliding noise of the lube, and the grunts of the two men.

Demitri's groans turned to the growls of a tiger, and claws shot into the cushions of the sofa. Leon felt the change want to rise in him, and he fought it down.

"Fuck," he whispered, then he said it louder as all control fled him.

What happened after that, he wasn't sure. He was riding Demitri's ass and laughing, Demitri swearing and shoving himself back against Leon. Leon felt his come shoot out of him, burying deep inside Demitri. Then Demitri turned around and grabbed Leon around the waist, pulling him down onto the sofa with him. They kissed and grappled, Demitri's claws thankfully once again human fingers.

Demitri held Leon around the neck while Demitri's mouth played in his. Leon surrendered himself, letting the other man kiss and stroke him, their lips and tongues frantic.

Demitri pushed Leon toward his still rampant cock, and Leon closed his mouth over it without thought. He suckled and played, swirling his tongue around the huge staff, until Demitri's fists clenched hard. Demitri hissed words Leon didn't understand, and then Leon's mouth filled with Demitri's semen.

Leon found himself cradled on Demitri's broad chest, the two men tangled on the sofa, sleep hurtling at him. "Shit," Leon murmured. "What the hell did I just do?"

"Made me damn happy," Demitri said, then sleep took both of them.

~ ~ ~

FELICIA slid off Remy's warm back as he halted in front of an out-cropping several miles from where they'd started. There hadn't been time to mark their trail, and she hoped Remy could find his way back to her last orange strip.

Her mind was fighting to get her to notice things—like that Remy had turned into a *lion*—but she suppressed it. The less she thought about what was happening, the better. She should be more worried about being in the middle of the desert in the middle of nowhere with dawn a few hours away and them not having nearly enough water to walk back to the Jeep. But such thoughts paled as Remy flowed back into his human form. He was stark naked.

Felicia stared in delight before she made herself avert her gaze. Remy was not as tall as his brother, but he was well built in the shoulders and chest department. Her fleeting glance took in hard biceps, narrow waist, strong thighs, and very nice, thick cock.

"It's all right, you can look," Remy said. When Felicia turned back, he was smiling, his eyes still lion gold instead of their usual green. "Are you all right?"

"I was just wondering if you were."

"This is natural for me." He reached out and touched her face—the Remy who didn't seem to notice the difference between men and women was suddenly comfortable touching her. "I know it must be scary for you."

"Confusing. But we can worry about it later. What about your tomb?"

Remy grinned. "That's what I love about you, Felicia, you never forget the essentials. This is what I found."

He took her to the pile of limestone chips strewn across the rocks, the lighter rubble shining under his flashlight's beam. He didn't seem to notice or be bothered by his nakedness, so Felicia pretended she didn't notice either. Her senses were screaming that a beautiful man she'd been in love with since she'd first met him was kneeling naked beside her, but she'd tamp down her feelings and be professional. She was good at that.

Remy brushed dust and pebbles from a gap between the desert floor and the outcropping. "You can see marks of tools. Barely."

Felicia forgot the strange night in a sudden rush of archaeological fever. "I think it *is* an opening. Nothing's ever been found out here. Oh my God, Remy, you're brilliant."

"Lucky. Damn lucky."

He was laughing. Felicia started laughing, too, and threw her arms around his neck. "You'll be famous."

"*We* will be. I can't do this without you."

Remy kissed her. He was still laughing. He pulled her to her feet and kept on kissing her. His lips were warm, silken, commanding. She did what she'd always longed to, ran her fingers through his hair as she kissed him back.

Remy suddenly stopped and pushed her away. He stared at her, his eyes reverting to their usual green.

"Felicia, I'm sorry." He backed a step, looking dismayed. "I didn't mean to push myself on you like that. It was—"

Felicia cut off his words by throwing her arms around his naked body and holding on. "Remy, just shut up," she said, and kissed him.

~ ~ ~

VAL woke between two warm, naked men who had curled up on either side of her. Leon was like a warm wall, head cushioned on his tanned arm. She liked his face, hard rather than handsome, unshaven whiskers darkening his jaw.

Demitri was all that was sinful, with his black hair falling like satin over his face, equally black hair curling on his chest. He lay on his back, his face turned away from her, one arm overhead. Both men snored.

The windows were lightening with the dawn. The overhead fan turned slowly, wafting cool air over the three bodies on the bed. The entire room smelled of sex.

I love these men, she thought. *Both of them.* Her love for Demitri was well honed, a polished diamond she'd treasured for years. Her love for Leon was new, sharp like the knife-edged shadows in the desert. She didn't know what they felt for her, but she loved them enough that she didn't care.

Oh, please, Valenarian sneered. *You're not that selfless. You want them to be madly in love with you, to do anything for you. You don't fool me.*

Val put her hands over her face. *Go away.*

No. This is too good to pass up.

Valerie tried to scream as she felt Valenarian push her aside. She tried to hold the last tattered remains of her sanity, but felt herself forced to let go as Valenarian pried her clinging fingers away one by one.

Ooo, nice. Valenarian propped herself on one elbow and gazed at the lush body of Demitri stretched beside her. He was aroused in his sleep, his cock stretching up to his navel.

Val leaned down and licked his cock. She tasted the remnants of his come—he and Leon must have been playing without her.

Demitri jumped, half-awake. He said nothing, but sleepily stroked her hair. Val smiled. He had no idea which manifestation of her pleasured him; he only felt the pleasure.

She toyed with him for a while, then she raised herself on hands and knees and straddled him. Demitri's half-closed eyes gleamed. He slid his hands to her hips and silently rocked up into her.

Val stroked her hands across his chest, letting her claws extend. Like she had in the meadow of Mount Olympus long ago, she marked him from neck to navel.

Demitri sucked in his breath and opened his eyes all the way. He grabbed her wrists in a strong grip, but he was too caught up in the sex to stop.

"That's it, lover," she whispered. "Do to me what you always wanted to."

Demitri held her down on him, his hips and hers moving in hard rhythm. His fingers bit into her wrists, anger in his eyes.

The movement of the bed partially woke Leon, but he only mumbled in his sleep and turned over, giving them a view of his delectable backside.

Val arched her brows at Demitri. "You want him."

"I had him," Demitri said. "He had me."

Val's entire body squeezed. "And I missed it. Tell me what he did to you."

Demitri complied. In a whisper of words from the language of old, he described how Leon had penetrated him and then gone down on him. He told her in graphic detail, using words modern humans had long ago abandoned.

It excited her. Val shuddered as Demitri spun out the tale, until she could clearly see Leon with every muscle tense, pushing and pushing between Demitri's spread legs.

She screamed her excitement, feeling Demitri's seed scalding her at the same time. She fell down on him, but Demitri wasn't finished. He rolled her over and pushed her facedown in the blankets. "Let her come back."

"No. You love me this way."

"You both have to be here—you both have to do this, or we're all lost."

Leon was awake now, blinking like a sleepy bear. "What the hell?"

Demitri had his hand on Val's neck. "Bring her back."

Val laughed into the pillows. "If you wanted Valerie so much, she'd be here. You are the one keeping her away."

She felt the weight of Demitri on top of her, his cock, hard once more, sliding inside her. He rode her furiously, his fingers in her hair, his body pinning hers. Dimly she heard Leon telling him to stop, swearing at him.

"She wants to be a demon, she can be," Demitri snarled. "I'm a demigod. A demon is my enemy."

"She's a woman we're trying to help," Leon protested.

Demitri's tiger's growl sounded in her ear. "She doesn't want help. She likes punishment. That's what she'll have."

Faster, harder. Demitri rode her more furiously than he ever had before, his strength and power completely overwhelming her. Demitri could have mastered Val any second, any time he wanted to. He'd been holding back.

Leon sat up straight. "Damn you, Demitri, don't make me stop you."

"You can't stop me." Demitri's voice had deepened, the god in him taking over. He was burning Val from the inside out, and she loved every minute of it. She heard herself screaming, begging him to punish her, heard Leon trying to hold Demitri back and not succeeding.

Then she heard the rumbling roar of an animal in fury, and Demitri was ripped from her. Val cried out and rolled over to see a huge bear standing on its hind legs at the foot of the bed, its razor-like claws extended.

Demitri faced it, still in human form, but with white-hot power flowing from his body. The bear towered over Demitri, its head brushing the ceiling. It was tawny brown, its neck ruff enormous, its black eyes alight with fury. It had huge teeth in its red mouth, lips curled back to reveal three-inch-long canines.

Val scrambled from the bed. As terrifying as the bear was, Demitri was still a god, and he could flatten Leon with the flick of a finger.

"No." Valenarian flung herself between the two, putting her back to the bear. "Don't kill him, Demitri. It's me you want to hurt. Don't let him die for that."

Demitri's eyes blazed black in the middle of the white light surrounding him. The tiger superimposed itself on him briefly, then the white took over again. "Bring Valerie back," he said in a terrible voice.

Damn it. She had to or Leon would attack Demitri, and Demitri would kill him.

"Fine, I'll let the wussy girl come back. All right?" Her voice shook as she squeezed her eyes shut.

Come out, Valerie. She sneered the name. *Your tame pets want you.*

Silence. Valenarian opened her eyes to find Demitri's power brighter.

Come back, you stupid bitch. Stop them from hurting each other.

Nothing happened.

"Shit," Valenarian said out loud. Behind her, Leon growled, a sound that shook the room.

Demitri's glow brightened. "Where is she?"

"I can't bring her back. I'm sorry, lover, she's gone."

Demitri's magic dampened with a suddenness that made Val's ears pop. Behind her, Leon shrank and became an upright, out-of-breath, pissed off human male.

"What are you talking about?" Demitri asked, his voice surprisingly steady.

"I can't reach her. Valerie—I mean, your little Goody Two-shoes lover. It looks like you're stuck with me."

Demitri came for her, rage on his face. Leon stepped in front of her. "Leave her alone," he said, his voice still holding the rumbling note of the bear. "The more you scare her, the more out of control she is."

Demitri stopped. His anger blazed from him, but he folded his massive arms and looked Val up and down. "If you're lying to me . . ."

"I'm not." Val shivered, wondering why she was afraid. She was Valenarian, the vengeance demon. No one could best her. "I'm not lying, Demitri. I'm Valenarian." She was powerful, and all men feared her. She folded her arms over her chest and started to cry.

~ ~ ~

WHEN Leon reached the dig that day, both Felicia and Remy looked exhausted but pleased with themselves. Sex? he wondered. Or some archaeological triumph?

Demitri and Val sat in the open-air tent on the site. They were sipping tea, and Demitri had hold of Val's hand. To an outside observer, they appeared as calm and unruffled as ever, but Leon saw the tension between them. The same tension rolled between himself and Demitri.

Valenarian was there to stay. Before they'd left the hotel in Luxor this morning, she'd smiled sadly at Leon and kissed him lightly on the lips. "Thank you for trying to protect me," she'd said. Her sadness made Leon feel worse than ever.

"Sorry I wasn't around last night," Leon said to Remy. "Anything missing today?"

"Missing?" Remy looked blank. "Oh, you mean from the storage room. I haven't gone over the inventory this morning. Come with me while I do it."

"Okay if Val and Demitri tag along?"

"Sure." Remy frowned at him. "What's up with you, anyway? Are you trying to get Val for yourself or keep them together?"

Leon answered evasively, guilt flushing him. He'd never lied to his brothers. "I'm trying to do what's best for Val."

"That's nice of you." Remy clapped Leon on the shoulder as Demitri and Val walked to them in response to Leon's beckoning. Val had wrapped her loose white scarf around her head again, her sunglasses glinting in the sunlight.

Demitri agreed without argument to accompany Remy and Leon back to the dig house. Val said nothing, but she walked demurely next to Demitri, Demitri's hand tight on her arm.

The demure act was just that—an act. Once she'd gotten over

her initial dismay that she couldn't make Valerie return, Valenarian had turned into a sexual fiend. It had taken them a long time to sate her, then clean up and dress to come to the dig.

Val looked over at Leon and smiled a red-lipped smile. He remembered her on her hands and knees under him not an hour ago, while he drove his cock into her wet pussy. Demitri had gotten behind Leon, his long cock rubbing between Leon's legs. That had been intense.

The four proceeded to the storage room, and Remy began checking the shelves. Felicia joined them, stifling her yawns as she marked off items on the clipboard.

Val chewed on the earpiece of her sunglasses, watching Felicia. "You seem tired today, sweetie. Did you two finally screw?"

Felicia jerked around, her face flooding with color. Remy looked up in astonishment.

"Val," Demitri said in a warning tone.

"Here's gratitude for you," Val went on. "I did my best to make her beautiful, and she's back looking like a withered stalk. He's not going to beg for you like that, darling. You need to listen to Val when she gives you advice."

Felicia looked as though she was torn between throwing the clipboard at Val or bursting into tears. Remy, always clueless about women, raised his brows at Felicia.

"What is she talking about?"

"I don't know," Felicia stammered.

Val rolled her eyes. Remy looked down at the clipboard in Felicia's hands. "What's next?"

Felicia managed to babble out the next item. Demitri followed Val as she wandered the shelves, but the demigod was smart enough not to say anything to her.

Remy and Felicia continued down the collection, and by the time they'd finished, Felicia had regained her composure. "Nothing missing," she said. "Nothing new, anyway."

Remy set the clipboard aside. "If you are wondering why we're so tired, it's because we went back out last night to where I thought I found the tomb. It took some searching, but we found it again." His grin was wide.

Felicia slanted him an alarmed look, but Remy held up his hand. "I trust my brother completely, and he'll vouch for his friends. I'm going back out tonight, and I'd be glad of your help."

"What about catching your thief?" Leon asked.

"Perhaps your friends could stand watch?"

"I'd rather see the tomb," Val said. She picked up Remy's clipboard and idly flipped through the pages. "I might be able to tell you whose tomb it was."

Remy looked surprised. "Are you an archaeologist? Or a historian?"

Val smiled at him. "I know things. Many things. Like who Hatshepsut's lover really was."

"Senenmut," Felicia said as she arranged something on a shelf.

"Do you really think that a woman who made herself king of Egypt would bestow her body on a mere man?" Val scoffed. "Hatshepsut was quite wild, especially in her younger years. Senenmut was a good and loyal friend, and kept up the pretense so she could enjoy herself."

"The jury is still out on that relationship," Remy said absently. "Not my period anyway. I wonder if the tomb I found is Roman."

"I shouldn't think so." Val turned the last pages on the clipboard and set it down. "More likely Eighteenth or early Nineteenth Dynasty."

"How do you know?"

"I told you, I know things."

"I wouldn't mind if you had a look at it," Remy said. "I don't want to tell anyone about it until I'm sure though. All right?"

Val touched her lips. "Your secret is safe with me."

"It's a long way out there," Remy said, glancing at Leon. "I only found it again because I . . ." He cleared his throat. "I used the same method I did when you and I were out earlier last night."

"They know," Leon said. He glanced at Felicia who had her arms tightly folded across her chest.

Remy nodded. "She knows, too. I showed her."

"Ah. So now she's in on the family secret."

"You turn into a lion, too?" Felicia asked Leon.

Val seated herself on the tabletop and crossed her ankles. "Leon can turn into any animal—lion or tiger or bear."

"Oh, my," Remy murmured.

"This morning he was a—what was that, Leon? I've never seen a bear like that before."

"A grizzly."

"Grizzly," Val repeated. "Very large and frightening. Demitri can only turn into a tiger." She smiled at him and tugged on one of her tight curls. "A very sexy tiger."

"I thought you were just a lion," Felicia said. "A were-lion. Like you were bitten by a lion and now have to change into one."

Remy burst out laughing, and Leon couldn't help a chuckle. "We're shifters," Remy explained. "Not were-anything. We have a talent to take on the shape of any animal, but we have to come into contact with it first, and touch it. When did you meet a grizzly, Leon?"

"Camping in the Rockies a few years ago."

"And you touched it?" Felicia looked awestruck.

"Carefully."

"Can everyone in your family do it?" Felicia asked.

"All four of us brothers can," Remy explained. "We have two other brothers, Thomas and Jean Marc. They're shifters, too. We get it from our father—our mother doesn't have the gift." He laughed a little. "You can imagine what the poor woman put up with when we were little."

"We're still making it up to her," Leon said.

"The talent runs in our father's line," Remy went on. "He wasn't sure where it came from, but there were Native Americans in our neck of the woods, long, long ago, who had the magic to turn into animals. Some call them witches or skinwalkers, but skinwalkers are evil mages, and these weren't like that. They learned the spirit of the animal, according to my grandfather, and could then take its shape. When the French came to Louisiana territory, and the Duprees settled in Fontaine, a Dupree married a Native American woman who had the gift, and we ended up with it."

"That's why we need to touch an animal before we can take its shape," Leon finished. He was surprised Remy was willing to give so much information to Felicia, but she listened with interest. Val was looking at the clipboard again, but Leon could tell she listened, too. "We have to learn the animal's spirit, its essence. Then our magic lets us become like it."

"And Demitri?" Felicia asked. "He's one of these shifters, too?"

Demitri shook his head. "I'm a different creature altogether."

"I'm certainly getting an education," Felicia said faintly.

"I don't change into anything," Val said. "Except a demon." She smiled broadly at Felicia, and Felicia smiled back, not an ounce of belief in her expression.

"If Val goes to the tomb tonight, I will accompany her," Demitri rumbled. "You'll have to find someone else to watch the storage room."

Remy chewed the inside of his cheek. "Felicia?"

Felicia looked disappointed, but she nodded. "I know there's no one else you can trust without admitting there's been thefts. But I want every detail of what you find, do you hear me?"

"Of course," Remy said. "I'll photograph what I can and make a map. Don't worry. You'll be in on everything."

Val handed the clipboard to Felicia. "You'll need this."

Felicia accepted it without a word. She sent Remy another glance, this one smoldering, but Remy's back was turned.

"Tell me honestly," Val said. "You two did screw last night, didn't you?"

Remy turned around, and this time he blushed as much as Felicia. "No. But I kissed her."

Val let out a sigh as she hopped to her feet. "Frigging finally. You two really need to think about more than old tombs."

She swept her scarf around her neck and slid on her sunglasses as she stepped out into the blinding sun. Demitri followed on her heels, the big man as enigmatic as ever. Leon came close behind.

"I wish you'd stay here," Remy said to Val, as he followed them out. "I don't like to think what would happen if the thief comes with only Felicia to guard the place."

"Oh, she'll be all right," Val said, walking away from him. "We're not dealing with a dangerous criminal."

"How do you know?" Leon asked.

Val turned and smiled sweetly at all three of them. "Because I know who did it."

"Who?" Demitri demanded.

"I'll tell you all about it tonight," she said, winking one dark blue eye. "We'll set a trap for the thief, with cute little Felicia as bait."

17

REMY drove them out into the desert in his Jeep. Val sat in the back, beside Demitri, who kept his strong arm around her. She laid her head back and let the night air stream over her face, feeling protected.

The illusion of protection was false, she knew. Demitri was trying to protect the world from Val, not the other way around. She knew that, in the long run, he wouldn't be able to save her. That thought lay heavy on her heart. Sweet Valerie had vanished into the recesses of Valenarian's psyche, holed up in whatever place Aphrodite had first found her.

Val had all of Valerie's memories—the tedium of day-to-day life in Aphrodite's temple, the relief when she was sent out to bring a couple together. If she'd had any gumption, Valenarian thought bitterly, Valerie would have simply refused to return from one of these assignments. Aphrodite might have killed her for disobeying, but wouldn't that have been better than her non-life inside the temple?

Valenarian was never going back to that. She lay her head on Demitri's shoulder as the miles rolled by, wishing that all those years ago she could have been what he wanted. He would have protected her if she'd suppressed her crazed need for vengeance and death. Aphrodite had managed to crush that out of her at least, but too late. Valenarian was still paying for sins committed three thousand years ago, and if the gods had their way, Demitri and Leon would pay for them, too.

The Jeep stopped at the end of a track that petered into nothingness. A bright orange piece of cloth moved on the rock-strewn ground ahead of them.

"On foot from here," Remy said. "I've driven us farther than I did last night, but it's still about a three-mile hike."

Demitri handed Val out of the Jeep like he would a royal princess from her coach, but his expression was far from admiring. He hadn't spoken much at all since they'd left the dig house.

"Don't worry about me, Remy," Val said. "I am in quite good shape, and I'm certain Demitri will carry me if I falter."

Demitri slanted her a silent look. Remy gave her an uncertain smile but unloaded water bottles and backpacks from the Jeep. He didn't give any to Val to carry, which she found amusing. He'd have readily handed over a load to Felicia. Felicia was definitely the woman for Remy.

Val ran her hand up Leon's well-muscled arm as he shouldered a large canteen. "If I get tired, Leon can always turn into a camel."

Leon's eyes glinted. "I only turn into carnivores, sweetheart."

Val chuckled, rose up on tiptoe, and kissed his cheek. She resumed her hold of Demitri's arm and smiled at Remy, who watched in confusion.

"Lead us on, Remy," she said.

Remy gave Leon another uncertain glance, but lifted his backpack and trudged away over the rocks.

Nothing grew in this desert. The Nile Valley could be green with farmer's fields and groves of trees, but where the life-giving waters were absent, the land was stark and dead. Val knew that oases bloomed farther to the west, where groundwater bubbled up from deep in the earth, and crops and palm trees once more ruled. But here in between, the ground was devoid of all life.

Val had always thought the Egyptian desert beautiful. The mountains cut sharply into the blue sky, and the sun dazzled overhead, the god Ra sailing it from horizon to horizon. This was her land, where she'd been spawned in a strange union between Heka and a half-demon, half-human woman. Val had been created as an enforcer, to ensure that philandering husbands were punished.

Made for a purpose, Val thought as she trudged across the desert with Demitri at her side. No thought for Val's own happiness. No thought for the fact that her tiny bit of human blood made her long for the things that humans did—love, warmth, happiness, family. She'd been an instrument of the gods, forgotten and abandoned when the old gods retreated. The Greco-Roman pantheon had all but swallowed the Egyptian gods, and they'd had no use for Val.

When the Copts came, they'd pushed out the pagan gods as well, erasing their names and turning the temples into monasteries. The powerful Greek pantheon found itself rendered powerless and retreated to Olympus, conceding defeat.

Recently, humans had begun studying the old gods again, not necessarily worshiping them, but remembering them and learning them anew. Life had stirred again among the pantheons, the gods never quite forgotten.

Remy finally said, "Here," and Leon set down his burdens with a grunt.

"It looks different during the day. What did you find?"

Remy crouched by a narrow slit between the ground and the wall of the outcropping. Limestone chips had flaked off here, a pile of them strewn on the desert floor. Remy pointed his flashlight into the hole, but the beam didn't penetrate very far.

"I think there's a step there. Lots of fill, of course. But I'm pretty sure this is a tomb, man-made."

Val sat on her heels and peered into the darkness. "That's it?"

"It might not look like much to you," Remy said patiently, an edge of excitement to his voice. "But when we remove the fill, who knows what we'll find?"

"Treasure?" Leon asked.

"It's not likely to be an intact tomb, not like Tutankhamun's. Most of the tombs were robbed long ago. But there might be wall paintings or reliefs, the sarcophagus, a mummy, writings." His eyes grew brighter as he warmed to his subject. "Another clue to the puzzle of ancient civilization. We don't know everything there is to know—we can't possibly. But if I could get a grant to excavate, to do a conservation project, way out here where no tourists come . . ."

Leon grinned. "Calm down, bro."

"Sorry. Let me take some photographs and then we'll go."

He sounded wistful. He wanted to know more about it, Val could tell. He was torn between the caution of his training and the natural excitement that had led him to this profession in the first place.

Val peered inside as Leon flashed his light around, but she saw nothing but rubble. She was pretty sure she knew what this place was: a secret tomb of one of the kings, placed out here because he knew the official tomb would be robbed very quickly. The mummy pulled out of the tomb in the Valley of the Kings would be a substitute, while the real pharaoh slept away undisturbed. Well, undisturbed until now.

"Why don't you shift into a worm or something and have a look?" Val asked Remy. "You're dying to know what's in there."

"Shifting doesn't work like that," Leon said. "You can't be something smaller than you really are—all your mass has to go somewhere."

"Maybe not a worm," Remy said, looking pointedly at Leon. "How about a snake?"

Leon grimaced. "I haven't done that in a long time."

"You can turn into a snake?" Val asked. "Mmm, think of *those* possibilities." Demitri, who'd watched in silence, scowled at her. She smiled serenely back at him.

"I still might be too big," Leon said.

"What kind of snake do you turn into?" Val asked him. "A cobra?"

"Python."

"When did you touch a python?" she asked. "Exploring a jungle?"

"Petting zoo when I was a kid."

"No one would touch the snake but Leon," Remy said. "So he learned its essence." He peered into the hole again. "You might fit. But I won't force you."

Leon sighed and started unlacing his boots. "Anything for you, little brother."

Val felt a twinge of concern. "Be careful."

Leon brushed the backs of his fingers over her cheek, gave Demitri a warning look, and continued to take off his clothes. Demitri slid his arm around Val's waist and pulled her against his warm body as Leon stood up, naked. Remy looked back and forth between the three of them, extremely puzzled.

~ ~ ~

LEON slid neatly through the slit and dropped a few feet to a hard surface. His snake eyes didn't see well in the dark, but he could feel things with his body. What he landed on was too even and sharp to be natural—definitely man-made and probably stairs.

It was cool down here, and his blood began to slow. Much better than up there in the heat and the open. He could curl up and take a long nap.

Leon forced his mind awake. The trouble with reptiles was that they liked two things, eating and sleeping. Mammals did, too, but the mammalian mind was a little sharper, a little more curious about things beyond food and rest. The snake couldn't care less what was down in this hole, only that it was a nice, dark place that might hold beetles and rats worth swallowing.

Leon made his long body uncurl and slide across the small area. Not much here except a pile of rubble blocking the stairs. He roamed across it then came to an indentation. Pressing the rubble aside with his head, he found a hole just wide enough for his body.

The snake wanted to go deeper into darkness, and Leon let it. Remy would want to know what was down there.

Gravity and Leon's sinuous body allowed him to slide down a long tube in the rubble, going down, down, down. At the bottom, Leon suddenly popped through another hole and fell several feet, to land with a splat on a stone floor.

The pain of that slapped him to awareness, and he stood up in his human form. It was pitch dark in here and hard to breathe. Leon morphed into a lynx, his eyes more attuned to the dark.

He couldn't see much in the pinpoint of light through the hole, but he saw colors and shapes, and his snake form had felt the smoothness of plaster.

It was cold down here, and smelled of death. The air supply couldn't be that great, either, despite the hole through the rubble to the surface. Leon rose into his human form again, and felt the rubble until he found the opening he'd made. He dove for it, turning into his snake form as he entered it.

Going uphill was a lot more work than coming down. Leon shoved himself up through the rubble, struggling to breathe. The snake was too damn big, and the chips of stone had collapsed a little as he came down. He shoved them aside with his broad nose, but the opening grew narrower as he ascended.

His head bumped a rock that didn't move. The sudden halt rippled down his long body, and Leon lay there, trying not to panic. The snake urged, *give up and sleep,* but Leon forced himself to stay alert.

He wished he *could* turn into a bug or worm, which could have found a way up through the cracks. But this python was the narrowest being he could manage. If he turned into anything else, including his human form, he'd be crushed to death by the fill.

Damn it, why had he been so anxious to dive down here? Showing off to Val, he thought. And Demitri. *I'm the big, bad shifter who can slither into holes no one else can. Idiot.*

He couldn't call out or signal his predicament. He could only lie here, unable to go up or down, until someone outside decided he'd been gone too long. And what could they do? No one else could get in here. They'd have to go back to the dig, get tools to pry him out, and by then, it might be too late.

The snake was cold, stymied, and shutting down. *Fuck,* the corner that was Leon's human brain thought. *What a stupid way to die.*

He fought to stay awake, fought to push farther into the rubble, but his struggles grew weaker. He knew his friends were within a few yards of him, which made the idiocy of it even harder to take.

His snake eyes closed, the thin film covering his orbs. It seemed to be lighter, but maybe that was heaven's gate. Would he enter the afterlife as a snake or a man? What was a snake's heaven like? All the mice you could eat and a steamy tropical jungle to hang out in? And would the mice you ate have their own afterlife, where they dined on boulder-sized hunks of cheese?

His mind was going. The light grew brighter and the rock in front of him suddenly dissolved into dust.

Leon popped his eyes open. The light wrapped itself around his snake body and slowly but surely pulled him out.

Leon traveled forward an inch at a time as though someone dragged him by a string. Rock scraped his skin, layers peeling from him as he went. He suddenly popped out of the hole at the top of the rubble and fell onto the cold step just inside the opening. The white light faded, and the yellow beam of a flashlight took its place.

"Leon," Demitri called, his voice rough with fear. "Can you make it the rest of the way?"

Leon grunted in pain as he flowed into this human form, his limbs aching, his skin smarting. What happened to the snake happened to him, and he'd been scraped and scratched all over. He put his fingers on the opening to the outside, slowly became a snake again, and flowed all the way out.

Demitri jumped aside as Leon slithered out of the hole and onto the ground. Leon had just enough strength to let the snake become human, then he lay on the ground, bloody, grimy, and panting.

Demitri crouched on one side of him, and Val knelt on the other.

"Are you all right?" Demitri's fingers skimmed Leon's back and arms, looking for injury. Val looked down at him, her midnight blue eyes wide with worry. Despite his pain and lingering fear, Leon's heart warmed.

"I think so," he croaked. He groaned as he sat up. "Y'all remind me never to do that again."

"I'm sorry," Remy said. "Damn, Leon, I'm so sorry."

"I was all right," Leon protested, though he knew he'd never reassure Remy. "Just a little stuck."

"A lot stuck," Val said. "Demitri saved your life."

Leon painfully pulled on his clothes then sat against the outcropping where he'd spent those agonizing moments in the dark. "How did you save me?" he asked Demitri. "All I saw was light."

"It's the magic of Apollo," Val said before Demitri could answer. "The power of the sun."

Leon drank deeply out of his canteen. "What's that supposed to mean?"

"I was sired by Apollo," Demitri said, looking off into the bright desert. "I have god-power, though not as much as my father does. The sun isn't just light, it's energy. I can manipulate it if I have to, though Apollo doesn't like it when I do."

"Why not?" Leon wiped his mouth. "Seems like it's damn useful."

"The Greek gods have always been jealous," Val said. She sat down at Leon's side and put her cool hand on his. He clasped it, knowing he'd come close to never seeing her again. "Gods guard their power well. Look what happened when Apollo's son Phaeton stole his chariot and drove it every which way. It scorched the earth. They have to be careful."

Remy snorted. "That's a myth made up by people who didn't understand weather cycles and climate change."

Val gave him an alarmed look. "Never say that. We're close to the gods here, and they get angry if you deny that they caused everything."

Demitri smiled a tight smile. "They'll say they created the weather cycles and climate change."

"Hanging out with you two is an education," Leon said. "Anyway, Remy, don't you want to know what's down there?"

"Did you see anything?"

"Felt it. Smooth walls, like they were plastered. Very smooth. The room I landed in wasn't big, maybe ten by ten, and one wall was covered with rubble. Other than that, the room was empty."

Remy's eyes lit up. "You must have landed in an antechamber."

"It's a long way down through the chips, though, and it's packed solid. It will take a backhoe to move it."

"We do it by hand and sift through every bit of fill."

"Are you serious? That will take forever."

"Doesn't matter. I'll write up a proposal on it, see if I can bring a team out. I won't be able to hide this for long, and I shouldn't. Even if I don't get to investigate it, someone else should."

Val laughed at him. "You sound so altruistic, but you know you want your name on this tomb. Don't worry, we'll make sure you get it all to yourself."

Demitri gave her a suspicious look. "How do you plan to go about that?"

"You and I are magical people, Demitri. We can reward humans we like, you know that."

"Not arbitrarily, and not without good reason."

"It's not arbitrary. He's kin of Leon, who is helping me. I can bestow rewards if I like. It's better than eviscerating people, isn't it?"

Remy looked startled, but Val smiled at him. "I'll reward you now," she said. "I'll tell you the name of your thief, but you have to promise me you won't send for the police."

"Why not? Stealing antiquities is a serious crime."

Val stood up, her slender thighs at Leon's eye level. "Promise me, Remy. Or I won't tell."

Remy looked at Leon for confirmation, and Leon shrugged. "She probably has a good reason."

"The only person I wouldn't turn in right away is Felicia," Remy said.

Val's smile widened. "Well, that's convenient."

Remy started to speak, then broke off. "You aren't seriously telling me *Felicia* has been stealing things, are you? She would never do that."

"Maybe she has a good reason," Val said. "I know Felicia has been doing it, Remy. But she loves you and doesn't want to hurt you. You need to promise me you'll be kind to her, or the vengeance demon in me might need to have one last fling."

Remy flushed. "I don't believe you. How could you possibly know?"

Leon got to his feet, sensing his brother's anger. "He has a point, Val. How do you know?"

"Simple. She changed the checklist that you keep on that clipboard. I looked over the sheets the first time you showed us the storage room. She's gotten clever—the reason you haven't noticed anything else missing is because she removed those pages from the inventory. You have no record of it, so you don't miss it. It will be a long time before someone figures out it's gone."

"But they *will* notice, eventually. And then I'm screwed."

"Maybe Felicia hopes to replace them," Val said in a reassuring voice. "You said that the stolen things weren't valuable information-wise, and you'd already photographed and recorded them. What's one more ushabti in a museum case full of them?"

Remy's scowl was fierce. "I don't believe you. You have no proof."

Leon moved to stand next to Val. "*Chere*, before we came out here, you said we could set a trap with Felicia as the bait."

"Because I knew she was listening."

Remy nodded reluctantly. "She was."

"I wanted to put her off guard. If we go back now, we'll likely catch her in the act."

"No," Remy said.

"I know you don't want it to be her," Val said. "You're in love with her. But she is going to need your understanding and love now more than ever. Use this as an opportunity to bring you closer together."

"What are you talking about? If she's been stealing from the dig . . ."

He trailed off, looking more unhappy than Leon had ever seen him look. Remy had always been the good Dupree, always agonizing over whether the right thing was the moral thing. Leon saw him agonizing now.

He put his hand on his brother's shoulder. "I'm sure there's a reasonable explanation. And Val could be wrong."

Val shook her head. "I'm not. She loves you, Remy, but she has some troubles of her own. She wasn't born an archaeology postdoc."

Remy's mouth closed in a tight line. He picked up his backpack and started walking back down their trail toward the Jeep. "Come on," he said over his shoulder. "Let's get this over with."

Val sighed and shook her head, but she turned to follow him. Demitri started after her, but Leon caught his arm and turned him back. Demitri looked him up and down with his dark eyes, the heat in them intense.

"Thanks, man," Leon said. "I thought I was dead."

Demitri didn't touch him, but his expression held relief. "I didn't want to lose you, too."

Leon reached out and squeezed the big man's shoulder. He turned to catch up with Val, and Demitri fell into step with him, putting his reassuring bulk at Leon's side.

18

FELICIA faced Remy with her head held high, but her heart beat swiftly with anger and dismay. Val had betrayed her. Felicia didn't know how Val had found out, but Val had told Remy out there in the desert that Felicia had been stealing from him.

When the four had returned, Remy hadn't spoken at all to Felicia. The other three had walked back to their own hired Jeep and roared off toward their hotel, leaving Remy and Felicia alone.

Felicia had started to ask Remy about the tomb, which could turn out to be an exciting find. Remy had regarded her stonily then quietly announced that Val thought Felicia was the thief.

"Please tell me she's wrong," he said.

"Do you believe her?"

Remy folded his arms. "I don't know. I don't want to. But she was convincing and told me I should confront you myself."

His green eyes fixed on her. Felicia couldn't read what was in them, and she realized that in spite of the five years she'd worked with Remy, she didn't truly know him. She'd had no idea he could turn into a lion, for one thing. She'd never met his family, never heard anything more than innocuous things about his life back in Louisiana. They'd talked about archaeology and good finds, research and theories, dreams and ambitions. Nothing about their true pasts, either of them.

Felicia drew a shaking breath. "She's not wrong."

Remy dissolved into rage. "Felicia, for God's sake, why? You of all people know how precious every artifact is, how—"

"Don't you dare lecture me!" Felicia stepped back and bumped against the table. She remembered Val sitting on it that afternoon, leafing through the pages of artifacts.

"Then tell me why," Remy demanded.

"Because I needed the money. Why do you think?"

"If you need money, why didn't you ask me for it? I could have floated you a loan."

"Sure, Remy, because you're rolling in money. I know you made it through school on scholarships and hard work. I know you came from a rough background. I also know how much a postdoc makes. You're lucky you can eat. You are the last person I'd ask for money."

"Stealing antiquities is better? Do you know what could happen to you? The best is you get tossed out of the country and not allowed back in. You'll lose your job and your reputation. No one will hire you ever again. And that's the best-case scenario. It's your career, Felicia. What the hell were you thinking?"

"I was thinking I needed the money," she ground out.

"For what? If you're in debt, there are programs. You can declare bankruptcy, you can do *something*. It's not that desperate."

"It isn't debt, Remy. It's medical bills. It's expenses way beyond my means, and I don't exactly get paid a lot myself."

"We get *some* insurance. And there's nothing wrong with you."

"It isn't for me." Felicia pressed her hands to her face, steeling herself to explain. "My mother is in a nursing home. She has Alzheimer's. She's only in her early sixties, and she's healthy otherwise. But nursing homes cost money, medicine costs money, food and clothes cost money, and I don't know where to get it."

Tears rolled down her cheeks, blurring Remy and the storage room and the shelves and shelves of potsherds.

"Jesus, Felicia, why didn't you tell me?"

"What could you have done? What can you do?"

Remy went silent, his eyes anguished. "I don't know. You're right, I'm useless as shit. But ripping off the dig isn't the answer. How can you help your mom if you're in prison?"

"Well, I was hoping I wouldn't get caught," she yelled.

"You would have eventually, damn it. Thank God I found out, not Habib. He'd have turned you over to the Egyptian police in a heartbeat."

"What are you going to do?"

"I don't know what the hell I'm going to do." Remy raked his hand through his hair, making it rumpled and adorable. "What did you do with the artifacts? Who did you sell them to?"

"No one, yet." Felicia wiped away tears with the back of her hand. "I lined up a buyer, but I haven't been able to bring myself to give him anything. He hasn't paid me anything either."

"Thank God for that. Where are they?"

"Under my bed."

Remy turned away, every line of his body strained. The man she loved had just found out she'd betrayed him. More tears rained down her face. Before this, she hadn't worried about losing Remy, because she'd been convinced he wasn't interested in her. But after last night, after kissing him out in the desert, after today when he'd talked to her like he assumed she'd work at his side the rest of her life, she understood what she'd thrown away. And it ripped her heart to pieces.

Remy heaved a long sigh. "Bring them back here and we'll put them away. No one needs to know about this, and we won't ever mention it again. All right?"

Felicia nodded, knowing she could do nothing else. The buyer had promised several thousand American dollars for the stuff, but she knew now she never could have gone through with it. Throwing away her career—and Remy's, too—for a few thousand dollars would have haunted her forever. Besides that, she had an emotional bond to every piece found on a dig, no matter how insignificant. It was a tie to the past that could never be replicated.

"I'll get them," she whispered. "I'm sorry, Remy."

Remy wouldn't look at her. "You bring them back, and I promise, no one has to know."

Felicia nodded again and walked blindly toward the door. Remy wouldn't punish her, wouldn't ruin her for this. He was a good enough friend for that. But she also knew, as she pushed her way out into the hot desert evening, that he would never forgive her.

~ ~ ~

"VALERIE is gone," Val said stubbornly in their suite in the small hotel outside the Valley of the Queens. "She's not coming back. She never existed in the first place."

Demitri looked into her beautiful dark blue eyes, the eyes that held the soul of Valenarian. A devious part of him was glad—he loved Valenarian, and she was back to stay.

But his rejoicing would be short-lived. Aphrodite would return in eleven more days to see if they'd succeeded in integrating both women at last.

"Val, *chere*." Leon caught her hand. "You know we're all going to die if you don't let the nice one come back, right?"

"I know that. There's nothing I can do about it. Valerie is gone."

Leon looked at Demitri. "How do we bring her back? More sex?"

Val ran her fingers through Leon's hair. "I like that idea."

"Deprive her of sex," Demitri said, his voice hard. "Valenarian likes it too much. Valerie was celibate."

"That would just drive me insane. I might turn into a wild killing machine if I don't have sex. You wouldn't want that, would you?" She smiled a dark smile.

"Be serious about this," Demitri snapped. "I don't want to lose you."

"Aw, it's sweet that you care."

Demitri glared at her. "You know how I feel about you. You've tortured me with it since the day I met you."

Val's smile vanished. "I'm the one who was tortured. What do you think it was like believing you'd never care for me, that you couldn't because of what I was?"

Leon cut in. "Could y'all save the walk down memory lane for another time? We need to figure out what to do."

"Find the pendant," Demitri said. "That must be the key."

"Where should we start looking?" Leon asked.

Demitri sank to the sofa with a sigh, stretching his arm behind Val's back. "Hell if I know."

"Well, I'm not giving up," Leon said. "If I have to go through every tomb out in that desert, I will. Remy might want to sift through it an inch at a time, but I don't care what it takes to find that pendant. Why don't you help with your Apollo sun magic?"

Demitri gave him a weary look. "It's not that simple. Nor is it a divining tool."

"Don't overwhelm me with your enthusiasm. Anyone would think you two had given up."

"Not quite," Demitri said.

"It's the gods, Leon," Val said, her voice tired. "They do what they want, and we can't stop them. They made me for a purpose, and when I broke away from that purpose, they sent Demitri to stop me and Aphrodite to destroy me."

Demitri closed his eyes, painful memories pushing their way into his head. "You'd gone insane. They had to stop you."

"But I'm not insane now. I haven't killed anyone since I met you, Demitri. Or hadn't you noticed?"

Demitri opened his eyes and looked sideways at her. "I did notice that, yes. But I stopped you that one time in Athens."

"I had no intention of killing the man. I wanted to frighten him, to make him go back to his wife where he belonged. I was finished with that, ready to pay, though I didn't know it at the time."

"And now?" Leon asked her.

"I want to get on with my life. But I'm a creature of the gods, and they don't want me to have a normal life. A vengeance demon who punishes unfaithful men? Untidy in the world of today, isn't it?"

Leon's mouth turned down, and his eyes took on the look of pain that he had too often. "But car bombs that kill children are fine," he muttered.

"The gods can't control that anymore," Val said. "But they can rid the world of me and feel like they're doing something."

"I'll talk to them," Leon said. "Testify for you."

Val gave a sharp laugh. "Give up, Leon. We do it their way, find the pendant or whatever and see what happens. Who knows? We might succeed."

"Your confidence overwhelms me, *chere*."

"Poor Leon. He's so young."

"Yeah, and since my life has been short so far, I'd like to make it last a little longer."

"Then we'll search for the pendant," Demitri said.

"Good."

Val leaned her head against Demitri's shoulder. "In the meantime, we should find some way to keep ourselves occupied."

Demitri's heart beat faster, and he exchanged a look with Leon. Leon's eyes sparkled, and Demitri let the warmth of sex run through his body.

"Come here," he said to Leon. "I have some interesting things in mind."

~ ~ ~

HOURS later, Leon woke blearily when his cell phone rang. "Hey," he answered.

"Leon." Remy's voice was strong. "You know that faience necklace that we found on the dig? The one that disappeared? Turns out Felicia doesn't have it, so I think a real thief took it."

Leon rubbed his eyes. "It didn't disappear, Remy. I'm sorry, I should have told you. Demitri borrowed it for a little while. I'll make sure you get it back."

"He did? Well, never mind. It's good to know it's safe at least. Anyway, I think I found out where it came from."

"Yeah?" Leon sat up. Beside him, Val and Demitri slumbered, Demitri's strong arm across Val's abdomen. "Where?"

"In the new tomb. I was poking around and—"

"You went back out there tonight? Remy, man, when do you sleep?"

"I'll sleep when I get back to the States. I was picking through the rubble at the entrance, and I found more faience beads, very much like what came off that necklace. So close it might be from the same necklace, but I won't know that until I see the whole thing again."

"You think the necklace was from that place?"

"Maybe. What I think is it's stuff that thieves dropped or threw away as they scrambled through the hole you found in the fill. I bet that was the remnants of a thieves' tunnel that they tried to fill in. Robbers after gold and silver wouldn't be interested in ceramic beads."

"Thanks for telling me. Maybe I can go out there in the morning with my friends and look around."

"You mean you don't want to come tonight?" Remy's tone was incredulous.

Leon did, but he didn't want to take Val out there on a false hope. Just because Remy found a few beads didn't mean this was the answer.

"I found something else," Remy continued. "It looks like part of a pendant, maybe a match to what was on the necklace."

"You're kidding. Bring it back with you. I'll meet you at your dig house."

"I can't do that. I can't take anything from this place until it's mapped and photographed and properly excavated. That won't happen until next season."

"Remy . . ."

"I've already broken enough rules coming out here again. I can't move so much as one piece of rock without recording it."

Leon swore to himself. "Fine. Let me come out there, then." The pendant might not be the one that matched theirs, but it didn't hurt to look. "How long you plan to be there?"

"As long as it takes. I'll need to be back at the dig by dawn."

Dawn was four hours away. "Hang on. I'll be right there, little brother." He punched off his phone.

Demitri proved hard to wake. The big man mumbled in his sleep and finally cracked open one eye. Leon hastily whispered what he wanted to do. No need to come or wake Val, he said. He'd dash out to Remy's tomb and back before Val missed him.

Demitri frowned at Leon but nodded. The necklace was tucked into a silk bag in his suitcase. Leon glanced into the pouch, then slid the pendant, pouch and all, into the pocket of his jacket.

It wasn't far from hotel to dig house, so Leon walked. He didn't know how he'd get out to Remy's find, but when he reached the dig house he found a Jeep parked in front with the keys in it. Since Remy was in charge of these vehicles, and he'd told Leon to meet him, Leon didn't feel odd climbing in, starting the thing, and driving off.

He'd memorized the way. Felicia's markers were stark under the starlit sky, and the moon, just past full, still sailed brightly overhead.

Leon saw a new Jeep trail that led to the outcropping and found his brother and another Jeep at the end of it. He parked a few yards away, to avoid disturbing a speck of dirt his brother thought important, and walked to him.

"Leon," Remy said, his face washed out with moonlight. "That was quick."

"I've learned how to be quick."

Leon walked around Remy's Jeep and saw that his brother had shoveled the opening wider. Remy's clothes were all dirty and misbuttoned—Leon guessed he'd widened the opening then morphed into something that could fit down there.

"What happened to not touching anything until the proper excavation?"

Remy looked away. "I couldn't stop myself. I had to know. I can fix it so no one can tell later."

"You were always good at getting away with shit. So show me this pendant."

"It's down here."

Remy stripped off and shrank down to the form of a large bobcat. Leon followed suit. The bobcat was the smallest shape any of the brothers could assume, and even then Leon looked like a bobcat that was born large and worked out. He lifted the pouch with the necklace between his teeth and followed Remy down into the hole he'd climbed out of earlier this evening.

The dust and stale air down there confused his sense of smell. Then again, he'd taken the form of a snake last time, and snakes processed smells differently. In any case, something had changed, and he couldn't put his finger on what.

The hole was much wider, showing that Remy had been working hard. Remy put his bobcat paws on the fill and wriggled his way into the hole. Leon felt a momentary twinge of fear as he followed, the memory of being stuck in here too fresh.

But the hole was now big enough that Remy and Leon could crawl through it without disturbing the packed rubble. At the bottom of the long shaft, Remy returned to his human form and picked up the big flashlights he'd left down here.

"This place is fantastic," he said, eagerly shining the light around the walls. "Intact paintings—they haven't been seen since the place was sealed. Doors in three of the walls, only one blocked up. Look at this."

Remy showed Leon what he hadn't been able to see in the dark, a rectangular doorway only half piled with rubble, a dark hole above it. "That room's even better. Want to see?"

"We don't have a lot of time," Leon said. "I need to look at the pendant, then we both need to get back."

"Oh, come on, Leon, it won't take that long. Let me show you."

Remy scrambled over the fill, not minding the rocks on his naked body. Leon sighed and followed. This had better be good.

They emerged into a larger room, and Leon beamed over the walls with the flashlight he'd grabbed from Remy's supplies. The walls were beautiful, painted in blue, red, and green. Gold glittered in the sudden light.

"They used real gold in their paints," Remy said. "And electrum, a mixture of silver and gold. I'm betting the thieves couldn't figure out how to get it off the walls, or else there was so much other treasure down here they didn't bother. You can see marks in the dust where stuff was piled."

Leon studied the empty room and the long rectangular stone box in the middle. "Is that where the mummy is?"

"It's a sarcophagus. Possibly one of many, because this is pretty close to the surface. A later burial, maybe. The mummy might still be here, but I'm not disturbing that to look." He lifted something from the floor. "Anyway, this is the pendant I found. Did you bring the rest of the necklace?"

Leon opened the pouch and carefully fished the broken pendant from it.

Remy held the other half up to it. "Looks like they match."

They did. Perfectly. The jagged edge of one lined up with the jagged edge of the other.

Leon took an excited breath. "Can I borrow this, Remy? I promise I'll bring it back when I'm done with it. In fact, you'll have the whole necklace to do what you want with it. I need this now, all right?"

"I told you, I can't disturb the site."

"Looks like you've disturbed it plenty. You must be more hyped about this place than you let on."

"It's my find. Mine. I'll do what I want with it."

Leon stared at him. "You feeling all right? Lack of air getting to you?"

"No. Who did you tell you were coming out here?"

"Just Demitri."

"Demitri. Ah, yes, my son."

Remy's voice changed, becoming deeper and fuller. A bright light filled the tomb, washing out the flashlight's beams. The light grew, as though the sun had started to rise inside the tomb.

Remy vanished. A man rose in his place, tall and muscular and beautiful. The perfection of the man's face was nearly blinding, his dark eyes burning like black holes in the brightness.

"What the fuck?"

"You wish to help the demon Valenarian, mortal man. I wish her to die. I'm a god. I win."

The necklace and pendant grew white-hot. Leon dropped them, the pendant's design burned now into his palm.

"You will stay here, human male, until I am finished."

"Fuck you. What did you do to Remy?"

"To the man whose form you trusted? Nothing. He is fast asleep in the house far away, dreaming troubled dreams of the woman he loves."

"Who the hell are you? And why are you trying to kill Val? She's been on the straight and narrow for thousands of years. Forgive and forget already."

"You have been alive merely thirty-two of those years. You cannot know."

"I know Val."

The god scoffed. "You have lain with Valenarian. Not the same thing. She will kill you in the end."

Leon thought of how Val's eyes moved from midnight dark to palest blue, from wicked glint to concerned caring. She was both women, and both women loved Demitri. Leon wasn't sure what Val thought of him, but her love for Demetri had been steadfast for thousands of years.

"You're the one who doesn't know Val."

The light flared, then started to fade. "Do not try to thwart the will of the gods. You will be safe here."

"Hey," Leon called as the light vanished. "I don't have any food down here."

"Then you'd better hope I kill her quickly." The voice faded with the light and then was gone, and Leon was left in absolute darkness.

19

DEMITRI woke as the sun touched the window. Val was cuddled up to his left side, but Leon had gone. Demitri rolled out of bed, careful to not wake Val, then showered and strolled out to the living room of their suite.

Leon wasn't there, either. Unalarmed, Demitri lifted the phone and ordered breakfast, then went back into the bedroom. He sat down on the bed and lifted Val's dark curls from her face.

"Wake up, sleepy."

Val blinked, then she stretched and smiled. "Hello, lover." She laced her arm around his waist. "Where's Leon?"

"I don't know." Demitri had the vague recollection of a dream— Leon standing over him, asking him something—but the vision faded as he reached for it. "He probably headed to the dig to check on his brother."

"He'll want to know what happened between Remy and Felicia. So do I." She yawned. "I like this. Waking up in a nest warmed my two lovers. I wish we could have this always."

"We will," Demitri said firmly. "We'll solve this puzzle, prove it to Aphrodite, and keep you with us."

She looked downcast. "You're too certain. She doesn't want that."

"I am certain. Now, get up. Breakfast will be here soon."

Demitri kissed her warm lips then left her to shower and dress. He let in the room service waiter and set up breakfast on the table, opening the newspapers from Cairo and London. News was much the same as always—war, death, rising prices, unemployment. Human newspapers often depressed him. There were good things going on in the world, too, pockets of humanity helping one another for no reward other than good feeling, but the newspapers didn't seem to be interested.

Val wandered out of the back and sat down at the table. She picked at her food, her gaze straying to the sunny window.

"I had a bad dream."

Demitri set aside the newspaper. It must have been the night for weird dreams. "What happened in it?"

"Nothing coherent. Just darkness. Heavy darkness. It scared me."

"It was just a dream."

"I don't dream like humans do. I relive memories, good or bad. This was different."

She looked pale and withdrawn. Demitri reached over and took her hand, startled to find it ice cold. "What's the matter, baby?"

"Nothing. Did Leon say where he was going?"

"Not to me." Again, the dream of Leon speaking to him teased him, but Demitri couldn't focus on it. "I woke up, and he was gone."

"We should find him."

Demitri nodded. "I think you're right."

They left the hotel and walked the short way to the dig, where they discovered Remy roaming around, supervising. Felicia glanced at them and away, her face strained.

"Leon didn't come here this morning," Remy said when they asked. "I haven't seen him since he left with you last night."

"Maybe he went back to Luxor," Val suggested.

"Without telling us?"

"That's not unusual for Leon," Remy said. "He sometimes disappears on his own, when he wants to think. It's been worse since he came back from Afghanistan."

"Do you think he'd go out to your tomb again?" Demitri asked him.

Remy looked blank. "I don't know what for. Anyway, all the Jeeps are accounted for, none missing. He wouldn't just go out there without supplies or without telling me. I'm sure of it."

He didn't look unduly worried. He seemed distracted by his work this morning and soon left them on their own.

"I'll be happier when I know where he is," Val said as they returned to the house.

"We'll go across to Luxor. He might be looking for the pendant in the souvenir shops."

Val hesitated. "You don't think he's gone home, do you? Aphrodite made it pretty clear that he'd die if he tried to help me and failed. He might have decided it was time to cut and run."

"It might not save him if he does."

"I know." Val rested her head on Demitri's shoulder. "I'm so sorry, Demitri. I dragged you into this; I dragged Leon into this. You don't deserve to be punished for my sins."

Demitri splayed his hand through her hair, loving the feel and scent of it. "I'll do anything to save you, Val. I don't care what happens to me."

"Do you care what happens to Leon?"

Demitri looked into her dark blue eyes. "Yes. Very much."

"Then we need to find him."

"I agree."

Demitri pulled her close, kissed her lips. They continued to the hotel, where they climbed into a taxi and had it take them to the ferry.

~ ~ ~

"FUCK," Leon repeated.

He had scrambled back through the half-filled doorway to the antechamber, using his flashlight to locate the canteens of water Remy had carted down here. Correction, the canteens Apollo—or whoever the hell the man had been—had carted down here.

The water was there, but the large hole in the rubble was gone. Leon's flashlight showed a solid wall of limestone chips, completely blocking his way out.

Leon swore a little longer. When his throat got dry, he started drinking water. It was a fallacy that a person should spare the water until they were thirsty. Leon could dehydrate very fast down here, and drinking as much water as possible right away was the smarter move.

He gulped down water until he was full and wiped his mouth. He calculated that he had enough water for a few days, even with keeping himself hydrated. It was cool in the tomb, but not freezing. And though the air was stale, it wasn't dead. There must be tiny shafts somewhere high above that ventilated the place.

That fact gave Leon hope that there was another way out. Did gods of the Greek pantheon know about exploring tombs? Leon remembered Remy showing him the detailed plans of tombs that had already been excavated and cleared. The simplest ones had an entrance, a stair straight down, another chamber, like the one he stood in, then another stair down to the main burial chamber. Some tombs were more elaborate, with long passages, more side rooms, and the tomb bending in an L-shape to fit the terrain in which it was dug. Leon had never seen any indication of a second way out.

"Doesn't mean there isn't one," he muttered. The tombs were sealed, Remy had said, after the main passage had been filled with rubble. But thieves through the ages had managed to find their way in and out.

Leon picked up the flashlight and started to explore. There was another door opposite the one the god disguised as Remy had taken him through. The fill was a little higher here, but the supplies he'd left in the antechamber included a trowel.

Leon used the small tool to work out a hole big enough to admit him. He scrambled through, swearing as the rocks peeled off some of his skin. On the other side, he held up the flashlight and stopped in astonishment.

A long passageway sloped away in front of him, open and unfilled. His flashlight beamed on walls and ceiling covered with painted images in blue, red, and green, outlined in black. Gold and silver glinted at him from the walls, bright and fresh.

Leon had a glimmer of understanding why Remy considered digging up ancient tombs a fine profession. The beauty of the art was incredible, and the thought that no one had looked at these images in thousands of years dizzying.

Leon shouldered the water he'd brought with him and started down the passage. It ran about a hundred yards before branching off in two directions, both side passages covered in just as many pictures. He shone his light into the dark maw of each passage, flipped a coin in his mind, and went right.

That passage led to a corridor with many rooms opening off it. Leon looked around him in wonder. It was silent so far under the earth, all this beauty hidden away under the stark surface of the desert.

"Remy's going to love this," he murmured. His words sounded flat, dead on the still air.

The place was a maze. Leon wiped sweat from his forehead and contemplated what to do. He didn't worry about getting lost—he could find his way back to the entrance, for all the good that would do. The trowel wouldn't cut through the huge rock fall that sealed up the only visible way out. He was stuck.

Leon's flashlight caught on a picture he hadn't noticed before in the myriad of musicians, dancers, men on thrones, workers in fields, and the like. It was of a small man with horns on his head, his face distorted to look like a lion's. The man pointed his right hand out in front of him, all fingers extended. The body seemed to shimmer when Leon's light passed over it, as though it were painted in the silver gold mixture called electrum.

A few feet down, Leon saw an identical picture, the arm pointing the same way. But at the end of the passage, the image appeared on the end wall, pointing left. Leon glanced that way then chose to turn right, as he had been.

His flashlight brushed a series of images so closely packed it was almost like animation. The little lion-faced man seemed to be waving his arms, his mouth open in a painted yell. At the end of this series, the arm pointed to Leon's left, his eye drawn large in a glare.

"Fine, I'll go left."

Leon started walking down the passage. When his light picked up a lion-faced man, he was still pointing that way down the passage. Leon kept walking. His feet ached from the stone floor, but he'd done tougher marches than this. At the end of this passage, the lion-headed man appeared again, his horns a little larger this time. He pointed right. Leon swung that way, and in the next image, the little man wore a large smile.

"I sure hope you're right," Leon muttered, and he kept walking, down into the dark.

~ ~ ~

THEY found no sign of Leon in Luxor. Val grew cold with worry. Demitri's Egyptian friends, which he seemed to have so many of, reported to him that Leon hadn't been seen returning to Luxor. Demitri's hotelier friend, Karim, knew the operator of the ferry line, who said Leon hadn't bought a ticket or disembarked from any of the ferries. Nor had he come across the bridge in a taxi. But Karim and his network would watch out for Leon and call Demitri if he was seen.

Val sat down on a bench outside Luxor Temple and clasped her hands. "What if he did go back out to Remy's tomb? He might have spent time in Afghanistan, but he doesn't know deserts like these."

"I'll find him." Demitri spoke in a determined voice.

Val reached up and took his hands. "We both have magic, Demitri. We can rip this place apart, stone by stone, until we find him. If anyone has hurt him, I'll peel their flesh from their bones."

"Which is exactly what Aphrodite wants you to do. Then she can kill you without remorse."

Val's anger stirred, black rage she'd kept suppressed for centuries. "Do you think she did this deliberately? Used him as bait to see how I'd react? Maybe that's why I met him in Cairo in the first place. Damn it, she knows how to twist the knife." She squeezed Demitri's hands in sudden worry. "She'll do the same to you."

"I won't let her, love."

"You're powerful, but you're still only half god."

Demitri leaned to her, his warmth comforting. "My mother's people were also very magical, a fact which the Greek gods tend to forget."

"Then help Leon."

Demitri touched her face. "Don't worry, love. I'll find him. And if he's hurt, the gods will learn what vengeance truly is."

~ ~ ~

FELICIA finished reshelving and rerecording the artifacts she'd taken from the room, marveling that she'd had the courage to take them in the first place. But her mother's care was expensive, and she'd been desperate. Felicia's sister, who lived half a mile from the nursing home where her mother was housed, tried to help, but her funds were limited, too. At least she could visit their mother every day, unlike Felicia, who was trying to build a career thousands of miles from home.

Remy hadn't spoken to Felicia at all since her confession that she'd taken the artifacts. She couldn't really blame him. The fact that he hadn't told her to pack up and go home was a miracle. But of course, he'd have to explain to the department why he'd dropped his second most experienced person from the team, which would lead to questions about how he'd let this happen in the first place. Remy was simply avoiding complications.

Felicia set the last article in place. The only thing missing was the faience necklace and pendant, but she hadn't taken that. She thought maybe Val had, but she had no idea why the woman would. Val didn't seem interested in antiquities, and she had Demitri to buy her gold and jewels. But Val was odd, and there was no telling why the woman did anything.

As Felicia finished restoring the checklist, Val and Demitri abruptly entered the storage room.

"Where's Remy?" Demitri demanded. His eyes were hard, his voice even harder.

Felicia dropped the clipboard. "At the dig. What's wrong?"

"Could you find your way back out to Remy's tomb if you had to?"

"Yes, I mapped it. Why?"

"Right now?"

"It's pretty hot right now. And you didn't answer. Why?"

"Can you take us?" Demitri was a big man, and his anger and power of command filled the room. Felicia had the sudden, strange impulse to fling herself on her knees and bow to him.

She resisted. "Remy would kill me. He's already pretty pissed at me."

"Thanks to me, I know," Val said in understanding. "But Leon might be trapped out there. We can't find him."

"Are you sure? Why would he go to the tomb without Remy?"

"He might have been lured there," Demitri snapped. "I need to check."

Worry welled up inside Felicia. The desert could be brutal, and if Leon was out alone, he could be in grave danger. None of the Jeeps was missing, so he'd have gone out there on foot—either human or in the form of whatever animal he'd chosen to become.

"We have to look," Demitri said. "Can you take us?"

Felicia bit her lip. In the desert, every minute counted. Remy was deep inside the dig today, on the other side of a rockfall that took time and ropes to climb over. By the time he got a message and came all the way back to the house, it could be too late for Leon.

She nodded. "I'll send word to Remy, but I'll drive you out right now."

Demitri gave her a curt nod, no thanks, and wrenched open the door.

"I'll stay here," Val announced.

Demitri turned back, rage on his face. Val stepped in front of him, meeting his awful gaze. Felicia had always thought Demitri handsome and reserved, but today something else shone in him, a strength and power she didn't understand.

"It might be safer for Leon if you rescue him by yourself," Val said quietly. "Besides, I can find Remy and tell him what's happened."

Demitri looked down at her for a long time. White light sparkled in his eyes, his face hard with brutal anger. Finally his gaze softened, and he bent down and kissed Val's lips. "I'll find him," he promised.

He turned and strode out. Felicia took the storage room key off her key ring and handed it to Val. "Make sure you lock up when you go find Remy."

Val accepted it with a sad look and a nod, and Felicia scurried out after Demitri.

The Jeeps were always kept stocked, so Felicia only had to grab a few more bottles of water before she started the engine and pulled away from the dig house.

Demitri was silent during the dusty ride into the desert. Felicia had never been very comfortable with him, and now he stared moodily into the distance, his emotions almost palpable. The sun was at its zenith, the heat intense. Felicia opened a water bottle one-handed and took a long drink.

"Why did you steal the artifacts?" Demitri asked her abruptly.

Felicia coughed. She closed the bottle and wiped her mouth. "Why do you want to know?"

Demitri turned his head, the flat black of his sunglasses trained on her. "You're a smart woman. You have integrity. There must have been a good reason."

"There was."

"Tell me."

He was like Val—Felicia had no desire to open her heart to him, but she found herself pouring out the story. She told him everything, about her mother and working her way through school, her sister's worries, Felicia's own fear that she'd have to give up the career she loved. When she finished, her mouth was bone-dry, and she took another long gulp of water.

"How much money will it take to keep your mother cared for in this place?"

Felicia gave a shaky laugh. "A lot. It's not a one-time deal—there are expenses every month."

Demitri's mouth flattened. "I asked you, how much?"

Felicia named the sum, unattainable in her opinion.

"I will open an account in your name in Chicago," he said. "I have business friends who will do this for me. You will have money there that you will use to pay for your mother's care."

Felicia jerked the steering wheel and the Jeep skittered off the track. With effort, she pulled it back in line. "You can't do that."

"I can do it easily. I will make one phone call when we return, and it will be done."

Felicia stared at him. Demitri returned to gazing at the desert in front of them. *I just snap my fingers, and all your problems are solved.*

"Why would you do this for me?"

He didn't look at her. "Remy is important to Leon, and you are important to Remy."

Felicia clenched the steering wheel. "That's taking friendship a long way. I can't let you do it."

"You can't stop me. I care very much for Leon, which is why we're driving out here to find him. It is the least I can do to repay you for your help."

"For driving the Jeep?"

"For not arguing or stalling, for helping us immediately even though you thought Remy would be unhappy with you. You understand essentials and have the courage to do what needs to be done."

"I'm that terrific, am I?"

"You do not deserve to worry unduly about your mother. I can easily provide the small sum you named and relieve those worries. Then you won't be tempted to steal worthless bits of clay and ruin your relationship with the man you love."

"They aren't worthless bits of clay."

"You put worth on them because of their connection with the past. That is your choice."

"You're an odd man, Demitri."

"I'm not a man."

With that strange comment, Demitri stopped talking, conversation over. He was silent the rest of the way to the tomb, and Felicia brooded on her own thoughts, not sure what to make of him.

20

VAL reported to Remy that his brother might be in trouble out in the desert, which started a flurry of activity. Remy wanted to rush off after Felicia, but Val cautioned him to slow down and carefully stock up with the tools he'd need for a rescue. Remy, his green eyes so like Leon's, nodded tersely and started shouting orders.

Not long after, two Jeeps roared off into the white desert. Val watched them depart, then she walked to the crossroads and talked a taxi driver into taking her back across the Nile to Luxor. The taxi dropped her at the hotel, where she procured a few things from her room, then walked to Luxor Temple.

Val tucked her head scarf more securely around her neck as she joined the throng of tourists entering the place. She walked along the aisles listlessly, not seeing the wonders the tour guides shouted about in several different languages.

Val left the group at the end of the temple and approached the antechambers in the rear. The tour guides didn't take people much beyond this point, declaring the crumbling inner sanctuary not as interesting as the preserved halls of Amenophis and Ramses the Great.

Val waited until the crowd had thinned a bit, then she ducked into the shadows of a ruined wall and removed her clothes. From her large handbag, she pulled out a thin dress of gauze that clasped at her right shoulder with a gold pin. She drew out a collar of gold and lapis lazuli and placed it around her neck, then slid gold bracelets onto her arms. She painted her eyes with eyeliner and dabbed scarlet on her lips. Barefoot, she stashed her bag and clothes under a pile of wall paintings from Roman times that had been removed from the more ancient temple.

"Look, Mum," a boy said in an English accent as she emerged. "That lady is dressed like Cleopatra."

The mother looked up, gaped at the paper-thin dress over Val's lush body, and abruptly dragged her son away. Val ignored them and turned to the sanctuary that housed a ruined statue of Amun.

Amun, one of the first gods of the Egyptian pantheon, had risen to great prominence during the Middle Kingdom. By the time of the New Kingdom, the time of Hatshepsut and Tuthmosis and Tutankhamun, Amun began to be conjoined with Ra, and a new manifestation rose—Amun-Ra, the all powerful, the sun god.

Val knelt at the base of the ruined statue and bent her head to the stone floor. "Your servant has come," she whispered in ancient Egyptian. "I give myself into your hands."

Nothing happened. Behind her, tourists still filed through the hypostyle hall, and in front of her, beyond the sanctuary, impatient traffic flowed. She heard the hum of a loudspeaker in the city followed by a muezzin calling for mid-afternoon prayer.

Slowly, slowly the sounds of the modern world faded. The temple walls began to solidify around her, as they had when she'd come with Demitri and Leon to call Aphrodite.

The god who answered Val was not the lovely Aphrodite. A beautiful marble statue appeared where Amun had once stood, but sculpted in the Greek mode. He was naked, perfect, his phallus erect, a coronet of laurel leaves resting on his head.

The white of the statue flushed pink, the marble faded, and the sun god of the Greeks stood in front of Val, his large toes just above her forehead.

"What is this?" His voice boomed through the temple, carrying the same timbre as Demitri's, but with an edge to it, a cruelty that Demitri lacked.

Val raised her head. "God of the sun, you want my life."

Apollo smiled, his beautiful face made even more beautiful. "I do. But I can't simply kill you, unfortunately. Aphrodite has claim on you until certain conditions are filled."

Val crossed her hands over her chest. "You gave her the chance to integrate me with the personality of Valerie, her servant. To render me harmless. But it won't work. I'm still Valenarian, and that's all I ever can be."

"I know that," Apollo said impatiently. "But Aphrodite likes her games. She likes to watch people fall in love. Very sweet. Sickeningly so. You must have grown tired of it over the years."

"Not really. I knew what it was to fall in love."

"Don't be maudlin." Apollo dragged Val to her feet with one great hand. He towered over her, twice her size, a god not willing to look quite like a normal human. "You seduced my son, who is an idiot for letting you."

"I love Demitri."

Apollo sneered. "You ruined him. He was happy and carefree until you found him."

"He found *me*, at Aphrodite's request. He seduced me and tricked me into Aphrodite's trap." Val smiled tiredly. "And I still love him."

"You know nothing about love."

"But I do. Demitri taught me everything there is to know about it." She gave him a mocking smile that she knew would cost her. "He certainly didn't learn it from you."

As predicted, Apollo's blow knocked her across the stones. "I do not discuss my son with whores."

Val wiped blood from her mouth. She wanted to taunt Apollo, to tell him there was a reason Apollo never got a Father's Day card from Demitri. Apollo had sired Demitri and deserted him, leaving his mother, a tiger shape shifter of the Indus Valley, to raise him. But Val didn't want Apollo's anger directed at Demitri.

"I want to spare him," she said. "And Leon. They don't deserve to die for me."

"They assisted you." Apollo scowled, his anger palpable. "And bedded you. And now Demitri cares for Leon, a mere mortal."

"Demitri is your son. Should he die for a whore like me? And Leon was caught in my wake, an innocent bystander."

Apollo's eyes narrowed. "What are you proposing?"

Val stood straight, facing him, not ready to kneel again. "I propose that I give myself up to you. I will let you destroy me, on two conditions."

"Conditions?" Apollo's voice rolled through the ancient room. "You put conditions on a god's will?"

"The first condition is that you spare Demitri and Leon," she said, ignoring him. "They should have no part in this."

"I am inclined to spare my son," Apollo answered. "I do care for him, whatever you may think. What is the second?"

"Give me time to do one thing. After that, you may do as you will."

"What is this one thing?"

"I want to make a journey." Val finally bowed her head in submission, something Valenarian was bad at, but she wanted this boon so much. "A short journey to make an offering, and then I will be ready."

Apollo went silent, his power filling up the temple. The old Egyptian gods were absent, perhaps not finding Val worthy of the bother. They'd made her, and they'd abandoned her.

Val did see a painting highlighted beyond Apollo's left leg, the black outline and coloring bright and fresh. The little god had horns in his curly hair and a lion's snout—Bes, the god who'd taken up carpet selling in Cairo and posing as a room service waiter at the hotel in Luxor. He was here to watch over her, though Val was skeptical about what he could do against the might of Apollo.

"Look at me, child of the dark," Apollo said.

Val raised her head, avoiding Apollo's direct gaze. She could die if she looked straight at him.

"I said look at me."

Val swallowed. She flicked her gaze briefly to Apollo's, finding black eyes that were like voids of darkness. A god's eyes could lead to many places. Demitri's eyes were warm and brown, and Leon's beautiful green. She'd never tired of looking at them.

"I'll take you there," Apollo said. "But you have to keep looking into my eyes."

Val drew a long breath, her body filling with fear. She said a silent good-bye to Demitri and Leon, her heart aching, then turned her head and looked at Apollo fully.

An impossibly bright light stabbed straight into her head, then the temple around Val disappeared. She felt herself floating, sickened, the power of the god tight around her.

Back in Luxor, the light cleared. The sanctuary was empty and deserted, the stump of a statue of Amun standing alone in its ruined chamber. The small British boy, who'd looked back to watch the lady in the see-through dress, rubbed his eyes. A sunbeam must have pierced them, he decided, and turned around to trot after his mother.

~ ~ ~

LEON reached the end of the long corridor, his bare feet throbbing. The passage ended in a wall painted with large bare-chested people in kilts, hunting and fishing, dancing and practicing with swords. No doors or corridors or stairs opened to either side—the wall was a dead end.

"I don't think this is the exit," Leon said, half to himself, half to the painting.

In the corner of the wall before him, the lion-faced god was depicted with his arms folded, a triumphant look on his face. Leon leaned to peer at him.

"Could you do something helpful like tell me the way out?"

Next to the small painted figure was a crack in the wall. Leon shone his flashlight on it, finding it regular and long, about a quarter of an inch across.

"Hidden door? Could I be so lucky?"

Leon opened the bag of supplies he carried and got out the trowel, his only tool. He poked this into the crack and tried to leverage it. He didn't have much hope, but suddenly the stone gave. He saw that this area of the wall was false, just plaster on very thin stone. He easily pushed the piece inward, opening a three-foot square.

He flashed the light inside, finding another room, but this one was different. It was filled from floor to ceiling with gleaming gold.

"Son of a bitch," he whispered.

His flashlight beam landed on gold boxes, chariot wheels, harnesses, jars, and other things Leon couldn't identify. The stash filled nearly every inch of space. It was incredible.

Very carefully, Leon climbed inside the room. He grabbed a box off the top of the pile and opened it. Inside lay long strands of gold laced with stones, some of which he identified as emeralds and lapis lazuli.

His mouth dry, Leon closed the box and opened another. He froze. The solid gold container held only one thing, the broken piece of a faience pendant.

Leon fumbled in the pack for the silk pouch. He dumped the beads into his palm, finding that the half of the pendant Apollo had handed him was now only a limestone pebble. He threw that aside and gingerly lifted the second half of the pendant from the box. He lined it up with the half he already had, and found a perfect match.

"Terrific," he said, his heart beating swiftly. "I've found the key. But I'm stuck in here and I can't use it."

Leon put the second piece of pendant back into his silk pouch with the necklace. He opened the first box again and extracted a gold chain, still gleaming and strong. He dropped that into the pouch with his beads, then he closed both boxes and put them back where he'd found them.

"Remy's name is made," he said. "That is, if I ever get out of here to tell him about it."

Leon crawled back out through the hole into the silent, empty corridor. He shone his light on the painted walls again, then he froze, his heart hammering.

"Well, shit."

No matter where he shone his light, no matter how hard he looked, he couldn't find any of the pictures of the lion-faced little god. All of his images had vanished.

~ ~ ~

To a woman who'd lived for three thousand years in a temple on magical Mount Olympus, southern Louisiana was an alien world. The narrow road Val found herself on angled through fields and was lined by a tangle of trees. The air was cooler than in Egypt but damp and clammy. It was night, but clouds overhead blotted out the stars and the moon.

A car rocketed down the strip of road, headlights slicing over Val. She was still wearing the nearly transparent shift from ancient Egypt, her gold collar and armbands winking in the sudden light. The car swerved sharply, then righted itself and hurried on.

A truck rumbled up behind her, breaks squealing as it slowed. A man's voice called from the truck's cab.

"Hey there, little lady. You need a ride?"

His accent was long and smooth, like Leon's. Val put Valenarian's smile on her lips.

"I do. Can you take me to a place called Fontaine?"

"Sure can. It's right on my way. Ain't you lucky."

Val kept smiling and waited until the man held the door open for her. He leered as she scrambled into the less than clean cab, then she settled herself while he climbed back into the driver's seat. A long shotgun rested across a rack in the back window, and by the smell of the clothes dumped behind the seat, he had recently killed an animal.

The truck roared out onto the road. The man was nothing like Leon—he had a scruffy beard and was thin, with a paunch where Leon's stomach was firm and tight.

"Do you know Leon Dupree?" she asked him.

"Can't say I do."

"I'm looking for his house."

"In Fontaine?"

"Yes. That's where he told me it was."

"He know you're coming?"

"No."

The man chuckled. "Well, I have a better idea. How's about you and me going to a place I know where we can have ourselves a fine time?"

"I'd rather go to Leon's house."

"Forget about Leon. If he wanted you to visit, he'd have given you directions. No, it's this guy's loss and Joss's lucky find."

"Who is Joss?"

"I am, darlin'. What's your name?"

"Val."

"Well, Val, honey, you lucked out hooking up with me. We'll have ourselves a mess of fun."

He really was wearisome. "I'd rather not," Val said.

Joss laughed again. "Well, you know what? This here's my truck, and you're in it. So we go where I say." He reached across the seat and put a sweaty hand on Val's thigh.

She moved in revulsion. "I don't think you should touch me."

"Why not? I don't see your Leon here to object. Just you in a see-through dress." Joss squeezed her leg, then slid his fingers down toward the join of her thighs.

"No, I really mean, *Don't touch me.*"

Val's body crackled with energy. Joss screamed as his hand became encased in sizzling lightning that traveled all the way up his arm. The truck swerved to the other side of the road, where a large semi was bearing down on them.

Joss wrenched his hand from Val and skidded the truck off into the dirt. They bounced across damp grass, past the semi, which honked at them, then back onto the pavement. Joss steered across to the right lane again, his hands shaking, then he pulled the truck off onto the narrow shoulder.

He was sweating and a damp patch stained his groin. "What the hell did you do, bitch? You almost killed us."

Val straightened her skirt. "Is Fontaine very far?"

"Couple miles," Joss panted.

Val smiled sweetly at him. "Then we should drive on, don't you think?"

Joss gulped, put the truck in gear, and steered back onto the road. He stomped on the gas pedal and peeled away, huddling against his door, as far as he could get from Val. Val rested her elbow on the passenger-side door and hummed a tune.

~ ~ ~

DEMITRI studied the stark outcropping that curved in to join a section of cliffs. Rivulets of water had carved these wadis eons ago, leaving limestone walls perfect for rock-cut tombs. The Valley of Kings was within reach of the living cities on the east side of the river, but this place Remy and Leon had found was miles beyond any village.

Demitri's magic was energy magic, not locating magic, so he'd needed the mortal woman to help him find the outcropping that looked like so many others. But now Demitri sensed the residue of strong magic here. Something had gone on in this place, which confirmed his conviction that Leon was down there somewhere.

Felicia opened the back of the Jeep and emerged with a shovel and pickax.

"Those will be too slow," Demitri said. He'd have to blast his way in. It would destroy much of the tomb and leave little for the archaeologists, but it could save Leon.

Felicia had just started chipping at the stone when another Jeep hurtled to a stop behind them, sending a cloud of dust into the blank sky. Remy leapt out, followed by Habib and some of the Egyptian workers.

"Leon's in there?" Remy demanded of Felicia.

"Demitri thinks so."

Remy grabbed the pickax from Felicia and started pounding away at the rock. Limestone chips flew, and Felicia turned away, coughing.

"What are you doing?" Habib demanded in British-accented English. "If that is a new tomb, as you say, we can't simply pummel our way into it."

"If my brother's down there, I can."

"How can he be? There is no way in, and the opening is too small. Stop and think, my friend."

Remy lowered the pick, his face bright red with sweat and anger. "If it was your brother down there, you'd be tearing the place apart with your hands."

Habib chewed on his lip, his dark brows drawn. The man was clearly torn between the burning need to preserve the tomb and the need to help Remy. "It's impossible that he was able to enter the tomb. He might be out in the desert, or fallen into a wadi. We need to coordinate a search for him."

"You do that," Remy said. "Meanwhile, I'm digging this hole."

Felicia stuck her shovel into the rubble Remy had dislodged and raked it away. Remy continued, with Felicia silently helping beside him. A few of the Egyptian workers grabbed their own tools and joined in.

Habib kept arguing. "Think about what you're doing. This is a piece of the past, a find undisturbed for centuries. We could do immeasurable damage to a pristine tomb."

Felicia straightened up. "A living man is more important than a ruin, no matter how intact. I'm sorry, Habib. You can kick me off the dig and send me home, but I'm not leaving until we know Leon's all right."

One of the Egyptian men, a thin man with hard brown skin, patted Remy's shoulder. "We find your brother. We work hard. Don't worry."

Habib looked pained, but he went back to his Jeep and pulled out a two-way radio. As he spoke rapidly into it, Demitri grabbed the pickax in Remy's hands.

Remy clung to the handle. "No. Don't stop me!"

"It will take you days to dig through that," Demitri snapped. "In that time, Leon could die."

"What the hell else do you expect me to do? That's my brother down there."

"You can stand back and let me work."

Remy raked a skeptical gaze over Demitri's expensive suit and silk shirt. Demitri felt the tiger welling inside him, felt his eyes go flat yellow, felt his teeth change to fangs. Remy stared at him, open-mouthed.

"I'm the only hope Leon has," Demitri growled. "Stand back if you don't want to be hurt."

"I think he's right, Remy," Felicia said. "He isn't like anyone I've ever met."

Remy took a reluctant step back. He told the diggers in Arabic that they should let Demitri try. The Egyptians looked just as skeptical as Remy, but they leaned on their shovels and waited to see what would happen.

Demitri shed his jacket and shirt. The sun was lowering to

the west, the god Ra sailing the orb on his boat into darkness. In Greece it had been Apollo's chariot dragging the sun to the other side of the world. One day from his chariot, Apollo had spied a tiger maiden of the Indus Valley and stopped to pay her a visit. The son of that union now stood in the middle of the Egyptian desert and reached out to the energy of the setting sun.

The power of the sun filled Demitri, coupled with the rage and strength of the tiger. Apollo would be angry at Demitri for stealing his sun magic, but at the moment Demitri didn't care. Once Leon was free and well, Apollo could punish Demitri as he pleased.

Fire built in Demitri's body and flowed through his veins. Hot wind rose around him, lifting his hair, raising the dust at his feet.

Remy grabbed Felicia and dragged her out of the way, and the Egyptians scrambled back to the Jeep. Habib watched from the driver's seat, his mouth open.

Demitri let the fire flow from his hands to the opening in the ground. The power didn't smash through the rock or dramatically break open the hole. It simply melted everything in its path.

The opening widened until it was at least ten feet in diameter, then the beam of sun magic started eating through the rubble fill. The fill was deep, probably thirty feet long, slanting all the way down into the earth.

Demitri burned steadily through it. He felt his body slowly changing to the tiger's, the animal's strength molding the fire to Demitri's needs. His mother's tiger people drew their power from the earth, not the sky. Demitri pulled on the heat of the earth far beneath him, coupling it with the sun's magic to melt the rock like ice before flame.

Smoke and steam came billowing out of the hole. When the smoke cleared, every piece of rubble and anything that might have been caught in it was gone.

"Leon," Remy bellowed into the hole. He glared at Demitri, coughing from the smoke. "I hope to God you didn't hurt him."

Demitri knew Leon hadn't been in the antechamber at the end

of the rock fill. As he'd drawn at his own magic, he'd sensed Leon's aura far away, at the very base of the tomb.

Demitri turned and leapt into the hole, the rest of his clothes shredding as he completed the change to his tiger. He ran down the revealed staircase, paws burning on the flame-hot stone. At the bottom, he used his massive strength to pull enough rubble from the blocked doorway to the right to let the tiger fit through.

He ran down the long corridors and around corners, following Leon's scent. As he got closer, he let out a snarling growl.

"Demitri?" Leon's warmly accented voice streamed through the passage. "Shit, was that you? I thought someone was trying to bury me alive."

Demitri ran straight at him. Leon was stark naked, his body covered with dirt, scrapes, bruises, and blood. Leon's flashlight spun away across the floor, lighting the tunnel like a strobe light, as Demitri leapt on him.

Demitri bore Leon to the ground and landed on top of him, licking his face. His heartbeat thrummed in relief. Leon was alive, and all right.

Demitri let his man shape displace the tiger, and then Demitri was kissing Leon. Leon laughed and kissed him back.

Another roar, and a lion came racing down the passage. Demitri rolled away in time to let the lion pounce on Leon. The lion looked anxiously into Leon's face, then started licking him with a long red tongue.

Leon shoved the lion off and sat up, wiping his face. "All right, all right. I'm happy you guys are glad I'm alive, but enough with the cat spit."

The lion rose to Remy's height, his eyes wide. "What the hell are you doing down here, Leon? Having a party?"

Leon let Demitri and Remy help him to his feet, then he enfolded Remy in a hug.

"You'll have a party when you see what's down here."

"No." Demitri stopped him. "We have to get out."

"It'll only take a minute. Remy, it's amazing, like all the stuff from King Tut's tomb. Gold shit all over the place."

Remy's eyes widened, the mania of the archaeologist taking over now that he knew Leon was safe. "This is an intact tomb? All these wall paintings *and* the original burial objects?"

"It was hidden behind a false wall," Leon said. "It's back here. I'll show you."

Demitri put a strong hand on Leon's shoulder. "No. We leave. Now."

"Just one second, Demitri. This is the kind of stuff Remy lives for."

Demitri shook his head. "I drew on the fires below the bedrock to burn my way in. I awakened them, and they're not ready to sleep again. We have to get out."

The ground started rocking. Demitri heard shouts up the long corridor, and Felicia's worried voice. "Remy?"

At the same time a large piece of the plastered ceiling fell to shatter around their feet.

21

LEON swore. He grabbed his bag, and Remy's arm as Remy started in the opposite direction of the way out.

"Wait," Remy protested. "Just let me look."

"Remy, damn it, if Demitri says this tomb is coming down, it's coming down."

"Let me at least take something . . ."

Demitri snarled and leapt at Remy. Remy paled as the tiger ran into him, shoving him toward the way out. Leon seized his brother's arm again and pulled him up the corridor. Demitri bounded past them, leading the way.

Felicia was in the antechamber, beaming her flashlight over the rubble that blocked the opening between them and her. The rocks were shaking and shifting. Demitri leapt over the blockage, then changed to his human form and pulled Leon over. Remy started to climb after Leon, but the rubble shuddered and buckled, and Remy slid back into the passage.

Felicia screamed and grabbed Remy's hands. Leon and Demitri

joined in. Remy slithered over the rocks, and the four of them fell together to the antechamber floor.

The shaking increased. Demitri pushed Leon ahead of him and up the stairs. Remy grabbed Felicia's hand, but just then the rubble in the opposite doors from the antechamber collapsed. The chamber quickly filled with limestone shards, piling on top of one another like an avalanche of stone. Felicia went down as the rocks poured over her.

Remy let out a terrible yell and grabbed her flailing arms. Demitri and Leon scrambled back down the stairs, Demitri's paws digging at the rapidly falling rock.

At last Felicia's body emerged, her eyes tightly closed. She coughed, trying to breathe. Remy reached down and hauled her up over his shoulder, then he sprinted up the stairs. Leon followed and Demitri came last. As they ran, the stairs buckled and fell behind them.

Remy burst out into the twilit desert first, followed by Leon. As Demitri leapt free, the ceiling above the stairs came down. Slowly the hole behind them collapsed on itself. The earthquake went on, dust rising into the sky. Those outside had retreated behind the Jeeps, some of the men on their knees, praying loudly.

Then everything stopped. Leon dropped to the ground, naked and dirty. Demitri flowed to his human form and fell next to him, dragging in deep breaths of clean night air.

Remy held Felicia in his arms, rocking her like she was a child.

"Oh, Remy," she sobbed. "I'm so sorry. Your tomb."

"It doesn't matter." Remy buried his face in her hair. "I almost lost you." He held her close, then he kissed her.

Leon gave a hoarse laugh. "Look at that." He scrubbed his hands through his dirty hair, still laughing. "Val's matchmaking finally worked."

He wanted to reach for Demitri, to fold the big man in his arms, to never let him go, but he had just enough reason to know it was a bad idea in front of Habib and the others. He restrained himself with effort.

"Where *is* Val?" Leon asked, glancing around. "She okay?"

"At the dig house," Demitri said, voice weak and rasping. "She's safe."

Leon let out his breath. "Good." He clasped Demitri's shoulder with his callused and dirty hand. "Thanks, Demitri. Again."

"I'll always come for you," Demitri said in a low voice. "Never doubt that."

Remy and Felicia were looking tenderly into each other's eyes. Leon let himself smooth his hand across Demitri's thigh, and Demitri rewarded him with a sinful look in his dark eyes. The celebration later would be worth waiting for.

~ ~ ~

VAL found her way to the small house at the end of a country road where Leon Dupree had spent his childhood. She stopped to take in the fading boards and trim, the porch lined with green plants, the carefully tended patch of lawn. Chairs were grouped on the porch so people could gather in the cool evening to watch the sun set.

Behind the screen door was a solid wood front door with a knocker. A button on the door frame had a carefully printed card stuck above it. "Doorbell out of order. Please knock."

Val plied the knocker. After a few moments, she heard footsteps inside, then a blind rattled in the front window and someone peered out.

The eyes disappeared, but the door didn't open. Val knocked again. She heard footsteps on the gravel path behind her and turned to see a woman in jeans and a sweatshirt come around the side of the house.

"There's no use you standing up there. That door's been busted forever. Come around back."

Val turned and walked down the porch stairs. The woman, whose eyes were so like Leon's, gaped at her.

"What the hell are you supposed to be?" the woman asked, giving her a suspicious glare. "The Queen of Sheba?"

"No, Sheba was Persian. I'm Egyptian. I'm a friend of Leon's."

Under the woman's stare, the shell of strength Val had been maintaining cracked and fell away. Tears poured down her cheeks, smearing her eyeliner, and she dropped to the porch stairs, burying her head in her hands.

"Oh, honey." The step sagged as Leon's mother sat next to her. A strong arm slid around her shoulders. "What's my son been up to? You come on inside and tell me all about it."

~ ~ ~

HABIB had to drive back to the dig house and return with clothes for Leon and Demitri, theirs now in shreds. Remy dressed again in the clothes he'd shed outside the tomb, but he never moved far from Felicia. They stood close together, and their arms were around each other whenever possible.

When Habib returned, Leon looked hopefully past him. "Did you bring Val?"

"Your friend Valerie? She wasn't at the house."

Demitri rose from the ground like a wary animal. "I left her at the dig house—she was setting off to take word to Remy that we'd come out here."

Habib shrugged. "She's not there now. I didn't see her, but I didn't look for her."

Leon's heart beat faster. "Why'd you leave her behind?" he demanded of Demitri.

"She insisted. Which was fine with me, because I knew she'd be safer there. Damn it."

Leon pulled on the pants and shirt Habib had brought and strode to the Jeeps. Demitri pushed past him, also now dressed. Before Habib or Remy could protest, Demitri slid himself behind the wheel of one of the Jeeps and started it up. Leon jumped into the passenger seat, and they roared off back to the dig house.

Val wasn't there. Leon raced through the house, questioning the students and workers who'd come in from the dig, but none had seen her except the housekeeper, who'd spotted her walking toward the crossroads. The housekeeper had assumed Val was returning to her hotel.

Leon and Demitri raced back to the hotel they'd stayed in near the Colossi, but she hadn't returned there.

"Are you looking for your lady?" A taxi driver lounged against his car at the hotel's entrance. "I took her to the ferry a couple of hours ago."

"Then you can take us there, too," Leon said. He scrambled into the taxi, and Demitri followed without a word.

"She's a beautiful woman," the taxi driver said as he sped toward the river. "I wouldn't let her get away, either."

The ticket seller at the ferry remembered Val. She'd definitely gone across. Demitri and Leon boarded the ferry, and when they disembarked, they questioned people on the other side. Yes, Val had come this way. One man had seen her take another taxi, one his uncle drove, in fact. He called his uncle on his cell phone and confirmed, after a maddeningly long conversation, that Val had been dropped off at their Luxor hotel.

Demitri and Leon hurried there and raced up to their private floor, but found the rooms empty.

"Her clothes are still here," Demitri said, looking through the closets. "And her suitcases. She's left everything behind. Except . . ."

"Except what?"

Demitri was looking into a empty square case. "She had Egyptian jewelry in here. Hers, from the time she first walked the earth. She's taken that."

"What for? To sell it?"

"I don't think so."

Demitri led the way out of the room again. He questioned Karim, who promised to discover whether Val took another taxi away from the hotel and, if so, where she'd gone.

Leon waited tensely with Demitri in the lobby. Demitri couldn't stop pacing, and Leon's knuckles whitened as he closed his fists.

Karim at last confirmed, with a worried look on his face, that Val had left the hotel, but not in a vehicle. She'd walked toward Luxor Temple.

"Bloody hell." Demitri swung away without thanks and dashed out the door. Leon followed.

"What has she done?" Leon demanded when he caught up with Demitri. "You know. Tell me, damn it."

"She's gone to call the gods. I don't know what she intended to do, but she's decided to take matters into her own hands."

"Shit." That couldn't be good. "Will they kill her?"

"Yes." The one word was grim, final.

"Damn it."

Demitri pushed through tourists streaming through Luxor Temple, heading to the chamber in the back where they'd performed the ritual to call Aphrodite. In the small sanctuary where the stump of statue stood in faded glory, Demitri found a small bundle of clothes that had been pushed behind a slab of wall painting.

He held them out to Leon. "Val's."

Leon touched the silk shirt that Val had worn, his shifter still smelling her scent on it. He picked up the shirt and rubbed it against his face.

Demitri's eyes were moist. "I love her more than anything in my life."

"I know. I'm in love with her, too."

Demitri raised his face to the darkening sky. "They took her." His voice filled with rage. "They took her from me. I let them do it once, but I'll not let them do it again."

His voice rang out, and the stones around them began to crumble. Chips of granite flaked from the walls, and people wandering the temple looked around fearfully.

Into that dramatic noise, Leon's cell phone chirped. Leon studied the readout incredulously. He flipped open the phone and put it to his ear.

"Mom?"

"Leon, what you been doing out there?" His mother's strident tones filled his ear. "I have your girlfriend, Val, here, sobbing in my kitchen. Answer me right, Leon. Did you get her pregnant?"

~ ~ ~

DEMITRI quickly and easily made all the arrangements to fly them back to New Orleans, even though most of the ticket offices were already closed for the day. He had friends in Luxor, he had money, and people fell all over themselves to please him.

They packed quickly in the hotel suite after Leon called Remy and told him they were leaving.

"She's in Fontaine?" Remy asked in surprise. "How the hell did she get there?"

"Don't ask me. We have to go to her. I'm sorry to run out on you."

"Hey, you have your own life. And you did find out what was happening to my artifacts. Thanks, Leon. If there's anything I can do . . ."

"You just keep digging up your bones and pottery. I'll be in touch."

Leon clicked off the phone and moodily stared out the hotel window. Luxor Temple had lit up for the night, the glow filtering into the room.

Demitri put his hands on Leon's shoulders, touched his forehead to Leon's neck. "I thought I'd lost you today."

"I was pretty sure you'd lost me, too."

He turned around to find Demitri an inch away from him, Demitri's hands still on his shoulders.

Leon wanted to melt into the man's touch. "I don't really get how I feel about you. It's not what I ever thought I'd feel for a guy. But when you knocked me over in that passage, I was so damn happy to see you. And not just because you'd come to get me out."

"I was happy to see you alive," Demitri said, his voice low.

"I knew right then I wanted to be with you. Always be with you, I mean. But I'm thinking that can't happen, can it?"

"Why not?"

"You're a rich, business-owning demigod. I'm a Cajun boy with no job and no money. I'm mortal, you're not."

"There might be ways around that."

"I'm not looking for a sugar daddy. I need my own life. I just want you in it. I'm not saying this very well."

Demitri's eyes were dark, pupils wide with longing. "So stop talking."

Leon found his mouth filled with Demitri's tongue. Leon snaked his arm around Demitri's back, his fingers sinking into Demitri's soft suit coat. Demitri licked Leon's mouth, his lips encouraging Leon to melt to him. Leon wasn't about to surrender, but he liked the comfort of the large, hard body in his arms.

Their plane left in three hours. Leon started to slide the coat from Demitri's shoulders. Demitri shrugged it off then skimmed Leon's shirt over his head.

Leon unbuckled Demitri's belt and unfastened his pants, sliding his hand inside to grip Demitri's penis. Demitri did the same to Leon, palm firm against Leon's cock.

They stroked each other and kissed. Leon's body started to tingle, excitement streaking through his desperate worry about Val. Being with Demitri didn't alleviate Leon's fears, but it gave him the strength to face them.

"Fuck me," he whispered to Demitri.

"We don't have time. Not to teach you."

"Suck me, then."

Demitri nodded. He pushed Leon's jeans down over his hips, still kissing him, hands stroking Leon's hard cock.

"Leon?"

The startled gurgle in Remy's voice sliced through the haze of

Leon's arousal. He jerked from Demitri to see Remy standing in the open door to the bedroom.

Demitri stepped away from Leon in silence. He zipped and fastened his pants without a word, his movements casual. As though getting caught stroking off another man didn't bother him in the slightest.

Leon's hands shook as he buttoned his jeans. Remy was frozen in place, his green eyes fixed in shock. Demitri slid sideways past the stunned Remy and out. He closed the bedroom door behind him, leaving the brothers alone.

"Leon?" Remy repeated.

Leon took a deep breath. "What are you doing here? I just talked to you at the dig. Didn't I?"

For a moment Remy looked like he couldn't remember how he'd gotten there or why he'd come. "I was heading here when you called me. I was going to offer you a ride to the airport, buy you something to eat on the way. I didn't think . . ." He trailed off. "What the hell did I just see?"

"Something I can't explain."

"I thought you were after Val. You've always chased ladies. I mean, really chased them. I guess it was all an act." The words were a question.

"It isn't an act. I'm not gay."

"You were kissing Demitri. And more."

"Yeah, I know."

Leon scrubbed his hand through his hair and turned away. Outside, Luxor Temple flared with light, an exotic backdrop to this bizarre situation.

Leon tried again. "It's not like I've always done this. Just with Demitri."

"What about Val? She's in love with him, isn't she?"

"Yes. And he is with her."

Remy scowled. "So what are you? Diversion?"

"Remy, will you shut up and let me explain?"

"I don't want to hear you explain." Remy folded his arms, his face red. "You're six years older than me. I never really knew you at all. You were off to the army when I was still in junior high. Hell, how did you make it through the army if you liked men?"

"Because this has never happened before," Leon said, exasperated. "I'm trying to tell you. I fell in love with Val, and I fell in love with Demitri." He stopped, his face heating. "We're having a threesome."

"Oh, holy shit."

"It happened, Remy, I didn't plan it. Now Val's in danger, and I need to get to her."

"So you're going back to Fontaine with your boyfriend—to find both of y'all's girlfriend? Have you lost your mind? You'll get run out of town. What's going to happen to Mom?"

"It's not going to matter if we don't help Val. She could die, and Demitri could die. And so can I."

Remy's angry look turned to bewilderment. "What the hell are you talking about?"

"You're a shifter, Remy, you know there's magic out there. You saw what Demitri did to get me out of the tomb. He's powerful, but there are beings out there even more powerful than he is, and right now they're after Val. She's the woman I love. I'll do anything I have to do to save her."

"Magic," Remy repeated. His forehead wrinkled, and he glanced at the closed door.

"If you want to believe I'm in love with the two of them because of some magic spell, you do that," Leon said irritably. "It doesn't change anything."

"No, I mean, you need magic. That's why you took the necklace and were looking for the pendant."

"Yeah. So?"

"Felicia knows about magic in ancient Egypt. She specialized in it."

"I know. She told us. What about it?"

Before Leon could answer, Demitri opened the door. He was fully dressed, his suit coat and tie immaculate, his hair pulled neatly into its ponytail. He might have been returning from a business meeting rather than having just been caught with his male lover.

"We need to go," he said with his usual calm command.

"Felicia's waiting in the car," Remy said without looking at Demitri. "You can talk to her about it as we go."

22

Val dressed in the clothes Lilianne Dupree gave her, a soft sweatshirt and blue jeans that cupped her bottom. Despite the warm air in the house, Val's fingers were cold, and her heart felt like there was a hole in it.

When she'd become Aphrodite's servant all those years ago, Valenarian had become an empty, numb shell. Now she hurt again, bad, the pain only mitigated by the fact that her actions would save Leon's and Demitri's lives.

She emerged into the kitchen, a big room with a large table, a huge refrigerator, and counters loaded with containers for bread, cookies, flour, spices. This was the heart of Leon's home, and Lilianne was its heartbeat.

"I just talked to Leon," Lilianne announced as Val emerged. "He's coming."

Val stopped. "You told him I was here?"

"Of course I did. He'd want to know."

Val bit her lip. She didn't want to see Leon again, didn't want to have to say good-bye to him. Better to make a clean break, a quick one.

She let out her breath. "It doesn't matter. The way humans travel, it will take him many hours to reach here."

"What do you mean, the way humans travel?"

"Leon is human—almost."

Lilianne looked at her sharply. "He told you?"

"That he's a shifter?" Val nodded. "He showed me."

Lilianne's brows drew together. "And that's all right with you?"

Val smiled. "I assure you, I am far stranger than he will ever be." She looked around. "I like it here, in his home."

"He doesn't live here anymore. He has a houseboat about a mile from here, when he isn't out roaming the world."

"But this is where he grew up, the house that made him the man he is." Val took the cup of coffee Lilianne handed her and cradled it wistfully. "Leon is a fine man."

Lilianne waved for Val to sit down, and the two women faced each other across the kitchen table. "Now, he wouldn't tell me, and I didn't press him," Lilianne said. "But did he get you in trouble, honey?"

"I am in the gravest trouble of my life, I'm afraid. But I'm trying to keep him out of it."

"No, I mean, did he knock you up?" When Val looked at her blankly, she tried again. "Get you pregnant? Are you having his baby?"

Val's eyes filled. "No. I can't have children."

Lilianne reached across the table and gripped Val's hand. "Oh, honey, I'm so sorry. Then what is it?"

Val wiped a tear from her cheek. "Nothing anyone can help. But I can take a few minutes to talk. Will you tell me about Leon? Please?"

~ ~ ~

NOT even Demitri's magic could change weather, airport waits, and flight delays. Leon was numb with exhaustion by the time they navigated through Frankfurt, JFK, DFW, and New Orleans. Leon drove out of New Orleans in a rented car, heading south for Fontaine and home. He wasn't sure what day it was anymore, though the clock in the car said it was eight in the evening.

He headed first for his mother's house. So much had happened to him since he'd left the little red house a wide-eyed eighteen-year-old, so sure he could go out and conquer the world. He'd experienced war and death, fear and fatigue, boredom and celebration, and returned burned out and restless.

After a few months of feeling ineffectual, he'd left to help Remy. He figured he'd kick around Egypt seeing the sights while he got his head out of his ass and figured out what he wanted to do with his life.

Then he'd met Val and Demitri, and here he was, as confused as ever. Leon knew what would make him happy, and he couldn't have it. Even if Val and Demitri were normal human beings, Remy's reaction was just a touch of what he'd have to face if he chose that path. Val and Demitri could be unconcerned because they were supernatural beings—demigods followed different rules, they said. Leon was mortal and had to live in the mortal world.

The house seemed small and strange to his eyes now. Leon led Demitri to the back door, following the glare of the porch light. The front door was still broken, he knew, despite the Dupree brothers' efforts to repair it. The damn thing would work for a while, then stick tight again, like it was trying to encourage visitors to go around back to the more welcoming kitchen door.

Lilianne opened the door before Leon could knock, and flung her arms around him. She held him in a tight hug and planted a kiss on his cheek.

"Where's Val?" Leon asked.

Lilianne glanced at Demitri beyond him. "She went to your houseboat. She said she wanted to see it." She hugged Leon up again. "Poor baby. She told me everything."

Leon hesitated. "Everything, everything?"

"Some of it was pretty hard to believe. But she told me about the three of you. Leon," she finished in an admonishing tone.

"Call Remy and commiserate. We have to find her."

Demitri bowed to Lilianne with his habitual elegance. "Mrs. Dupree. I look forward to seeing you again."

Leon's mother softened, but Leon turned to leave, in a hurry to find Val. "Come on," he called irritably behind him, then strode back out into the night.

Leon's younger brother Jean Marc had been taking care of the houseboat in Leon's absence, but he wasn't there when Demitri and Leon pulled up to it. Leon led the way across the small gangplank to the boat, where they found lights on inside and the door unlocked.

Val turned from the middle of the bright kitchen, where she was making sandwiches. She looked at them with tired eyes, her dark hair mussed.

"I hoped it would be all over before you got here," she said.

Demitri took the bread knife from her hand and set it on Leon's counter. "You hoped all what would be over?"

Val sighed. She put the last piece of bread over the cheese and tuna sandwiches and wiped her hands. "Apollo promised he'd spare you if I came to him voluntarily. Which I will do."

"No," Demitri growled, and Leon echoed him.

"Don't argue with me. It's done. The idea that I could ever be anything but Valenarian was foolish. You tried, and I love you both for trying. But I refuse to let you die because of me."

"We didn't try everything." Leon upended his backpack on the couch and extracted the pouch. He poured the beads and pendant pieces onto the counter and started threading them on the gold chain.

Val stared at it. "You found the other piece of the pendant."

"It was in Remy's tomb. That little god—what's his name? Bes—showed me where it was."

Val raised her dark brows skeptically. "So you put the necklace on me and I'll be better?"

"Not quite." Demitri slid off his coat and slung it over the back of a chair, then loosened his tie.

Leon continued stringing the necklace. "Felicia finally found the spell people used this kind of necklace for. Like Demitri said, it can either be a curse to break someone, or a spell of wholeness if you reverse it." He put the last bead in place and lifted the necklace. "It requires an incantation, the will to make it work, and a joining."

Val smiled through the sadness in her eyes. "Joining. Do you mean sex?"

Demitri leaned his ass on the back of the couch. "Semen is used in many rituals, the stuff of life. The vagina is powerful, too. The cradle of life."

"Very philosophical." Val's lips curved.

"I'm not letting you go until we try," Leon said, and Demitri nodded in agreement.

She laughed, sounding more like Valenarian again. "Oh, all right. You never had to persuade me very hard to couple with you, you know. What do we have to do, my lovers?"

~ ~ ~

THE ritual was simple and beautiful. Val recognized the ancient Egyptian words for wellness and healing, for joining soul and body.

Demitri and Leon undressed her in the moonlit bedroom, then slicked her body with fragrant oils Demitri had brought. Leon placed the necklace with the broken pendant around her neck, and Demitri fastened it in place.

The two men touched her all over, smoothing her skin, kneading her shoulders, relaxing her. Leon's bedroom was small, at the end of the boat, and the dank smell of the river came through the window. But Val loved the dampness and even the slight hardness of the bed, because Leon's aura permeated it. This was his home, and she'd fallen instantly in love with it.

Leon took off his clothes and let Val and Demitri oil him next. They were going to be three slippery people, Val thought with inward amusement. Last, they rubbed the oil on Demitri, Val loving the feel of his slick erection beneath her palms.

The two men stood side by side, muscular, shining with oil, rampant and ready. Val licked her lips. "A girl couldn't ask for a better send-off."

"Stop talking about leaving us," Demitri said sternly. "We're starting."

Step one was for Leon to lie faceup on the bed. His cock stood stiffly upward, held in place with his thumb while he laced his other hand behind his head. Val had at first thought the ritual would be double penetration, which made her pulse race, but Demitri told her it wouldn't be that straightforward.

"Even vanilla sex is fine with me," she said. She lifted her breasts in her hands, liking how both men's gazes were drawn to her as she flicked her fingers across her nipples. "You know I don't mind."

"That's one thing I love about you, Val," Leon said, smiling.

"Can we get on with this?" Demitri growled.

"Fuck you," Leon said softly.

"That was the idea."

Val lay down next to Leon and watched Demitri climb onto him, his cock hanging hard between his legs. Leon slid his hand over Demitri's balls to his ass, showing Val that he'd learned how to ready Demitri to receive him.

Demitri unbound his hair, shaking it out over his shoulders. The dark-eyed man looked disheveled and wild, like he had when Val first met him. She'd gotten wet just looking at him, and when he'd first pressed his big body over hers, she'd thought she'd die of happiness.

Demitri lowered himself onto Leon's slick and waiting cock, his own in hard erection. Leon's face changed as Demitri slid onto him. His hands went to Demitri's thighs, fingertips indenting oiled skin.

"Fuck, he's tight," Leon moaned. "Oh, damn it, Demitri. I love you."

Demitri flushed, his eyes flicking coffee brown to tiger yellow. "You're not so bad yourself, my Leon."

Val leaned to Leon and kissed him. He snaked his hand through her hair, kissing her with the passion Demitri was making him feel.

"Mmm, lover, I could come just watching you."

"Not yet, baby," Demitri whispered. "Not just yet."

Val's body crawled with heat. "Better hurry then. My pussy is dripping wet."

Leon groaned and thrust up into Demitri, who let out a noise of pleasure. Demitri started suggesting dirty things he wanted to do to Leon, and then Val, and then Leon again. Demitri had learned to be sophisticated and sleek around his hotelier friends, but he was just as raw and untamed as he ever was. He'd always been a god at sex.

"I'm going to come," Leon moaned. "Too soon. Oh, God."

Demitri chanted words in ancient Egyptian, and Val felt the necklace warm around her throat. The broken piece of pendant lay on the table next to the bed, waiting.

Leon shouted as he came, thrusting his hips high. Demitri grunted with it, eyes closed, losing the thread of the incantation.

Demitri fell forward on his hands and knees, sliding off Leon, then he grabbed the oil and started rubbing it on Leon's cock again, bringing him once more full and ready.

Demitri slammed the oil back onto the table and flipped Val to her hands and knees. She didn't protest as Demitri slid himself inside her quim, his cock fully extended. Leon watched with half-closed eyes, stroking his own staff, as Demitri fucked Val hard.

Val screamed and scrabbled on the bed. Demitri was so erect, fucking her so fast, and the feeling was too joyous to handle.

Demitri panted behind her, sweat dripping to her bare back. "You ready?" Demitri said breathlessly to Leon.

Leon nodded. He rose up as Demitri slid out of Val, making her cry out in disappointment. But almost instantly she was filled with Leon, his wide cock opening her, his hips pumping himself into her.

It was glorious. Leon rode her for a minute, then Demitri took over, then Leon, then Demitri. Val climaxed, screaming, begging for them to stop—begging for them to never stop. She whimpered as she wound down, but they kept on, one after the other, until she rose to climax again and again.

A human woman couldn't have taken it. Not with Demitri, not with Leon, not for as long as they shared her. Valenarian loved it, coming over and over again, shoving herself back them, begging them to hurry when they slowed to switch places.

Leon came first. He cried out as his semen scalded Val inside, his voice ringing in the little room. He fell onto the bed beside her, breathing hard, watching while Demitri rose over Val again.

Demitri shoved himself into Val, pumping a little longer before Val felt his seed shoot far inside her. She climaxed once again, and they collapsed together, sweating and laughing.

What happened after that, Val wasn't sure. She slid into profound sleep, and when she woke, Demitri and Leon lay tangled with her, the two men protectively on either side of her. The clock on the nightstand told her it was two in the morning, and the moon had vanished.

She sighed. If only she could have this forever. Val's joy subsided, her sadness returning. They were sweet to try to save her, and she wouldn't forget it, but she knew it was futile. The will of the gods couldn't be thwarted, and she could only save them if she gave them up.

Val lay tiredly, amazed at how much of her energy they'd taken. Demitri had sometimes ridden Val all night and all the next day without either of them tiring, but this ritual seemed to zap their strength.

The necklace was warm, uncomfortably so, but Val didn't dare take it off. If it burned her, so be it. To move it might void the ritual, and Demitri said it couldn't be done a second time.

Demitri opened his eyes. They were sin-dark, warm, tender, and he smiled at her like he had long ago. Her heart ached.

"I love you, Demitri," she whispered. "I always have."

"I love you too, baby." Demitri kissed her lips, then he reached over her and shook Leon. "Wake up. We're not finished, yet."

Leon rubbed his eyes and yawned. "You two have stamina."

"That's why you love us," Val said softly, running her hands through his short hair.

"You bet it is." Leon kissed her then rose on his elbow and looked at Demitri. "I'm ready anytime you are."

"Good," Demitri said, his eyes burning. Then he reached for the bottle of oil.

23

Now I'm going where I've never gone before, Leon thought as he turned facedown and let Demitri slide oiled fingers between his buttocks. Val lay beside Leon, watching with her midnight blue eyes, her breasts firm and dark-tipped.

Demitri's touch felt weird, the fingers playing with him wide and a man's, not slender and female. Leon had played with wands with women before, but never had he experienced a man tucking one slick finger inside him. He moved, clamping down.

"Relax," Demitri murmured. "Feel it. Enjoy it."

Val touching his hair helped. Leon wriggled his hips once, then forced himself to open.

"There you go." Demitri slid a second finger inside. He didn't move them, simply rested them there until Leon became used to it.

Leon relaxed a little, then hissed in a breath as Demitri added a third finger.

"Quietly," Demitri said, his voice soothing. "You're opening for me."

Val bit the knuckle of her thumb, her nipples hard little points. She took Leon's hand and slid it between her legs, showing him how excited she was.

Leon's body warmed as he played his thumb across Val's clit, as he opened to Demitri's touch. As Leon smiled at Val, Demitri slid his fourth finger inside.

"Shit," Leon gasped. "Oh, man, that's good. I never knew . . ."

Val licked her red lips. "You never had Demitri. He's wonderful, isn't he, lover?"

"Damn straight."

Demitri leaned down, covering Leon with his warm body. "Are you ready for me?"

Something dark twisted in Leon's belly. "I am." He reached up and touched Demitri's long hair. "Lover."

Demitri chuckled. He eased his fingers out of Leon, then pulled Leon's hips back to meet the blunt end of his cock.

Leon tensed, but Demitri's warm hand smoothed his back. "Look at Val," Demitri said. "Focus on her, not me."

Leon couldn't help one glance at Demitri behind him, cock huge and ready, before he closed his eyes. He opened them and focused his gaze on Val's beautiful face as instructed, and Demitri slid rapidly inside.

Leon thought he was coming apart. He cried out, his jaw clenching, but Val was there, kissing him. She moved so she sat at the head of the bed, her thighs spread while Demitri started to fuck him.

"I'm doing this for you, you know, *chere*," Leon said, touching the moist curls at her pussy.

Val grinned. "Sure, I believe you. Every bit of this is for me."

"It is, love. If Demitri has to screw me every night for a year in order to save you, I'll have to put up with it."

"You're a shit, Leon."

"Love you, too, babe."

"Shut up," Demitri said. "Feel me, asshole. Do you love it?"

"Hell yes." Leon groaned into Val's thigh, his body jolting with Demitri's thrusts.

The man was good. Demitri knew exactly how to give and take, never hurting, never letting up. He rode Leon hard and fast, and at the same time made Leon feel the most ecstasy he'd ever felt.

When Demitri pulled out, Leon made a noise of vast disappointment. "What the hell?" Demitri wasn't following the plan.

"Get yourself inside Val," Demitri said.

Yes.

Val scrambled to obey. She lay down under Leon and grabbed Leon's cock, guiding it into her. In seconds, Leon was buried inside her, and at the same time, Demitri pressed back into Leon.

Double penetration. No wonder Val begged for it. Leon couldn't think, couldn't do anything but *feel*. Val was warmly squeezing his cock, her beautiful lips within reach of his. Demitri filled him from behind, his huge, beautiful cock fucking him and making him feel things Leon had never been aware he could.

Leon felt complete. Whole. For the first time since he'd drifted away from home, he felt like he belonged. He belonged to these two people, a beautiful woman and a gorgeous man.

It didn't even matter that they weren't really human. Right now they were simply Val and Demitri, two people, who both amazingly loved Leon Dupree.

Dark sensation swamped him, cutting off all thoughts. He heard himself screaming, felt burning heat flush his body, felt a searing pain as the necklace Val wore sizzled his skin.

Leon came. He was pounding into Val, filling her before he even realized it. At the same time, a scalding heat filled him from behind. Demitri's come, the semen of a demigod.

Leon fell, limp, spent, happy. Demitri lifted Leon out of the way, then he held Val down on the bed and slid his already erect cock inside her. Val laughed, her hips dancing. Demitri held her close, pressing her hard against him. When Demitri finished and rose, the outline of her necklace was burned onto his skin as well.

They all bore the mark now. The faience beads were hot, smoking, but Val didn't say a word. Her eyes were filled with pain, but she remained silent, holding it in.

Demitri lifted the broken piece of pendant. He fitted it against the mark of the other piece on Leon's chest. Leon winced as the piece burned into his skin.

Demitri did the same to his own chest, marking it, then he laid the pendant piece on Val.

She screamed. The hot pendant fitted right against the other broken piece, and the two halves fused together.

Except they didn't. Demitri held them together, cursing, commanding them to become whole, but the pendant remained broken. Val was writhing and screaming, the necklace red-hot.

"Stop!" Leon shouted. "You're killing her."

Demitri stared at Val a moment, then he ripped the necklace from her and dropped it to the floor. Val put her hands over her face and wept in anguish.

Leon grabbed the oil and started rubbing the soothing liquid over the burns. "It's all right, *chere*. It's over."

Demitri gently touched the seared outline between Val's breasts. His voice was full of sorrow. "I'm sorry, baby. I was so sure it would work."

"Damn it, we can't give up," Leon said.

Tears silently trickled down Demitri's face. "It's not working—it's only causing her more agony."

Val gave Leon a watery smile. "Thank you, Leon. You tried."

Leon felt his own face wet. "I'm not ready to lose you. Damn it, Val, I just found you."

"I'm sorry," she whispered. "I love you both."

"No," Leon said again.

His words cut off as bright light filled the dark room. It became sunlit as day, though the clock proclaimed it was still the middle of the night.

"Your time is up," the god Apollo said as his body manifested.

He was naked, muscular, handsome, and wore a circlet of leaves on his head. He pointed a long finger at Val. "Valenarian, it is time for your sacrifice."

Demitri threw the bottle of oil at him. Apollo flicked his fingers and the bottle shattered, sending shards of glass and steaming oil across the floor.

Demitri was on his feet, his tearstained face dark with rage. "She has until the new moon. You have no right."

Apollo regarded him disapprovingly. "She is a creature of the gods, as you are. We can take her anytime we wish. And you. Remember that."

"Fuck you."

"Is that any way to speak to your father?"

Val slid out from under Leon and to her feet. Leon rose beside her, putting his body protectively between her and Apollo.

"It's all right," Val told him. "I made my choice, made the agreement. I'll go."

"Like hell," Leon growled.

Apollo's voice turned weary. "If they interfere, they die."

"Please." Val stepped in front of Leon and placed her hands on his broad shoulders. Her touch was smooth and cool. "I'm doing this so you that will be spared. You and Demitri."

"I don't give a damn why you're doing it," Leon began.

"I know about the gods, Leon. They can exact terrible vengeance, especially on mortals who thwart them. Let me do this for you."

Demitri snatched the necklace off the floor. It had cooled, no longer burning. "So, you're saying that you'll give up your life so that we may live?" He said the words slowly, as though each one was significant.

Val nodded. "Giving it gladly. Aphrodite's bargain was unfair. I will let myself be punished, and you and Leon may live out your lives without fear."

Demitri's anger vanished. To Leon's astonishment the big man laughed, then he brandished the necklace in the air.

"Aphrodite!" he shouted. "I call upon you to tend your servant. Come to me!"

Apollo swelled, his light filling the room until Leon felt his skin burning. "What have you done?" the god demanded.

"What have *you* done, Father?" Demitri laughed. "You've lost."

Val glared at Demitri. "Stop. Don't make him kill you."

"He won't."

Before Leon could ask what he meant, the room filled with another light, this one slightly paler, like moonlight. A sweet scent followed along with a faint ringing of chimes.

Aphrodite appeared by the window, wearing the thin Egyptian gown she'd worn in Luxor Temple. Bangles whispered on her arms, and she smiled.

"My creature has passed the test," she said. "Release her to me."

Apollo gave her an incredulous look. "*Your* test?"

"Did you really think I'd let you kill Val without impunity? I gave her a puzzle that would test her resources and her courage. I wanted to see whether she'd make the ultimate sacrifice in order to save those she loved. And she did it." Aphrodite beamed at Val, her beauty making Leon's eyes ache.

"What if I hadn't passed?" Val asked in a small voice.

"Then you would have perished," Aphrodite said. "And Leon and Demitri with you."

The heat and the sun-brightness in the room increased. "We did not agree on the test," Apollo rumbled. "She offered her life to me, and I will take it. You may have the mortal Leon as compensation. I know how you like beautiful males."

Aphrodite hissed, her power suddenly intense. "Reminding me of Adonis is not the way to placate me."

"I don't wish to placate you. I want my sacrifice." Apollo held out his hand, and a band of light laced around Val's throat.

Val screamed, and Leon threw himself in front of her. Demitri slammed himself protectively over them both, taking the full brunt of the light. He threw back his head in wordless agony, then his face went gray and still. Demitri fell to the floor, and the light vanished. Val dropped to her knees beside him, a horrible keening coming from her throat.

Apollo froze, arm still raised, looking down at the body of his son. "You bitch, look what you made me do."

"You did it yourself," Aphrodite said tartly. "What a waste."

"Wait a minute, are you saying he's dead?" Leon knelt quickly on Demitri's other side. He couldn't tell whether Demitri breathed or not, couldn't find a pulse.

Val flung herself across Demitri's chest, weeping. His own pulse racing, Leon pushed her gently away and laid Demitri flat on the floor. He pulled Demitri's head back, laced his hands together, and started CPR.

"What is he doing?" Apollo asked.

"Trying to save his life," Leon snarled. "Now get the fuck out of my house."

"Val," Apollo snapped. "Come with me now."

Aphrodite's power filled the room. "I said no."

Apollo's power expanded to meet hers. The houseboat began to rock, too weak to contain the volatile magic of gods. Leon's few pieces of furniture crumbled into dust.

"Stop," Val shouted. She leapt to her feet. Leon was sweating, still pumping at Demitri's chest.

I can't save them both, Leon thought, and he felt tears trickle down his cheeks. *I'm not strong enough to save them both.*

He heard Valenarian screech. Out of the corner of his eye, Leon saw her change from beautiful woman to creature of brilliant light. Her teeth were sharp as a lion's, her claws like those of a grizzly. She flew at Apollo, snarling invectives, her claws bent to kill.

"Val, no!" Aphrodite shouted, but Val was already attacking Apollo.

Val's aura was flushed with rage, her need for vengeance crack-ling in the air. Only this time she wasn't taking vengeance on a wronged woman's behalf—she was trying to destroy the being who'd killed her mate. But she couldn't destroy him—he was a god who would crush her like a fly.

A long, low growl sounded from the veranda that overlooked the river. *Now what?* Leon thought distractedly. Sweat poured down his face, but he couldn't stop pumping Demitri's chest. *Damn you, Demitri, breathe!*

Glass broke as a huge tiger sprang through the windows and went straight for Apollo. Val rolled quickly out of the way and became human-shaped again, her midnight blue eyes wide.

The tiger fought Apollo, the two of them rolling over and over, tearing a hole in the bedroom wall and tumbling through it into the living room. The tiger snarled and bit, and Apollo could barely dodge its blows.

Finally Apollo scrambled to his feet and faced the tiger, panting. He looked less like a powerful god and more like a handsome hu-man who'd been in a fight. His lip bled and his cheeks bore claw marks. His laurel coronet hung askew, and torn leaves were scat-tered over Leon's drab carpet.

Apollo stared at the tiger in something close to terror. The tiger rose on its hind feet, its huge head touching the ceiling, and sud-denly it became a woman.

She had long black hair, large dark eyes, melonlike breasts, and four strong arms tipped with long fingernails. She was as beautiful as Aphrodite, but in a wild way. This woman had never been civilized.

"You killed my son," she hissed. The language she spoke was alien to Leon, but somehow he understood it.

"I didn't mean to."

The woman whirled so fast she was a blur. When she stopped, sixteen red gashes had been torn across Apollo's chest. "You gave him to me, and you are not allowed to take him back," the woman said. "That is the way of the universe."

Apollo lifted his massive hands. "Fine. I'll take Valenarian and go."

The woman hissed again and flames burst from the tips of her fingers. "You will take no one. Be gone, and do not return."

Apollo stared at the woman a moment longer, his face ashen. "You win," he said, then his voice dropped to a mutter. "Again."

Light flashed, and Apollo disappeared, fallen laurel leaves and all. The brightness in the room dimmed, Leon's lamps illuminating the broken wall and furniture, Demitri lying lifeless, and the three women standing upright over him.

The black-haired tiger woman knelt next to Demitri, her look turning to concern and deep love.

"My son," she whispered, and touched his forehead. "Come back to me."

Demitri heaved a sudden breath and opened his eyes. Leon backed away, his hands aching from pushing Demitri's chest.

Demitri blinked a few times, his gaze confused, then he focused on the woman and sat up in amazement. "What the hell just happened?"

Val crouched next to Leon, her eyes wide. "Apollo killed you. He was aiming for me. I'm so sorry."

"I remember now." Demitri ran his fingers through his hair. "That was death?"

"Take it easy," Leon said. "You were gone for a while. You need to get checked out."

"I'm a demigod," Demitri said, his voice hoarse. He reached up and clasped the woman's hand. "You brought me back."

"I did." She ran a fond hand through his hair. "Be well, my son. And be happy."

"You're Demitri's mother?" Leon asked.

Val looked at the woman with great respect. "I've always wondered about you."

"I am called Kalika, a daughter of Kali. I come from the tiger people of the Indus Valley."

Val's eyes sparkled, a hint of her old smile returning. "You're a wronged woman, then. Apollo left you high and dry with a baby to raise. Would you like me to exact a little vengeance?"

Kalika laughed gently. "Apollo did not leave me. He fled me when I finished with him. I seduced him because I wanted his seed. I knew that a divine son I bore would be special and magical." She stroked Demitri's hair again. "I was right."

Demitri struggled to his feet, leaning heavily on Leon, but his strength was returning quickly. He reached out to take his mother's hand. "Thank you."

Kalika brushed his cheek then kissed it. "These are the creatures you love?"

"This is Val and Leon."

"A demon and a shifter. Such interesting company." Kalika lifted her brows, but her dark eyes were warm. She rested her hands on Leon's and Val's heads. "But if you love them, I will give them each a gift."

Heat seared through Leon, and he cried out in sudden pain. Val gasped beside him.

"What did you do?" Demitri demanded.

"Valenarian will no longer worry about her demon becoming impossible to control. She nearly cured herself by her great love for both of you, but I simply gave it an extra guarantee."

"And Leon?" Demitri asked.

"He will be able to stay with you as long as he wants, and retreat either to Olympus or to my valley when you are both weary of the world."

"You made him immortal?"

"Semi-immortal. He will answer to the same laws as you—the gods alone will be able to cause his death."

Leon looked at her in amazement. "That makes no sense. How could you make me immortal?"

"I have many powers, shifter. I must go now. My time outside my valley is limited."

She hugged Demitri, love in her eyes. Then she hugged Val and, last, Leon. It felt very strange to have four arms around him, but it also felt protective.

Kalika kissed Demitri again, shifted back into the huge tiger, bounded past the staring Aphrodite, and leapt out the window. Light flashed, and she was gone.

"Goodness," Aphrodite said, blowing out her breath. "How very unusual." She put her head on one side, studying Demitri. "What was it like to have a mother with four arms?"

Demitri shrugged. "I never thought it was odd. Two-armed women looked wrong to me until I got used to it."

Aphrodite's beautiful face clouded. "I'm not used to anyone not thinking me supremely beautiful."

"Oh, I think you beautiful." Demitri grinned. "For a two-armed woman."

Aphrodite frowned, not mollified. "Put the necklace on Val. We need to finish this."

Leon lifted the necklace from where Demitri had dropped it and hung it again around Val's neck. It fitted against the burn marks on her skin.

Demitri found the broken pendant and held it against the other piece. The necklace heated again, then a light appeared between the two cracks. The light grew in intensity, then faded just as quickly. The pendant sealed together.

The necklace dropped, cool and whole, against Val's chest, and the burn marks on her skin vanished. The burn marks disappeared from Leon and Demitri at the same time.

Leon sagged in relief. "Welcome back, *chere*."

Demitri wrapped his arms around Val from behind, tugging her back against him. "I love you, Val. Innocent woman or crazed demon, it doesn't matter."

"Very touching," Aphrodite said. "But that's all over. She is one being again. Be happy, Val." Her voice gentled. "I'll miss you."

Val looked at her in surprise. Val's eyes were blue now, a shade between the demon darkness and the sky blue that had been Valerie's color. "I thought you were going to take me back to the temple."

"No, dear. You served me well, but you need this life." Aphrodite gave a breathy little laugh. "Besides, I don't want that tiger woman coming to chastise me for taking you from her son. She's quite . . . formidable."

Leon grinned at Demitri. "Your mom's the greatest. Bet she and my mom would get along just fine."

Val gave them both a wistful look. "I always wanted a mom."

Leon hugged her. "Now you have two."

"I'll be going now," Aphrodite said loudly.

Val broke from Demitri and Leon and went to her. She knelt at Aphrodite's feet and bowed in true supplication. "Thank you. You have given me the greatest gift."

Aphrodite smiled, appeased, and lifted Val to her feet. Aphrodite hugged her suddenly, looking almost warm and human. "Be well, my dear. Now I will give you another gift." She kissed Val's forehead, and Val's body flooded with sudden light.

Leon started for her, but the light faded, Aphrodite smiled at them, and dissolved into mist.

24

Because the battle had destroyed much of the interior of Leon's houseboat, Val got to discover the joys of decorating. She and Leon's mother went shopping the next afternoon, and Val learned how much fun it could be to pick out new furniture, curtains, pillows, towels, and other little bits to make Leon's house a home. Leon, who'd been repairing the bedroom wall, looked on with a pained expression as they unloaded everything, but Demitri lounged on the back terrace in bathing trunks and left the women to it.

Lilianne seemed a bit pensive about the relationship between Leon, Demitri, and Val, but she softened as Val chattered about it like it was the most natural thing in the world.

"I just want you to be happy," Lilianne told Leon.

"I am happy, Mom."

Demitri rose languidly from the sunny porch and strolled back inside. His trunks clung to his muscular body, and he'd pulled his hair back into its sleek ponytail.

"I understand," he said to Lilianne in a rumbling voice. "All mothers want their sons to be happy. And safe."

Val arranged the mountain of cushions on the new sofa she'd bought and stepped back to admire her work. "Demitri's very rich. He's paying for all this. Does that help?"

"Money is not my biggest concern," Lilianne said.

"The neighbors can think what they want," Leon told her. He fetched two cold beers from the refrigerator and handed one bottle to Demitri.

"My neighbors aren't my concern either. If they're too nosy, they deserve to be shocked."

"Then what?" Leon asked.

"I'm concerned about you." Lilianne looked straight into her son's green eyes. "I want you to be all right. Are you?"

Leon nodded. "I'm getting a lot better. I was lonely, Mom, even when I was home. Now I'm not."

Demitri broke in. "Leon wants to be a doctor."

Leon stared at him in amazement. "I do?"

"You rushed off to Egypt to nurse insect bites at Remy's dig. You were drawn to medicine in the army, but you never had the money to go to school. As Val said, I'm quite well off. I am happy to fund your education."

"Just like that?"

"Just like that. If you want it."

Leon studied him for a long time. "Let me think about it."

Demitri shrugged his bare shoulders. "All right."

Lilianne looked on with a strange expression on her face. "Well, don't decide until after Remy's wedding. I want the family to be together for that."

Val smiled to herself. Remy had called this morning with the news that he'd asked Felicia to marry him. Val could cross that matchmaking chore off her list.

Leon chuckled. "Don't worry. I want to be here for that, too. I want to make damn sure it happens."

Lilianne hugged her son, then impulsively hugged Demitri. Demitri returned the hug, looking surprised.

"It's unusual," Lilianne said to Val as Val walked her out to her car. "But then, I had an unusual marriage myself. It's not every girl who falls in love with a shape shifter."

"And you had four sons, all of them shape shifters also."

Lilianne laughed. "I did. It was a challenge, I won't lie. But a happy one."

Val waved her off and returned to the house. Leon had his arms around Demitri's bare torso and was kissing him.

"I put brand new sheets on the bed," Val said. "Want to try them out?"

Demitri gestured with his beer bottle, which was sweating in the humid air. "Lead the way."

~ ~ ~

Much later, as the sun set, Val lay happily tangled with the two men she loved. Both were awake—Demitri lay stretched out full length on her right, while Leon hemmed her in on the left. Val liked being sandwiched.

Leon was lazily stroking her skin. The faience necklace still hung between her breasts, her reminder of what she'd gone through to find her way to love.

Demitri kissed her cheek, his hand coming up to play with her breast, his dark eyes sinful. "You never told us, Val," he murmured. "What was the gift Aphrodite gave you?"

"Children."

Both men's eyes popped open. Val resisted the urge to laugh at them.

"Sometime in the future, you two will be fathers," she explained. "They'll be unusual children, certainly. Probably shape shifters, likely magical."

"And a handful." Leon started to grin. "Like me and my brothers."

"What did your mother call it? A challenge, but a happy one."

Leon's laughter shook the bed. "That was a nice way to put it."

Demitri's eyes warmed. "When my friends Nico and Andreas left me to marry, I was lonely. They were like my family, and I thought I'd never have a family of my own. You both have given me so much."

Val traced Demitri's cheek with her hand. "You made me fall in love with you such a long time ago. I've never stopped. You saved my life by letting me love you."

Leon propped himself on his elbow. "And I've been drifting around trying to figure out what I wanted and not finding it. Thank you for towing me to a safe harbor."

"Anytime," Val said. She ran her tongue across her lower lip. "I'd like to tow you somewhere now."

"Haven't had enough, have you?"

"I'll never have enough of you two," Val said.

Leon guided her hand down to his already erect cock. "Tow away, *chere*."

Demitri rose, his big body filling the bed. "Ride him," he instructed. "I'm going to enter you, too."

Val shivered in delight. She'd been longing for this.

"Anything you say, lover," she said, drawing her finger across Demitri's cheek.

She kissed Demitri, then lowered herself onto Leon. She laughed in joy to feel Demitri's chest against her back. His strong arms enclosed both Val and Leon as he entered her, holding them both safe.

ABOUT THE AUTHOR

Allyson James writes bestselling and award-winning romances, mysteries, and mainstream fiction under several pseudonyms. Her books have hit the *USA Today* bestseller list, and have won several Romantic Times Reviewer's Choice awards, and Romance Writers of America's RITA award. She lives in the warm Southwest with her husband and cats, and spends most of her time in the world of her stories. More about Allyson's books can be found on her website: www.allysonjames.com. Or contact Allyson via e-mail at allysonjames@cox.net.